THE JACKAL WAR

WILL KINNEBREW

THE JACKAL WAR

Design Vault Press, LLC
www.designvaultpress.com

First Edition: August 2019
ISBN: 978-0-9768974-5-3

Books by Will Kinnebrew

Marshal Law
Satan's Brand
The Jackal War

For Lisa, who walks the trail with me.

"For he is God's minister to you for good. But if you do evil, be afraid; for he does not bear the sword in vain; for he is God's minister, an avenger to execute wrath on him who practices evil."

Romans 13:4

FORWARD

When I was young, I spent countless hours tending the family garden in the hot Mississippi sun, turning the soil and plucking weeds. The weeds were persistent and always seemed to return, sometimes by the very next morning. Left alone, the weeds would undoubtedly have taken over the garden, robbing the soil of valuable nutrients and choking the life from the wonderful fruit-bearing plants we'd worked so hard to cultivate.

Over the years, I've come to understand that evil is like a weed; it needs no help to thrive, and will therefore grow out of control when fed. The battle to defeat either—weed or evil—is won daily through vigilance and discipline, creating a hostile environment in which growth cannot take place.

The first step in winning any battle is to recognize the enemy and understand its character. Peter tells us that Satan prowls around like a roaring lion, seeking someone to devour. Yet in his desperation to gain a toehold in our lives, the Father of Lies isn't above disguising himself as something good. The Apostle Paul wrote that Satan masquerades as an angel of light. That revelation alone should be warning enough to carefully consider what we embrace in this world.

We must acknowledge that we are at war, and that every day is another battle. We should celebrate our victories over the enemy, just as we should mourn our losses and repent, praying for forgiveness and strength for the battles ahead. We must be on the lookout for deception, however sincere it may appear to be. The longer we allow weeds to thrive in our lives, the more difficult they become to remove.

CHAPTER 1

Spring in the Rocky Mountains was always a season full of surprise. In times past, small mountain towns anxiously waited for bright sunny days that would bring smiles and tan lines while farmers and ranchers merely found more light to work by, ending their day when the sun disappeared from the sky. The Pandemic and subsequent Fall was a cancer to many small communities, especially in the high country. Even the larger resort areas became ghost towns. Vacations were nonexistent and travel only occurred out of necessity. Not long after the United States' decisive victory at the battle of Washington, American exceptionalism and patriotism began to return. Even the enemy was forced to take a step back and recognize the characteristics of a champion, one that continued to defeat any and all challengers. But as time passed, memories of the chaos and violence softened. Many people forgot who to blame and—like a weed that quickly took root in a garden—evil returned once more.

Creede was never large, even in its heyday of a mining town, and by the turn of the twenty-first century, rural isolation coupled with a lack of area jobs caused the population to drop significantly. The once thriving mining town had been reduced to less than four hundred people. By the time the Battle of Salida was history, Creede had become just another mountain ghost town.

The beauty of the mountains surrounded the statutory town of

Creede, and it was without question a high-country paradise. However, the season of spring was as volatile at eight thousand seven hundred and ninety-nine feet as any month during the dead of winter. After the battle in Washington D.C., a new era of westward expansion began and towns like Creede, Telluride and Gunnison filled the dreams of many who longed for the promise of cheap land and the return to a simpler way of life. The events of previous years had ended society's addiction to technology, and people adjusted accordingly. To survive in remote areas, men and women learned to take on different roles, returning to the habits of their forefathers. The hunter gatherer re-emerged as the primary activity of people living in these isolated areas. Vegetable gardens and food canned for winter replaced the weekly trip to the local grocery, and once the chores were done, children turned their attention to games; they played outside, engaging their imaginations.

A weathered piece of wood swayed back and forth in the breeze from the post of a gated entry. The heavy slab hung from two one-foot sections of logging chain, just as it had for years, preserved by the high-mountain climate. It was cracked in several places and seemed to be holding on for dear life. The grain of the wood along the edges had become rough and dry, bleached to a soft gray by the sun. Uneven letters newly painted in white read *Death Valley*.

In a dry dusty field beyond the sign stood a young boy wearing an Oklahoma Sooners jersey, facing the road to Mammoth Mountain. At four feet, five and a half inches, he stood proudly, holding a stick twice his height. At the end of the stick were the remnants of a faded flag. It was tattered and torn, but the letters OU were still legible. At either end of the field were goal posts fashioned from two-by-fours tied to t-posts that, with much sweat and effort, had been driven into the rocky ground.

The young Sooner leaned his flag against a goalpost and stared down the field at his opposition, cradling a football under his arm. He took one step and then another, quickly building up speed. As he raced toward the others, he yelled, "ROUGH HOOOUSE!"

Two defenders ran toward the young Sooner fan. One wore a faded version of the crimson, gray and white of the Alabama Tide, the other a stained burnt orange of the Texas Longhorns.

"ROUGH HOOOUSE!" they yelled in return as they challenged the boy with the ball.

The Sooner slowed to a trot when the defenders drew near; as they committed to the tackle, he planted one foot, slipped to the right and spun out of each defender's grasp, sprinting for the goal. Both Texas and Alabama sprawled on the dried, powdery dirt of the Rocky Mountains. The Sooner turned to gloat over his opponents eating dust; he performed a cocky, high-step dance in his final approach to the goal line.

Suddenly, in a flash of gold, an unseen defender sprinted from the brush. In desperation, he dove across the dusty field and scooped the Sooner's legs from under him, landing the boy wearing crimson and cream hard on his back, three yards shy of the goal line.

The defender in gold jumped to his feet and high fived Bama and Texas as they approached. "Never underestimate the underdog!" he shouted.

They all laughed, except for the Sooner, who was slow to get up.

"Sorry I'm late, guys. Mom made me split wood."

"Dammit, Brett—coming off the sideline is illegal! You can't hit like that."

"Sorry, Fuzzy. But that cocky high step had to be stopped. It ain't right. I couldn't let you score like that. Besides, it's rough house. Our job is to tackle; your job is to not get tackled. That's all. And quit your cussin'. Mom hears you and we'll be chopping wood all day for weeks."

"Don't call me Fuzzy," the Sooner growled, clenching his fists. "I hate that name."

"You want me to call you Zachariah, then?"

Brett had called his little brother Fuzzy since he was four years old. The younger boy had developed a thick head of black curly hair at an early age, earning him the name. He'd never taken to it, and Brett often used the nickname to get a rise out of his little brother.

"No! I hate that name, too. You've got a cool football name. It ain't fair! Why'd they name me Zachariah? I want a cool football name, too. Something like Baker or Colt. Or maybe Eli. Anything but Zachariah."

"Papaw's name was Zachariah. You're named after him."

"I know, but it's lame."

Brett paused for a moment; he didn't want to be overly hard on his little brother. "Just shorten it, then. How about Zack? Yeah, you know—Zack."

Zachariah stood lost in thought with hands in his pockets, kicking the dust and prodding the ground. He glanced up at his big brother with a grin. "Yeah," he said. "That's okay, I guess. I can handle that."

"I sure wish Dad would get back," Brett said with a sigh.

"Me too," said the young Sooner fan.

Shortly after the families had moved to Creede, one of the dads found a DVD library of old college football games at the high school coach's office. They were able to watch most of the games using four panels from a solar system they salvaged from an abandoned ranch house. They connected the panels to several tractor batteries from the local hardware store, and for several months were able to watch a couple of games a week—depending on how long the sun shone. Their dads taught them the fundamentals of football and built a roughly made sandlot field as a place to play. Because of the limited number of players, Brett's dad taught them to play Rough House, which was a game of everyone against the other.

The rules were simple.

From the point where the ball was downed, the downed player turned his back on the other players and blindly threw the ball over his head, allowing someone else to run with the ball. The object was to avoid tackle and score a touchdown.

One week earlier, their fathers had been forced to leave them in Creede and, much like the Native Americans of old, head into the backcountry in search of subsistence for the families. As the women and children performed their chores of gathering wood and preparing the garden for planting, the men saddled their horses, loaded their rifles and rode into the wilderness in pursuit of new hunting grounds.

Their first mistake the previous year had been a lack of concern for resources. Their relentless pursuit of local game—conveniently close to home—had pressured wildlife to abandon the area. The men's second mistake would prove to be their last. Survival for those accustomed to living in the security of a community was defined by three criteria: shelter, water and food.

War had never crossed their minds.

Four boys idled for a moment as Brett took the ball from his little brother. Brett was thirteen and well on his way to becoming a man, as evidenced by several hairs on his chin that he refused to shave. The team he had chosen was his dad's alma mater. Both boys adored their father, but Brett was allowed to pick first based on seniority; he chose his dad's Golden Eagles of Southern Mississippi. His dad would never admit it, but Brett was pretty confident of whom he'd been named after.

Little brother Zack picked Oklahoma because they were the only team that had beaten the Crimson Tide since 2017, and that had only occurred because of a rainy day in Tuscaloosa, when a third-string freshman had picked up a fumbled punt and ran it into the end zone with less than a minute on the clock. That was the last game recorded in the library annals at the school. It was the last game before the Fall, and if not for these boys on the sandlot field, it might well have been the last football game ever played.

Brett took the ball and nodded at Jimmy, who was wearing the Longhorn Jersey.

"Go deep."

Jimmy took off at a dead run for the opposite end of the field. Zack and Eddie gave chase. Brett waited several seconds, drew back his arm and let the ball fly. The ball rolled off his fingers and arced through the air in a perfect spiral. A gust of wind lifted the ball from behind, pushing it higher and farther than he'd ever imagined possible. The three younger boys chased the ball, trying to run under it and catch it before it hit the ground. But the field was too short, and they were too slow. The ball sailed far beyond the sprinting boys and hit the ground at the edge of the woods near the opposite end of the field. It bounced three times and disappeared into the trees.

Brett smiled proudly as the three boys lost sight of the ball. They all slowed to a walk and came to a stop at the edge of the trees. Zack turned to Brett with hands raised in the air and shouted, "Are you happy now?"

Zack turned to Eddie and Jimmy.

"Mister Big Shot thinks he has to show off that arm every chance he gets."

The high weeds and grass were perfect camouflage for the brown football. Jimmy stepped into the brush and started to inch his way through the grass, pushing the brush aside as he scanned the ground.

"No way it could've gone far," he insisted. "C'mon guys, spread out."

"Yeah, we gotta find it," Eddie chimed in. "It's the only ball we have left."

The four boys waded into the brush and, thanks to the height and density of the shrubs and young pine trees, lost sight of each other almost immediately.

After several minutes, Jimmy held the ball high over his head and shouted, "Found it!"

The boys were working their way back to Death Valley when Jimmy stopped midstep. "Who's that?"

Eddie and Zack peered through the trees as six men on horseback emerged from the woods behind where Brett had been standing only moments ago. Eddie started to move forward, but Zack grabbed his shirt to hold him back.

"Hold on. Dad taught me to spy on strangers before I meet them. Let's wait and see what they do."

"Aw, C'mon Fuzzy," Eddie replied with a cat-like grin. "They're cowboys. They can't be bad guys."

"Don't call me that, Edward. You know I can pound you."

In an act of defiance, Eddie stepped from the safety of the woods to approach the strangers. "C'mon, Jimmy," he called over his shoulder. "Let's show him."

Jimmy stole an uncertain glance at Zack and followed Eddie with a shrug. As they jogged across the field, the riders turned their horses and urged their mounts to meet the boys. The two parties met in the middle of the field, where two of the men dismounted. Nestled in the trees, Zack strained to hear what they said.

"What are you boys doin' out here in the middle of nowhere?"

"Not much, mister. Just playing a little football."

"Just the two of you? Where's the ball?"

"We were just passing and kicking it around. We lost it over in those bushes."

The two men extended their hands to the boys, smiling genially. "Well, that brings back some memories," chuckled one. "Name's Rowdy Stone. This is Dan." He hooked a thumb over his shoulder. "The four yahoos still on their horses are Matt, Johnny, Luke and Mark."

The boys shook hands with the two men on the ground and nodded to the others on horseback.

"You boys live around here?"

Eddie grinned, feeling more comfortable with the cowboys. He slipped a hand behind his back and gave Zack the finger.

"Yessir. We live in town. Our moms are home, but our dads left a week ago to find new hunting ground."

The big cowboy—Rowdy—smiled at Eddie and gave his friends a casual wink. The two men climbed back into their saddles. "Well, heck," Rowdy said. "How 'bout you two hop aboard one of these horses and we'll take you home. Maybe we can help your moms with some of the chores around the house."

Eddie reached up a hand and Rowdy pulled him onto the back of his horse. Eddie turned back to flash a grin across the field at Zack, but his effort was wasted; though he looked hard into the woods, scrutinizing the area from tree to tree, Zack wasn't there.

CHAPTER 2

Sam slowly opened his eyes. He blinked several times at the gray clouds passing overhead. They seemed to spin and swirl as he tried to rise. His head began to pound, forcing him back onto the hard ground.

Cold... so cold.

The retired marshal shivered, trying to move one hand slowly and deliberately. He stretched stiff fingers, moving them back and forth. He squeezed them into a fist, and then extended them once more to get the blood flowing. His head throbbed. With careful movements, he examined his scalp for the source of pain. His fingers came to a rest on a swollen cut just above his hairline. A glance nearby found a chunk of granite that must have caused the gash.

It was impossible to say how long Sam had been there, unconscious on the frozen ground, but it was long enough to leave him very stiff. He rolled to one side and groaned when a burning pain shot through his hip. He laid flat again and gazed into the sky as a snowflake landed softly on his face. Sam explored his side, just above his hip. He felt the wound with trembling fingertips and then turned his attention to his back.

Two holes... good. In and out.

Sam heard leaves rustling to one side and reached instinctively for his sidearm. The Glock wasn't there. He checked the cross-draw rig on his other side; the Ruger was missing as well. His last hope was a Bianchi Nighthawk, a knife his dad had given him for high-school graduation. It was there, thank God. He drew the cold blade of Solingen steel and rolled to his belly, teeth grinding with pain. He raised his head cautiously to peer over the short juniper brush surrounding him, scanning the trees for whatever had rustled the leaves.

Movement caught his eye just beyond the tree line across the meadow. Something thrashed on the ground there, as if wounded. He gathered his legs beneath him and rose with care. The whimper of an animal caught his attention.

Tango!

Abandoning caution, Sam staggered toward the trees. Tango recognized Sam and struggled to rise but pain won the battle; the black wolf let his head return to the frozen ground with a whine. Sam knelt at Tango's side, comforting the huge animal with gentle strokes. Combing fingers through coarse fur, Sam searched for a wound; it didn't take long to find one. Tango flinched as calloused fingers glanced over the hole of a small-caliber round above the shoulder, below the spine. It was the area of an animal hunters often referred to as *no man's land*. Luckily for Tango, the bullet had entered slightly above his vital organs and below the spinal cord, leaving arteries that fed the rear proximities untouched.

He would survive.

"Shh, boy. Rest for now," he whispered. "I know it hurts, but you'll be okay."

Sam had found Tango tangled in wire as a mere cub. He'd nursed the pup back to health, and the pair had been inseparable ever since. Tango had grown rapidly, proving to be a formidable asset during the Battle of Washington, striking fear into the hearts of the enemy with his howl.

Sam's platoon of patriots had come to be known as the Howlers, owing their success against the United Nations' Peace Enforcers largely to the black wolf. The 'Peace' Enforcers were more of a war party that slaughtered anyone who stood against them. Tango would let his presence be known to the enemy with an eerie cry; Sam's men had made sport of joining the chorus, giving the opposition fair warning of who and what they were about to face.

The days and months following the battle had been kind to Tango;

food was plentiful, and it had been a while since the wolf missed a meal. He'd grown to an enormous size, even by wolf standards.

Sam's touch, his soothing voice, put the wolf at ease now. "Hang in there, friend."

Rising to survey his situation, Sam returned to the spot where he'd awakened only moments ago and tried to piece together how he'd come to be there. His memory came up blank, though a disconcerting thought struck like lightning.

Where was Patton?

The wind was barely noticeable as the snow fell. Sam needed to hurry, he knew. His tracks were visible enough in the soft earth, but it wouldn't be long before the snow covered them. Holding his side, his head pounding, he limped around the shrubbery and found where he'd fallen after being shot. A steep ledge to the south left little doubt which direction he'd traveled from. And from the looks of the tracks, he'd been chasing something. Or was it some*one*?

Where are you, Patton?

The only time Patton had ever left Sam was under duress by two thieves who had confronted Sam over dinner one evening. They'd been brazened and rude to their host, so Sam had taught them some manners. The next morning, Patton had disappeared from the corral. Sam had been forced to track the thieves down on a borrowed horse. In a small valley south of Pagosa Springs, the thieves managed to ambush Sam, shooting him in the chest. He'd been wearing his Kevlar vest, yet even still, the impact of the rifle slug had put him down for days. If not for a good Samaritan named Kuruk—Chief of the Jicarilla Apache—Sam might've lost track of Patton forever.

Where are you, boy?

Sam continued down the trail, observing the gray winter forest of bare aspen and green spruce. The snowfall was becoming more persistent; Sam knew he'd soon need shelter. He rounded a curve in the trail and froze; his heart sank at what lay before him on the ground.

Limping toward the big horse, Sam ground his teeth. He fell to his knees at Patton's side, rubbing the horse's neck beneath a long beautiful mane. Tears filled his eyes, hot and angry.

Patton's remains were stiff, his skin cold. His eyes remained open, though the life had left them and no longer shined. Sam sensed movement behind him and turned quickly as Tango staggered to Patton's side and curled into a ball beside him.

Sam wiped his eyes and tried to redirect his sadness by collecting whatever gear he could find. He would freeze to death if he failed to focus on survival. His bags had been thrown aside and emptied on to the ground. His rifles were missing, along with all the ammunition he'd kept in his pack.

On the ground beside Patton's head was the hat Sam had worn for more than a decade. Its crown had been crushed during the fall, the brim no longer a crisp, sweeping line from front to back. Sam bent at the waist to recover the hat. The sweat of a dozen years stained the band, along with fresh mud from the trail. He pushed the crown back into place and tried to re-shape the crumbled mess as best he could; his efforts resulted in an old worn out hat with a floppy brim.

Kinda like me, he thought.

He perched the misshapen hat on his head, shared a few moments of reverent silence with his dead horse and began to inventory his remaining supplies.

His mind wandered as he sat next to his old friend. Life had been a blur since the Fall, and death seemed to follow Sam wherever he went. The Pandemic had left him empty and alone, stealing his wife and unborn daughter. Alone became a way of life then, isolation his comfort. His only joy had come from his horse, Patton.

Then one night, as he closed his eyes and slipped into a dream, he'd seen a face. She'd seemed so vivid, so real. Her jeweled eyes, her raven-black hair…

Jennifer!

It was more than a dream; it was a vision—a vision he couldn't have escaped, even if he'd wanted to. And given any kind of choice, Sam would have gladly remained in that vision forever.

During one of his many pursuits of solitude, Sam had unwittingly landed on a path that could only be explained by fate. He found Theresa and the girls in the Ouachita Mountains one cold February morning, and the events that followed were nothing short of incredible.

The girls told Sam an unbelievable story, one that—however unbelievable—had been confirmed the next day when he faced off with six assassins in the basin of the Illinois River. A story that had unveiled a conspiracy involving treachery and treason at the highest levels of government. Corrupt government officials had thrown the U.S. Constitution on the auction block, and the highest bidder was ready to destroy everything it stood for.

A fierce battle in Salida, Colorado proved to the world that the USA wasn't ready to be conquered just yet. That sentiment was reaffirmed just two years later, when the United Nations attempted to take control of Washington D.C.

After the Battle of Washington, Sam had retired. He and Jennifer moved west from Oklahoma to a ranch outside of Pagosa Springs, Colorado. Much of the remaining population had moved to more densely populated areas, abandoning their homes and personal treasures for the security of numbers and the conveniences of city life. Sam had purchased a secluded piece of land by merely settling delinquent taxes on behalf of the previous owner.

The beautiful ranch property consisted of a horse barn with stables, a large log-cabin style lodge and four smaller cabins that were perfect for the girls—Theresa, Elise, Tiffany and Sara. Before the Fall, an outfitter for guided hunting had run the six-hundred and forty-acre ranch. Located west of Pagosa Springs along the Piedra River, the property was hemmed in on two sides by hundreds of thousands of acres of National Forest. Sam's favorite feature of the ranch property was its own private hot spring.

Sam and Jennifer found every excuse to take long rides and relish the peace that seemed to naturally come with the solitude of the high country. A peace that was much needed after the destruction evil forces had brought upon them.

On one particular trip, they discovered a steep path through the National Forest that led to what Sam called *the top of the world.* From that vantage, it seemed they could follow the Continental Divide just about anywhere. And indeed, they had often ridden along the Divide, traveling until sunset and spending the night by a fire. When it burned down to little more than glowing embers, they fell asleep under an incredible galaxy of stars, which danced in unison across the sky. Sam usually woke before sunrise to coax the fire back to flame. He'd have a pot of coffee ready when Jennifer crawled from her bedding. The two often rested against their saddles, cuddled in their bedrolls as a golden slice of warmth appeared at the top of the Rockies, chasing the stars from the sky.

Two days earlier, the ranch had been bustling with excitement as Jennifer and the girls prepared for their first trip to town in weeks. It was early May, and Sam was itching to get lost on a trail in the high lonesome. After months of shorter days and snowy weather, he suffered a horrible case of cabin fever. He missed gazing at an infinite horizon. He longed to see what was over the next mountain. So, on a beautiful sunny day, Sam saddled Patton and loaded a pack with two days' supplies, including an old take-down fly rod and tackle.

Excited to get out of the pasture, Patton seemed determined to race Tango to the top of the world. Melting snow still covered the landscape then, and the trail had been slick as they made their way up the mountain. When the trail opened into a meadow, Sam was surprised to see a herd of wild horses grazing. Patton snorted, nickered and moved his front feet back and forth, unsure of what to make of the wild animals. Sam remembered smiling and rubbing the neck of the big horse as the herd lifted its heads in unison to confront the strangers in their midst.

After the Pandemic, many farms and ranches had been abandoned, leaving the animals to live off the land. Gates were left open whenever possible, and livestock took advantage of their newfound freedom. Animals that managed to survive the first few winters migrated to lower elevations, finding their way to the rich grass and warmer temperatures of the prairies. Surprised by the sight of wild horses at this elevation, Sam had begun to think of turning a profit and improving his own stock. This was the first wild herd Sam had seen since leaving Oklahoma, and the herd looked to have come from warmbloods or draft horses. The animals were large by most standards, some as tall as Patton.

The boss mare was—a tall bay roan—kept a watchful eye in Sam's direction as a lone stallion guarded the edge of the herd, ready to challenge a threat or announce a retreat.

Contrary to popular belief, horses were usually led by the boss mare while the alpha stallion played a more defensive role; she was the boss, he the protector.

This herd consisted of about forty mature horses with numerous fillies and colts of various sizes and ages. All seemed healthy and of good confirmation. Sam took note of his location, referencing the mountain peaks in hopes that he might return soon for a roundup. He coaxed Patton forward with a click of his tongue and they moved through the meadow at a safe distance, careful not to spook the herd.

Early that afternoon, Sam had camped near the upper Piedra River and caught several trout. Tango stretched his legs by running down a couple of grouse on his own. They'd risen early the next morning and headed up the trail to Turkey Creek Lake. As the trio reached the trail's crest, the sun hovered over the Rockies to the east; still stiff from the night chill, Sam embraced the warmth of the sun. They relaxed for a while at the top of the trail, enjoying the view of a vast world below. An hour later, they reached the lake.

Sam pieced together his packable fly rod. After carefully choosing his bait, Sam began to work his way around the lake, flipping the rod back and forth. For a variety of reasons, Sam was grateful for his retirement; this new hobby—fly fishing and tying his own flies—was one of them.

With each extension of his arm, he unfolded the line gracefully over the water. His *cone headed wooly booger* lure came to rest on the smooth, glass-like surface next to the base of a large boulder. The still surface of the lake seemed to retreat for a moment as if drawing a breath for the inevitable.

Suddenly, the water churned violently as Sam firmly set the hook. The stillness of the lake erupted with an explosive splash as a magnificent cutthroat twisted and turned in a futile attempt to escape Sam's hook.

By mid-morning, Sam was roasting trout over a fire. The morning sun felt wonderful at this altitude; he reclined against a rock with a comfortably angled face and bathed in the sun's warmth. The comfort of the bright glowing orb might've filled him with peace, if not for a sudden nagging sense that something was amiss. What or when was a mystery.

Sam shook off his unease as the sun approached its own summit in the sky. A glance over his shoulder found dark gray clouds to the north-west; a storm was building, and while forty-five degrees seemed warm enough in the sun, it was still winter—even in May—at this altitude. Severe weather wasn't just a possibility in the high country; it was a probability that should never be taken lightly.

He watched the clouds for a moment, hoping the storm would move more eastward. It didn't take long to determine that he'd see no such luck. Returning to where Patton was grazing, Sam began to pack up his tackle. A chilling north wind fought its way across the mountain range, raising goosebumps on his arms.

Eyes darting around the landscape, Sam frowned. Aside from the weather, he saw no cause for alarm. Yet there remained a feeling that something was wrong. "Let's cut this short and hunker down in the canyon by the river," he said aloud. Patton snorted in agreement.

Sam secured his pack across Patton's back, swung his leg into the saddle and headed down the narrow trail they had traveled earlier. The path was hemmed in by a tree line on one side and a steep ledge on the other.

Tango remained in a meadow by the lake, distracted by a colony of marmots. Sam knew he would soon catch up. As he and Patton slowly worked their way down the canyon, they rounded a bend in the trail.

And then, in a split second, the world around them seemed to explode.

Caught by surprise, Sam was thrown to the rocky ground. Years of training and muscle memory found Sam instinctively reaching for his Glock, yet before his thumb could break the leather snap on his holster, he was already unconscious.

CHAPTER 3

The line between youthful ambition and tombstone courage is thin. Unfortunately, both lead to serious harm in the wrong situation. The young Apache lifted his head to face his tormentors as blood ran from his lips to his chin and patted to the ground. His hands and feet were bound by rope, stretched painfully behind him around a large stone. His struggle was useless, but his spirit was to be admired. The wind was cold on his bare skin, but the young man stood defiantly. He'd been lured in by pieces of women's clothing and deer blood. With honor as his guide, the noble scout had ridden into a trap with the good intentions of a hero.

He never imagined becoming a victim.

The assassin caressed the dark skin of the Apache brave with the edge of a knife and teased him with the point of the blade. The brave spat in his face, drawing only an evil grin from his tormentor. The rest of the assassin's team looked on wordlessly, enamored by the ritual of *death by a thousand cuts* and relishing the reaction of each wound. Each cut a little longer, a little deeper than the one before it. The blade moved a little slower each time, drawing out the pain that much longer. However spirited, the brave's defiance was short-lived; his stoic demeanor soon turned to screams of pain.

By noon the team of assassins had begun to take turns. They laughed at the boy's cries while carving into his flesh, falling silent when the young man finally passed out.

The team's leader held up a hand to halt the process. "We'll wait until he awakens," he advised.

"Let's just kill him and be done with it," said one. "Why does it have to take so long?"

"The ritual of *death by a thousand cuts* isn't about the killing of an infidel. It's about becoming Eru Olorun, or Allah's slave."

"Allah's slave?"

"Yes. We—you and I—are Allah's slaves, or servants. The body of the infidel represents all that stands against Allah, each cut a symbolic victory over the infidel. It matters not how long we take; only that we remain diligent, patient and ultimately successful in serving our master."

He could've mentioned that the ritual wasn't of Islamic origin—that it had been borrowed and adapted in recent years from the ancient Chinese tradition—but what was the point? The young men under his charge were idiots.

"But why stop when he passes out?"

A sigh of disgust. "What use is a cut if the infidel isn't awake to feel it? Each cut teaches the infidel to fear Allah more and reveals to us the value of the Jihad. His suffering is our reward."

"But he'll eventually be unconscious, anyway."

Another of his men chimed in. "And he'll eventually die, either way, right?"

"And that is the lesson we must learn. Cut the infidel and take control of his will. Control his pain, his fear. Show him that his life and death are in the palm of your hand."

Both men turned toward the Apache brave, who was now stirring. He lifted his head and grinned with a blood-filled mouth.

"You can kill me and call it whatever you want, but there's no mistaking what you are."

"What *I* am?" the assassin sneered. He circled the brave tied to the stone. "Tell me, young man; what exactly am I?"

The brave leaned forward with teeth clenched, blood dripping from his lips. "You're nothing but a coward. A thug hiding behind a withering cult. A bunch of Jackals!"

The assassin's face darkened, his patience with the brave slipping away. He flipped the long-bladed knife in his hand and plunged it deep into the young man's gut, twisting it sideways. He watched the boy's eyes widen, his face contorting with pain.

"There now, how's that? Sticks and stones, ya know." The assassin withdrew his knife and wiped it clean on the young man's shirt. He turned to address the others, who'd been watching intently. "He's dead and doesn't even know it."

His gaze returned to the young man. "Coyotes will gnaw at your legs before you take your last breath," he promised, twirling the knife as he spoke. "You could live for days like this. Or, you may apologize and beg forgiveness. I will kill you swiftly and be done with it."

The brave's head hung forward; he peered up at the assassin from under the strands of his long black hair. Smiling through the blood and pain, he began to laugh. "I'm already forgiven, Jackal. You can take your cult and burn in hell."

The assassin leaned forward and snatched the young man's long black hair, wrapped it around his hand and lifted it tightly over the infidel's bloody head. With the long-bladed knife, he made a slow, deliberate cut across the brave's hairline. The boy screamed. The assassin took his time, making a gruesome display of cutting a flap of skin and peeling back the young man's scalp.

"Isn't this how you savages like to do it?" he hissed. He stepped back for a moment, allowing the brave to catch his breath before continuing the torment. He buried a finger in one of the boy's wounds, grinning all the while.

As the butchering continued, even the assassin's men couldn't help but have second thoughts about a god who promote such carnage. The team leader yanked harder on the boy's hair, lifting it high and drawing his blade across the remaining flap of skin; what used to be the top of the young man's head ripped free and dangled from a bloody hand. Abandoning his knife for the moment, the assassin peeled the boy's skin down the back of his head as if skinning a rabbit.

The Apache brave was barely conscious, his head bobbing forward on his chest with blood dripping into a large puddle at his feet. He tried to mumble something, and the assassin leaned in close.

"Excuse me? I didn't quite catch that."

Somewhere downwind at the base of the canyon, a coyote howled. As its song faded in the distance, another yipped and howled a chorus of its own. Soon, the air was filled with nature's refrain as a dozen voices responded to the smell of the young man's blood.

"See? Your dinner date will be here any minute."

The young man tried to speak again, but his words fell away as the life flowed from his body.

"C'mon, man. You got to speak up."

As the assassin leaned close to the brave, he heard something behind him—something that sounded out of place. Almost like the *thunk* of an axe against a rotten tree. He hesitated and turned his head slightly; another *thunk*, followed by one more. Coyotes continued to cry in the distance as the sun fell behind the mountains to the west.

The assassin turned to face three large men standing over the bodies of his team. Each held a modern version of a tomahawk, constructed from durable steel with a razor-sharp blade. On the opposing end was a forged tactical point, designed to penetrate and pry open doors and windows—even skulls, if need be. The obvious leader of the three slipped his tomahawk into a holster at his side, and the two younger men followed suit. He then transitioned to a rifle that hung from his neck on a single-point sling, leveling it at the assassin's chest.

"Drop the knife," the man said coldly.

The enormous man wore the coat of a silver tip grizzly bear; it fit snugly on his oversized shoulders. His skin was dark, his hair long and silver. It hung halfway down his back and blended with the fur of the bear. Beside him stood two more men, almost as tall but much younger.

The assassin's gaze flicked to the rifle he'd leaned against a tree just a few steps away.

Kuruk gestured with his own rifle and repeated himself with more conviction. "Drop the knife!"

The assassin hesitated. "Do you intend to let me live?"

"You won't see another sunrise."

"Then, I'd just as soon die with a weapon in my hand."

Without hesitation, Kuruk aimed his rifle and squeezed the trigger. The assassin's blade flew from his hand, as did two of his fingers. The man dropped to his knees and clutched his right hand with the left. Kuruk stepped forward and kicked the knife across the clearing, out of reach for the man in black.

"You don't deserve the opportunity to die with honor, but I'll give you the same choice you offered my friend. Tell me what's going on—what is your mission—and I'll make your death a swift one."

The assassin still clutched his hand as Kuruk yanked him to his feet.

The huge Indian nodded to his men. "Eli, take him for me. Put him on the ground and tie his hands to that tree."

As Eli obeyed his father, Kuruk turned his attention to his friend, the brave who lay dying against the large stone. Kuruk drew his knife and cut the ropes, lowering the young man gingerly to the ground.

"My brother," the brave wheezed, coughing up a mouthful of blood.

"Shh," Kuruk whispered and placed a hand on the dying man's chest. "Nakota, you've always been brave. We will honor your journey with the great warriors who have gone before you. Now, rest my friend. We'll take it from here."

Perhaps finding comfort in Kuruk's words, Nakota smiled. Moments later, pain in Nakota's gut stole the smile from his face as he took his last breath.

Kuruk's head dropped against his chest. "Father, please accept this young man into your presence," he whispered. "And please, forgive me for what I'm about to do."

His chest heaving with emotion, Kuruk rose, drawing his knife from its sheath. He strode to the assassin tied to the tree and squatted to face him. He rested the point of his blade on the tip of the Jackal's nose.

"Now, it's your turn."

CHAPTER 4

The candlelight flickered across the beautiful wood-grained walls of the Moon Dog Lodge. Jennifer watched the shadows battle back and forth in a dance of darkness versus light. She was exhausted, yet her mind refused to rest. She and the girls had returned from Pagosa four days ago, and Sam was now long overdue. He was supposed to have camped and fished for a couple of days while the weather was warm. Since a snowstorm blew in from the northwest, he ought to have returned by now. With every passing hour, Jennifer became more fearful that something had happened.

She threw her covers aside and tiptoed down the hall, past the spare bedroom. The cold floor against her bare feet sent a chill up her legs. The lodge was heated through a geothermal system powered by a hot spring near the home. The structure maintained a temperature of sixty-five degrees inside, even during the coldest of winter days. Yet now, as Jennifer reached the first floor, the temperature was significantly cooler inside than normal. When her foot touched the bottom stair, she went rigid.

The front door was partially open, and the cold breeze whistling through the gap gave her more than one reason to chill.

Coffee?

The aroma of a freshly brewed pot drifted through the lodge.

Sam? she thought, her heart thumping wildly in her chest. *Has he returned? Better not take any chances.*

She stepped into the kitchen; the wood stove was stoked with a percolator boiling on top. Jennifer reached beneath the kitchen table where a Glock 43 9mm was secured for home defense. She leveled the gun in a combat-ready position, just as Sam had taught her, and returned to the entryway at the foot of the stairs. With her handgun held at the ready, Jennifer opened the door and slipped through the opening.

In the darkness, she could just make out the shapes of three men on the front porch, sitting in chairs like they owned the place. The one closest to her lifted a coffee cup to his lips. Jennifer remained hidden in the doorway; using the frame as cover, she leaned out and leveled her weapon on the form closest to her.

"Show me your hands!" she barked.

All three men jumped. The closest man's hands shot straight up and out, as if shocked by a cattle prod; his coffee cup sailed into the air, drenching his two companions.

With a flick of a switch, Jennifer turned on the porch lights. Not for the first time, she felt a stab of gratitude for the lodge's power system, which was fed by solar panels and a hydroelectric water wheel in the nearby Piedra River.

"Hell, woman!" Kuruk snapped. "That was uncalled for."

Jennifer lowered her Glock with a giggle.

Kuruk rose to wipe the coffee from his coat. His two traveling companions, equally drenched, followed suit. Eli was Kuruk's son, Bendigo his nephew. While they were cousins, the two young men could easily pass for brothers. Both were as tall as Kuruk, and just as strong, but long and lean with a litheness that came with youth. Their movements were smooth and agile, betraying years of training in the old ways of the warrior, pathfinder and scout.

"I'm not used to company in the middle of the night," Jennifer grumbled, mostly in jest. "Especially company that leaves the door open and then helps themselves to my coffee. A man could get shot for less, you know."

"And here I was thinking I was being considerate, letting you guys sleep till sunup." Kuruk snickered, then frowned. "Sorry about the door."

"What's going on?" Jennifer asked. "It's the middle of the night and you're—" A terrible thought cut her off in midsentence. Something must've happened. Her heart sank, her eyes widened. "It's Sam, isn't it? Is he okay?"

"I don't know. I thought he'd be here," Kuruk replied. "We came to warn him."

"Warn him?"

"Yeah, one of our scouts came up missing the other day; we tracked him into a remote canyon. A pack of Jackals was torturing him with the *death by a thousand cuts*."

"Jackals… as in the assassins? I thought we were done with all that insanity."

"I'm afraid not. Evil never goes away. It may hide for a while but it's always there."

Jennifer shook her head sadly. "What happened to the scout?"

"Well, he… he didn't make it. But neither did they. After some persuading, their leader gave us some disturbing intel. He said after the Battle of D.C., many of the surviving assassins found a safe haven to wait."

"Wait for what?"

"An opportunity, a new leader—who knows?" His eyes narrowed. "Where is Sam, anyway? I noticed Patton wasn't in the stockade."

"I don't know. He left five days ago packed for just two days. He wanted to fish up at Turkey Creek Lake while the weather was nice."

"Damn," Kuruk replied, shaking his head.

"What?"

"I'm sure he'll be fine, but I need two things right now."

Jennifer nodded in a daze.

"We need some supplies for several days. Food and ammo."

"Ammo? What exactly is going on, Kuruk?"

"Jennifer, I'm not going to pretend this isn't serious. The Jackals are back, and they're hunting anyone involved in the Battle of Washington. I don't have all the details, but these guys are different. It's not just one ego-crazed tyrant, this time. They've formed a council, of sorts; an entire congress of Akhzam's and Mahannad's followers. They plan to destroy as many communities as possible and target the foot soldiers before they have a chance to assemble and grow in strength. And they've started with the Howlers."

"Just how is this different than before?"

"Their mission before was to start at the top. If they controlled the head, the body would follow. They underestimated the resolve of the American people; they didn't plan for an uprising. Their mission now is to kill anyone who's ever gotten in their way. Everyone west of the Mississippi is in danger."

"They have that many men?"

"I'm not sure, but they have new tactics. They've spent the last three years learning to blend, pretending to be something they're not so that people will embrace them. They no longer wear the black uniform of the assassins; their new uniform is a cowboy hat and boots. They've learned to say *yes ma'am* and *no ma'am* and chat politely until you let your guard down; then, they torture you with a thousand cuts and take your head as a trophy."

Jennifer cupped her mouth in her hand. "This is insane. It makes absolutely no sense. The cutting death… I've never heard of it being used here. Back when they were collecting people and building their numbers, they tortured people right and left. But *death by a thousand cuts*? I've always thought that was eastern folklore."

"I'm afraid not. They must be desperate. Time is short for those who are lost, and evil wants to take a large toll before the end."

Jennifer sat in silence for a moment, trying to process all this. She heard footsteps in the stairwell and turned just as Theresa poked her head through the door.

"Hey y'all. What's everyone up so early for?"

Kuruk's eyes flicked to Theresa, but he continued to speak to Jennifer. "I need one more thing. You and the girls need to leave. You can't stay here on the ranch. I'm surprised we found you first."

"Where are we supposed to go?"

"You'll be safe on the reservation. I don't believe the enemy has the guts to go there; there's simply too much resistance waiting for them. They're a cowardly bunch; they don't like victims who fight back."

Theresa looked surprised. "Okay, I'm obviously out of the loop.

What's going—"

Before she could finish, Jennifer cut off her question. "No time, hun. I'll explain on the way. Go wake the others and get packed. I'll be up in a minute."

Theresa glanced at Eli and smiled. The tall Apache brave returned the gesture with a nod and smile of his own. Jennifer looked at her daughter and cleared her throat.

"Okay, you two can visit while I help Kuruk with supplies."

"Bendigo, come with me," Kuruk said with a smile and wink. "I'll need your help carrying something."

Elise, Tiffany and Sara were all up by now, standing at the top of the stairs. Seeing the lovely young ladies as he stepped inside, Bendigo stumbled in the entryway. Kuruk smirked knowingly. When the young man dared to glance at his uncle, the smirk was replaced with a stern gaze.

"Boy, it's neither the time nor the place."

Bendigo dipped his head slightly in embarrassment and turned away, but not before stealing a glimpse of Elise from under the brim of his hat. The young men had become frequent visitors of the Moon Dog Ranch over the past year; naturally, the rituals of courting were in full bloom. Their recent encounter with the Jackals made the boys realize that the ones who'd become dear to them were now in danger.

Jennifer led the three men through the kitchen, into Sam's converted man cave. It had once been a trophy room for the hunting lodge, complete with a walk-in gun vault large enough to double as a safe room.

Jennifer entered a series of numbers on a keypad set into the door. A barely audible *click* signaled the release of bolts securing the door to the wall. She spun the wheel, which disengaged the bolts from slots in the wall; with a loud clunk, the enormous steel door broke free to swing open on well-oiled hinges. The three men followed Jennifer into the safe room, pausing in the doorway to admire the amazing collection of firearms displayed within. Eli and Bendigo went so far as to gape, in awe of the sheer variety of weapons. Similarly, Kuruk's eyes widened. He turned to Jennifer.

"You've been holding out on me."

"I know," she replied, cringing guiltily. "The safe room was here when we bought the place. The owners must've abandoned it a very long time ago; the door was sealed when we moved in. No one could open it."

"Well, obviously somebody managed," Kuruk remarked with a chuckle.

"Well, yeah. I was dusting several days after we were getting settled and found a little metal tab hidden in a crack in that log." Jennifer pointed to a spot on the timber wall, behind which the safe was hidden. "It had the magic numbers scratched into it."

Turning to leave, Jennifer glanced back at Kuruk. "Help yourselves to whatever you need. I have some packing to do."

Jennifer headed upstairs to the bedroom, where she shoveled clothes into a backpack normally reserved for her mountain excursions with Sam. Moments later, she strode into the bathroom and peered into the mirror. She splashed some water on her cheeks, pulled her long black-and-silver hair into a ponytail. She needed to get her head straight.

It was time to prepare for another war.

She'd dealt with this evil far too long; she was tired of it. She finished packing the bare essentials and returned to the man cave, where Kuruk lingered.

"Sent the boys to prepare the horses," he said.

Jennifer approached him, coming to a halt squarely in front of him. "I'm not going to hide somewhere while Sam is in trouble. I know where he's gone, and I'm going to find him."

"Jennifer," Kuruk replied in a kind voice, "I can't allow that. The Jackals could be closing in on us right now. You won't survive a confrontation with them alone. I don't even want to think about what they'd do to you."

"Well, come with me then. Hell, let's all go."

Kuruk frowned.

"These girls are adults now, and they're as tough as nails. They were raised in the same kind of place those Jackals came from; I'd put my money on them in a fight any day."

Abruptly, Bendigo slid to a halt just outside the door, chest heaving. "Hey, boss. We've got company!"

CHAPTER 5

Sam gazed back at the big horse that lay lifeless and cold. His hurt was deep like a knife in the gut, and as the snow began to cover his old friend, a rage unlike any he'd felt in years welled up within. Patton had carried him through the battles of Salida and Washington as enemies of the United States joined forces to drive a spike through Lady Liberty's heart. Their mission to destroy the world's last hope for freedom had been thwarted by an unexpected rallying of the people, Americans from all walks of life. Patriots no longer divided by politics, fighting for the preservation of all that was good and righteous. Fighting not only for survival, but for the destruction of evil.

Patton had been a cocky little colt when Sam found him, yet they forged a bond over time that went deeper than the superficial role of pet and master. They moved as one with uncanny precision, as if each shared thoughts with the other. Alone, they were formidable; together, they'd been unstoppable.

Sam examined Patton's body and identified four bullet wounds, each inflicted from a different vector. Scanning the rocks at the edge of the bluff, he discovered several empty .223 casings. He found more at various positions within the nearby trees.

They had known he was coming, and they had waited. They killed his horse and pilfered his belongings, leaving Sam for dead.

"Why didn't they finish the job?" he whispered to no one.

Sam couldn't remember anything. Everything from Turkey Creek Lake and beyond was foggy, as if he'd slept through it all. He glanced at Tango, who raised his head in response.

The devil dog scared them away, Sam surmised. "Assassins," he said aloud.

His suspicion was confirmed after surveying the other tracks for several minutes. Six horses. A whole damn pack of Jackals. But why here? Why now?

"I wish we still had that pager," Sam mumbled to himself as Tango cocked his head to one side.

During the Battle of Salida, the good guys had discovered the Jackals—assassins masquerading as UN Peace Enforcers—were communicating via technology from the nineties. The enemy had found a way to bounce analogue signals to and from specific pagers using abandoned cell towers; agents with the Secret Service had reverse engineered the technology and provided Sam with a pager. After the battle of Washington and the ultimate surrender of the United Nations, President Bradshaw and the Joint Chiefs of Staff ordered the towers to be destroyed. They couldn't risk American technology being used against its own people again—at least, not until the government had rebuilt the infrastructure and amassed the manpower to secure it.

This time, I'm on my own, he realized.

Sam looked past the steep ledge to the valley below. There, a string of six men on horseback was barely visible in the fading light. He lifted his head to the sky and began to howl, just as he and his band of Howlers had done several years before to strike fear into the hearts of ISIS assassins. The assassins had earned the nickname 'Jackals' because they traveled in packs, preying on the weak and innocent. Their fear of the devil dog was rooted in a belief that dying in the jaws of the demonic beast would prevent their souls from entering paradise.

Sam's howl was long and loud. He gathered his breath and howled again and again until it became a horrible scream, and in the failing light of the dreary day, Tango joined the chorus. The two wounded warriors cried a melody worthy of terror for anyone listening in the valley below. Sam squinted down at the six dots below. They'd hunkered like quail in the scrub, hiding in fear. When Tango let loose another howl, they spurred their horses into a run, fleeing the terror of his song.

Darkness came quickly, and so did the storm. As night settled over the high country, wind began to drive heavy snow across the mountains, creating swirling walls of ice. What remained of Sam's gear lay scattered about. Racing against the weather, he gathered what he could into his saddlebag. In near darkness, he picked his way down a trail with Tango on his heels. He kept his eyes peeled for anything they could use for shelter. The terrain soon leveled, and Sam noticed two large boulders set back against the canyon wall. He limped over. With snow pelting and wind howling at their backs, Sam and Tango crawled between the rocks and tried to get as comfortable as possible.

The temperature was dropping rapidly, and Sam was already feeling the early symptoms of hypothermia. Peeking his head through the opening between the boulders, he felt a significant difference in cold with the wind chill. Moving around would help combat the cold, he knew.

Abandoning the boulders for the moment, Sam found a large spruce tree nearby. He collected an armload of dry twigs and sticks from beneath its protective limbs, shivering all the while. Like many evergreens found in the Rocky Mountains, the spruce's limbs grew close together and produced thick green needles year-round. In a pinch, the trees provided adequate shelter from a storm while keeping the tinder at its base fairly dry. But it wouldn't be enough shelter from these high winds, and certainly not the freezing temperatures of this particular storm. Sam collected tinder until it was too dark to continue, stacking his fire materials near the entrance of the boulder shelter.

Tango was curled just inside the opening. The ferocious black wolf seemed to grimace as he moved. He whined a small protest but allowed Sam to pass through the narrow opening.

"Oh, c'mon, sissy," Sam snickered in passing. "We've been through worse than this."

Sam pilfered a small leather pouch from his saddlebag and blew into his hands before attempting to untie the knotted strings. Inside, the bag contained a fire starter kit, complete with quick fuel discs. With numbing hands, he placed the fuel and sticks against the canyon wall at the back of the alcove created by the boulders. Within seconds, he had a small fire going. He fed twigs to the fire until he had a good bed of coals.

Sam was exhausted and sore, but it was time to tend to their wounds; he'd put it off as long as he dared. Methodically, he teased a few coals from the fire to cool. He then retrieved a small metal tin from his saddlebag and carefully removed its contents, which were wrapped in wax paper, and slid the parcel next to the coals.

Sam gave Tango an affectionate scratch on the snout. "Brother, I'm going to show you how to treat a wound."

The wolf looked at him as if he understood and licked the bullet hole in his tough hide.

"Okay, fair enough," Sam chuckled. "You have your way, and I have mine."

Sam scooped the coals into the bottom of his tin. With a stick about the size of his index finger, he ground the coals into a fine ash. Next, he sliced almost half the contents of the wax paper and dropped it into the can of ashes.

Sam continued to talk to Tango to keep his mind busy.

"This is spirit clay from the hot springs in Pagosa Springs. It's full of healing minerals, along with some boiled willow bark, which I added myself. I learned this remedy from our old friend, Kuruk."

Tango's ears perked up at the sound of Kuruk's name.

"Yeah, I know. I miss him, too. He's a long way off right now, I'm afraid."

Sam mixed the clay with the ground ash until they became a uniform gray paste. The concoction had the same rotten-egg, Sulphur-like smell as the water that bubbled from the hot springs near Pagosa. He scooped a healthy portion onto the end of a finger and gently packed his entry wound with the poultice. He did the same for the exit wound on the backside of his hip. Sam dug a roll of gauze from his saddlebag and dressed each of his wounds. He turned to Tango.

"Your turn."

Sam applied the poultice to the wolf's wound before the animal had a chance to argue. The wolf whined for a second but lay still long enough for Sam to finish. When he was done, Sam fed the fire and then crawled from the safety of his boulder shelter once more. He returned seconds later with the tin packed to the rim with snow; this he positioned over the fire to melt. He drank some and offered the rest to Tango. He repeated the process several times until he and Tango had satisfied their thirst.

Realizing there was nothing more he could do, Sam leaned against the canyon wall and watched snow swirl above through a gap in the boulders. The fire caused an updraft between the boulders, which gusted the snowfall away from the opening.

Small favors.

Sam thought about Patton. Though saddened, he realized that all warriors must eventually move on to the happy hunting ground. Patton had lived a good life; Sam was grateful to have been a part of it. Inevitably, his thoughts turned to Jennifer. He longed to be in her arms, to feel her warm skin against his. She was the only woman he'd ever loved.

Sam watched the flickering glow of fire dancing off the swirling snowflakes above and tried not to think. For a while, anyway. The dazzling lightshow mesmerized him, eventually lulling him to sleep.

Spring in the high country was a far more tedious affair than in the flatland. Violent and unpredictable, the weather shifted from one extreme to another within hours, sometimes even minutes. Tonight's storm reinforced the seriousness of his situation.

The blizzard persisted through the night, blanketing the mountains in deep snow. The boulders had provided a perfect windbreak, but as the fire turned to embers and faded to ash, the snow soon found its way into the shelter. Sam shivered beneath the thin blanket he'd salvaged from his gear. Weak, wounded and freezing, he crawled to what remained of his tinder stash and returned with an armload of twigs and sticks. Tango lifted his head for a second and then returned it to rest on his paws. Sam stacked the tinder around another quick fuel disc; within seconds, he'd coaxed the small fire back to life.

As the fire warmed the small enclosure, Sam began to drift off to sleep again. This time, sleep was restless, filled with violent images—men dressed in the black uniform of Islamic assassins.

"Jackals," Sam muttered in his sleep. At the sound of his voice, Tango twitched his ears. Sam's dream was vivid with the smell of gunpowder and death. He rolled and twisted as he slept, but eventually the dreams faded and he rested easy.

The sun had chased the clouds from the sky, the chill from the air, when Sam's eyes finally opened. He awoke to water dripping on one cheek as snow from the ledge above melted. He checked the dressings on his wounds and repacked them with the clay-and-ash poultice. It would probably be useless to repack Tango's wound, he realized; the wolf had licked the previous night's packing from his wound, leaving the gaping hole to scab over.

"We need something to eat, little brother. We won't last another day in this cold without some calories."

Suddenly, Tango raised his ears and peered through the opening of the shelter. Sam froze and listened. High above them on the mountain, the lone cry of a coyote pierced the morning silence. As the call faded, the chorus of a pack joined the song. They howled and cackled an announcement to the world: they'd had found a meal!

Sam's eyes widened. "Patton!"

He crawled from the opening between the boulders, grimacing in pain as he got to his feet. He limped along the trail, struggling for a foothold in the melting snow, slipping where it had turned to mud. The racket of hungry scavengers drew closer, zeroing in on the scent of the dead horse.

Sam all but crawled the last few yards up the hill. There, the terrain leveled near the trail where Patton's carcass lay. The wind blew down the mountain into Sam's face, so he knew the dogs would be unlikely to smell his approach. He picked up a solid branch and gripped it like a baseball bat.

"Here goes nothing," he hissed.

With no more forethought, Sam stormed into the clearing, where the coyotes had gathered to feast.

"No!" he shouted.

The dogs raised their heads to look at Sam and froze. For a long moment, time seemed to stand still. Sam expected them to run at any second, but they held their ground. The dog closest to Sam glared at the intrusion, growling deep in its throat. It took a step toward Sam, then another. The others moved in coordination with their leader. As the pack drew closer, the dogs instinctively fanned out, peeling off at the edges to flank Sam.

Sam wielded the branch like a club with one hand and brandished his knife with the other. "Come on, you sons of bitches! If it's death you want, it's death you'll have!"

As the alpha launched forth, a black missile exploded from the brush behind Sam and crashed into the first three animals, sending them tumbling. The black wolf snatched up the closest coyote by its throat and snapped its neck with a mighty twist. Tango dropped the limp carcass like a rag and stood over the body. With fangs bared and fur standing on end, the huge animal began to growl.

Sam fell still at Tango's display of incredible ferociousness. The pack's attention was all on Tango now; three of the larger males circled the lone wolf, waiting for an opening to strike. They'd all but forgotten about Sam. When one circled too close to Sam, the man let his Nighthawk fly; its honed blade struck squarely between the coyote's ribs, buried to the hilt.

The remaining pack now sensed that both Tango and Sam were threats. Noiselessly, they surrounded man and wolf. Sam cocked back his branch as another dog lunged. The club connected with the side of the dog's skull, sending the animal to the ground with its lower jaw broken and dangling uselessly. Rather than put the pack on warning, its cries of pain seemed to drive them into a frenzy of bloodlust. With teeth bared, the remaining coyotes charged. Each met a swift end by club, or worse, in the crushing jaws of Tango the wolf.

CHAPTER 6

Kuruk bolted down the hallway with a speed that seemed unlikely for a man his size. "Where and how many?" he demanded, flipping lights off from room to room throughout the lodge.

"Two teams," Bendigo replied. "One's moving up the road from the south. The other's positioned in the woods to the east."

Kuruk turned to Jennifer. "Where are the horses?"

"We put them out to graze in the back pasture this afternoon."

"Damn. Ours are at the barn, but we only have three. I don't think we can outrun them doubled up."

"What if we outfox them?"

"What do you mean?"

"We have canoes behind the barn, next to the river."

Kuruk nodded. "We'll cause a distraction. Take the river to Chimney Rock. They'll help you get to the reservation. Get the girls to the barn, right now. Move on my signal!"

Jennifer noted the urgency in Kuruk's voice with dread. Her heart pounding, she gathered the girls with their backpacks and weapons and led them to the back door of the lodge. She looked across the room to Kuruk, who waited by a fuse box near the kitchen door. The Apache gave her a thumbs up and she nodded; they were ready.

Kuruk threw the main switch. The lights went out immediately, engulfing the lodge in a blanket of darkness. The only light came from the stars above now, and those who were watching from the distant trees would be lost for a minute as their eyes adjusted.

Jennifer and the girls darted down the driveway and across the corral, slipping noiselessly to the rear of the barn. Jennifer and Sara took one canoe while Theresa, Elise and Tiffany took the other. With snow melting rapidly in the high country, the river raged beside them.

Once the girls were settled in, Jennifer looked each in the eye and whispered, "I love you, girls. Be careful." Without waiting for a reply, she gave the canoe a shove and watched it glide into the current.

Jennifer was gathering her own gear when she heard shouts from Kuruk and the boys. She let Sara clamber into the canoe and handed her a paddle. In the cover of darkness, she and Sara pushed off the bank and began to paddle quietly after the girls. As they rounded the bend in the river, shots rang out upstream; she could only pray the ruse had worked.

The current picked up speed as the river narrowed through steep canyon walls. The canoe rose and fell with the undulating whitewater. The riverbank sped by, and with each second, Jennifer realized she could only be moving farther from Sam.

For well over an hour, Jennifer and Sara fought the river, struggling to keep the canoe upright and pointed in the right direction. They paddled furiously through rough water, yet even when the current finally slowed, Theresa's canoe remained nowhere to be seen. Jennifer couldn't help but worry.

Had their canoe capsized?

Had they been captured?

No, she told herself. *They're better than that.*

Jennifer clung to her confidence in the girls; they were more experienced in the outdoors than most, after all, and had navigated this river countless times.

But never at night, her doubt whispered.

They were adults now, she reminded herself. They had fended for themselves after escaping a compound in Arkansas, years before. They had endured a lifetime of turmoil, yet evil was still knocking on the door. There was still so much to lose.

Shadows appeared over the river ahead; they were about to cross under the highway. If the enemy was waiting to ambush her, this was where they'd spring their trap. Fortunately, nothing happened.

Minutes later, she and Sara drifted past a large and familiar farm. Once upon a time, this farm had been responsible for much of the local produce. Abandoned after the Fall, the buildings now sagged on their foundations, broken windows gaped dark and empty. The former owners had succumbed to the plague, all but one. The sole survivor had fled the isolation of the high-country farm in trade for the security of city life in Denver.

For the first time, Jennifer wondered if her retreat into the high country with Sam had been a mistake. Not that it mattered now.

The moon cast an eerie glow on the valley. With no sign of the other canoe, Jennifer and Sara paddled on. A warm southern breeze caught the long, thin branches of a willow thicket on the river's edge, rocking the leaves back and forth in a hypnotic cadence. Two miles farther downstream, Jennifer spotted an opening in the trees that looked like a good place to land. She and Sara beached the canoe and dragged it several yards into the willows, where they covered it with leaves and dead branches. Once Jennifer was confident it was well hidden, they slung their rifles and packs over their shoulders and began to hike the riverbank toward a copse of trees.

As they approached a clearing, Jennifer slowed and changed her stride pattern—toe to heel, just as Sam had taught her. She motioned for Sara to imitate her steps, and the younger woman didn't hesitate. In low light, one relied more on motion than shape, Jennifer knew; rapid movement would catch the attention of even the most untrained eye.

Slow down, Sam had told her. *Make every movement count, and rest beside good cover.*

Jennifer paused beside a particularly large cottonwood with Sara on her tail. The moon was now high in the mountain sky, providing enough light to see quite clearly. Several yards beyond the cottonwood, Jennifer could plainly see a trail that wound toward a farm. Still no sign of the girls, though.

Somewhere to the northwest, a coyote howled; soon, the chorus of its pack joined in. It was a chilling sound that took over her thoughts for a moment. Sam was out there, somewhere. What if he was hurt? What if—

Focus, dammit.

Jennifer leaned in to whisper to Sara. "Let's follow the trail and see if we can spot any sign of Theresa and the girls around the farm."

Jennifer unslung her M-4 and pointed the muzzle forward with the stock nestled in the pocket of her shoulder. With her thumb, she casually moved the safety lever from *safe* to *fire*. Likewise, Sara made her weapon ready. The two advanced on the farm, keeping their rifles low but ready for business. When they reached the edge of a field, they took cover. Jennifer dropped to one knee and gestured for Sara to take refuge by a nearby tree.

"Take a break," she whispered. "We won't go any farther until we can see better."

Sara nodded and leaned back against the tree. Jennifer settled in to watch the farmhouse. Her thoughts drifted to more of Sam's training.

Don't let low light fool you. If you look directly at something long enough, you'll see something that isn't there. Look away, then look back. Look to the right or left of what you actually want to see. Trick your mind into seeing around the darkness.

Sam had been right, of course. She remembered one night under a full moon when he'd taken her to a meadow close to the ranch.

"Look. There, across the field," he'd said. "There's a man standing by that tall pine, watching us."

Jennifer hadn't seen anything at first; it wasn't until she'd squinted her eyes that she finally saw him.

"There—did you see him move? "

"Yes," Jennifer had whispered, the hairs on the back of her neck standing at attention.

"He's walking toward us, now. Be very still. Can you see him?"

"Yes. I see him."

Jennifer had watched intently. The dark shape of a man certainly appeared to be walking toward them, yet as time passed, the man hadn't come any closer.

Sam rested a hand on her shoulder and whispered, "Close your eyes for a second, and relax."

She did.

"Okay, now open them. Look across the meadow at the largest pine tree. Now look back to the spot the man was, only focus just to the left of him.

Jennifer complied, shaking her head a second later. "Where did he go?" It dawned on her then that she'd been looking at a tree stump the entire time.

"Don't let low light fool you," Sam had said, and she could still hear his words.

Focus, she kept telling herself.

To keep her eyes sharp in the moonlight, she trained her gaze to the left or right of points in the field, rather than directly at any one point. She did this several times until she was confident that the field before her contained no immediate threat.

Jennifer turned her attention to the farmhouse. It was a dilapidated, two-story home that had seen better days. Her eyes drifted toward the barn but snapped back when something caught her eye in a second-story window of the house.

Was that a flash of light? "Sara, did you see that?"

"See what?"

"Watch the house and tell me if you see anything."

Jennifer sighted through her rifle scope to see if she could detect anything. She trained the scope from one side of the house to the other, letting it come to rest on the window from which she thought she'd seen the light. The scope was already straining her eye; she was about to give up when it happened again.

"There," she hissed. "Did you see that?"

"Yeah, but it's gone now."

"It isn't gone. I think it might be a candle or maybe a fire flickering against the back wall."

"What do we do?"

"Nothing. It would be crazy for the two of us to check the place out in the dark. Let's move back into the willows and stay hidden until morning."

"What if it's the girls?"
Jennifer shrugged in the darkness. "What if it isn't?"

CHAPTER 7

The wooded trail winding behind the neighborhood was as soft as baby powder. It had been cleared of limbs and other debris from four boys running up and down it daily. The trees blurred past as Zack hurtled down the path, surging behind broken-down cars and trucks once clear of the woods. He paused to catch his breath behind a decaying repair shop, and then was off again.

These guys are bad. I know they're bad.

The foreboding thoughts pushed the boy to move even faster. Images of what these men could do to his mom and little sister sent his blood into a boil. He'd heard stories of men like these around the campfire, stories about wars and assassins, the horrible things they did.

Zack had to warn the others. He caught an occasional glimpse of the riders between homes and buildings along the way, but the horses were just too fast. His lungs burned, his legs cramped with exertion. The exposed root of an aspen snagged a foot, sending him tumbling down the trail. He lay still for a moment to regain his composure; once he'd caught his breath, Zack took off again. He could see the roof of his home through the trees now; as he got closer, a man's voice could be heard.

"Yes, I hear you, ma'am. What was your name? Lisa, is it? I know these are tough times. We're just passing through and thought we might offer a hand."

Zack inched closer to the property. The one named Rowdy stood on the front porch with two of his men beside him. Jimmy and Eddie stood nearby in the yard, kicking at the grass with their hands in their pockets. Zack's mom wasn't alone; Jimmy's mother stood just behind her in the doorway. Little Emily—Zack's three-year-old sister—clung to her mother's leg.

"Sir, please understand. I appreciate the offer, but the answer is no. Besides, we don't have the enough food for y'all. It's hard enough providing for ourselves."

Zack dropped to all fours and crawled toward a rock garden at the edge of the yard.

"Well, I hate to be pushy," the man was saying, "but your boys here told us that your husbands are gonna be gone for a while. We just thought we could lend a hand till they get back. We won't be no trouble. Heck, if your men approve when they get back, we might even stick around to be a part of your little community, here."

"I'm afraid we can't agree to that. We're not going to give you room and board when you're obviously capable of working and providing for yourselves. There are only three families here in Creede, so there are plenty of places to stay. Just pick an empty house and get to work."

Zack was proud of his mom for standing up to these men. Maybe they'd move to the other side of town or—better yet—leave town altogether.

Man, I wish Dad was here.

Rowdy spat on the porch and grinned. "Miss, I'm afraid that is not in my nature. Work, that is. I'd rather someone else do it for me." He casually reached into his coat to unholster a 1911 Colt .45. He raised the barrel until it hovered mere inches from Lisa's face.

"Go on, Brenda," she hissed over her shoulder.

Jimmy's mom retreated into the house with Emily in tow.

Rowdy sighed. "Matt, go get her, would you? And see if there's anyone else inside, while you're at it."

Zack squeezed his eyes shut frantically, as if the power of his will could make this nightmare go away. But when he opened them again, his hopes sagged.

Matt had returned not only with Jimmy's mom, but Eddie's as well;

he shoved them down the porch steps. They remained on the ground where they'd fallen, too afraid to move.

Zack's mom stood quietly, her gaze fixed beyond the gun barrel into Rowdy Stone's cold eyes. She had no doubt that he was capable of doing terrible things to get what he wanted. She trembled as she forced her lips to form the words.

"What do you want?" she managed to say.

Rowdy laughed and holstered his gun. "See, that wasn't so hard! Let's all be nice—you be nice, I be nice." His eyes traveled down her curves. "But, damn. You are a pretty one. And your little girl? Well, we need to make sure these kids are raised up proper. What you ladies need to realize is that your men—your husbands, the providers of your families—won't be coming home. I know it's an inconvenience, but it's shoot-dead-gum kind of ironic that they went on a hunting trip, and darn their luck—they became the hunted. What's most convenient to us, though, is their trail led us straight to your little Eden, here. So blame them, if you're going to blame anybody. I just do what I do."

Lisa's face was pale. A primal part of her wanted to make a run for it, but she knew how that would end.

"Now this is what's going to happen," Rowdy was saying. "I'm gonna to take you inside for a bit, and we're going to continue being nice to each other. And then I'm gonna leave with your daughter, and whatever the hell else I want. But don't worry—she'll be well taken care of."

Rowdy paused for a moment and turned to face his men. "Boys, kill the rest."

Matt and Luke had already drawn their guns; they were firing even before Zack knew what was happening. The scene was surreal yet covered in a haze, like the clouded stuff of bad dreams. The gunshots seemed far away as Jimmy and Eddie fell lifeless to the ground.

Rowdy leaned casually against a bannister, delegating his evil deeds with the ease of someone born to it. The group leader smiled as his men executed his orders without question, without emotion.

Fear pinned Zack to the ground behind the largest rock in the garden. Jimmy's mom lay lifeless on the lawn, Eddie bleeding out nearby. Zack squeezed his eyes shut again, as tight as he could. His hands pressed tightly over his ears to muffle the sound of gunfire, the unbearable cries of his little sister.

When everything settled, Rowdy took Lisa by the arm and led her back into the house. "I'll be back in a few," he told his men. "Take care of the little girl, and don't let her out of your sight. We'll save her for the Captain."

Zack peered over the rock just as his mom was shoved through the front door by the large cowboy. Zack wanted to move. He wanted to help but his feet betrayed him. That, or they saved him. Hard to say in the heat of the moment.

Suddenly, a series of shots resounded from inside the home. Rowdy burst through the front door and rolled across the porch. Another shot rang from inside and parts of the door flew into the yard. Rowdy darted off the porch just as Brett stepped through the door with his dad's shotgun. He sighted down the barrel at one of the cowboys and pulled the trigger; a load of double-aught buckshot hit Johnny square in the chest, unseating him from his horse. He hit the ground as Zack's older brother racked the action of the pump shotgun and fired another round, this one all but removing Dan's arm.

Frozen, Zack watched as Rowdy drew his Colt and calmly fired two rounds from behind a tree, putting a stop to Brett's revenge. The first round tore through the boy's shoulder, spinning Brett under the impact and knocking him to one knee. He was still holding the shotgun in one hand, trying to raise the barrel, when the second round hit. Zack's older brother collapsed with the shotgun still clenched in one hand; he died with his finger on the trigger.

Rowdy circled Lisa and spread his arms wide. "Any more surprises, lady? Huh? Anyone else just waiting to take a shot at us? I'm down two men, now. Dammit!"

Lisa's chin fell to her chest. "There's no one left," she whimpered.

Dan sat in the grass cradling what was left of his arm in his lap. Rowdy examined the damage, shaking his head. "And then there's you. What am I supposed to do with you, now?"

"Awe, c'mon, man. I can still ride. I got one good arm."

"You weren't worth a damn with two good arms."

Rowdy raised his Colt and before Dan could mutter a word of protest, a hole appeared between his eyes. He slumped like a dirty blanket onto the grass.

Rowdy stepped over Dan's corpse, assessing the rest of the damage. He eyed his remaining men. "Tie the girl up, and don't take your eyes off her. Take turns on watch, and one of you needs to recon the area and round up food and supplies. We'll stay here tonight, then head south to meet up with the Captain."

As Zack lay curled behind the rocks, crying noiselessly, Rowdy grabbed the boy's mother again and shoved her back inside. Zack knew he needed to move in case the men started to look around, so he returned to the woods. At the intersection of three trails, he sat on a log. The junction was marked by three logs with a firepit in the middle. At this spot, the boys had met every morning to plan the day.

Zack cradled his head in his hands and let the tears flow. He would never see his friends again. His brother, either. Not here at the junction, not anywhere.

Zack thought of his Mom and little sister Emily. There was only one chance for their survival now, he realized. And it rested on his shoulders. Afraid but determined, he made his way down the trail toward Jimmy's house, four houses down from his own. He figured it would be a while before one of the cowboys made it that far. Staying to one side of the back yard, Zack kept a hand on the wooden privacy fence and approached the side entrance to the garage.

He turned the knob gingerly, glancing around. The garage's overhead door was closed; he felt safe to enter. Since they had arrived in Creede, he and his friends had made a habit of rummaging through abandoned homes and businesses to scavenge anything useful for survival. Once a fitting home for SUVs and soccer-mom minivans, garages had become secondary storage spaces for anything that could withstand freezing temperatures. It was no surprise that Jimmy's was crammed with stuff.

Zack opened the entry door and emerged into the kitchen. He slipped through the living room and made his way upstairs to Jimmy's room. He and his buddy were about the same size, so Zack threw a cold-weather jacket, gloves and a Yankees ball cap into a pile. He found a backpack hanging from a hook on the wall and carried it into the master bedroom and opened the closet.

He peered inside, his mouth agape. This walk-in closet was huge, bigger than his bedroom at home. It was supposed to be a secret, but Jimmy had told Zack where his dad hid his guns and ammunition. Against the back wall was a large wardrobe. Zack opened its doors and frowned. Instead of firearms, the wardrobe was crammed with women's dresses and evening gowns.

What the heck? Was Jimmy fibbing to me all along?

Zack lingered in front of the cabinet, trying to make sense of the dresses. Why had Jimmy's mom even bothered to keep them? They had no use in this world. More importantly though, where were the guns? Despite a meticulous search of the closet, he found nothing that could be used as a weapon. Abandoning the master suite, he returned to the hallway. As he approached the stairwell, the front doorknob turned downstairs. He dropped to the floor just as the door swung open.

Zack peeked between the bannisters as the barrel of a gun appeared in the doorway, followed by a man wearing a cowboy hat. The armed intruder did a quick scan of the rooms downstairs before he bothered to look up. If Zack had been armed, the guy would've been toast. At least, that's what Zack told himself.

The boy ducked low and crawled back into the master bedroom. His body trembling, he slipped into the closet and closed the door behind him. There, he could only pray that he wouldn't be found. The odds were stacked against him, he knew.

On hands and knees, Zack burrowed beneath clothes that hung neatly from the rod above. He curled into a ball facing the door.

The heavy sound of boots on stair treads rumbled through the house. The cowboy started at the other end of the hall. Zack could hear him rummaging through drawers and tossing furniture in search of supplies. Another door opened—this one only a room away—and the sound of boots on tile told Zack the cowboy was in the bathroom. He was coming closer; it was only a matter of time before he found Zack. The boy looked around the closet and then noticed something; there, at the back of the wardrobe, was a series of scratches on the wall. He'd missed them before; maybe it was the lighting from this angle that brought them out now. It didn't take much to figure out they'd been left by someone moving the wardrobe.

The boy grabbed the back edge of the wardrobe and pulled. Nothing moved.

The bathroom door closed; Zack knew he had mere seconds before the cowboy opened the closet door. In desperation, he threw his whole body against the wardrobe and drove with his legs; the heavy piece of furniture moved, revealing an opening in the wall behind it. Zack pushed his head into the space; nothing but an unwelcoming black hole, but it sure beat the alternative. He squeezed his shoulders inside and within seconds had wormed through the crack, heaving the wardrobe back against the wall with all his might.

Zack stood in total darkness now, knees wobbling. Helpless to do anything else, he could only listen, wait and pray. He'd lost track of the boots when they ventured onto carpet, so he was startled when they clapped into the master bathroom, not twenty feet away. Drawers slammed, cabinet doors clattered.

And then, all was quiet.

Zack didn't dare to move; his heart had jumped into his throat. He'd almost convinced himself the intruder was gone when the closet door opened. The sound of clothes hangers sliding back and forth on galvanized rods was like fingernails on a chalkboard.

"Nothing!" the man grumbled—to no one, as far as Zack could tell. "This place wasn't worth the ammo, much less the trouble of killin' anyone. These folks don't have drugs, booze or guns."

Zack closed his eyes tightly and tried to become invisible as the cowboy opened the wardrobe.

"Damn!" The wardrobe doors rattled and slammed mere feet from Zack. He jumped and held his breath, barely managing to stifle a cry.

The footfalls stormed from the closet and faded. Zack began to breathe as they thumped downstairs. Five minutes in darkness with the angel of death hovering just out of arm's reach was hard for a ten-year-old to handle, yet in the darkness is where he chose to remain for the next hour.

Zack braced his feet against the heavy wardrobe and heaved until it moved. He pushed again, creating a gap large enough for light to get through. He squinted into the space behind him, and as his eyes adjusted to the light, it dawned on him that he wasn't in a simple crawl space where a timid, unprepared father hid his hunting rifles and handguns; this was the war room.

A room where a warrior prepared for battle.

CHAPTER 8

Sam stood with the club in one hand and the knife in the other; blood and fur were matted to both. Tango looked left and right for another attack but found none. Sam collapsed to his knees and clutched his side, trying to catch his breath. He leaned on the club like a crutch. Both man and dog breathed a sigh of relief. The mountain grew silent again, with no memory of the raging bloodbath that had just occurred.

From all directions, scavengers converged on the scene in hopes of an easy meal. Angrily, Sam lifted himself up to shoo a crow away from Patton's carcass.

"Thanks, old boy," he muttered. "You saved me once again."

Never before had Sam considered eating a coyote; yet under the circumstances, the fresh meat of a scavenger was as welcome as an Angus sirloin.

Sam rested only for a moment before setting about skinning one of the coyotes. In minutes, he'd removed the hide and draped it over a low-hanging limb. He then began cutting strips of meat from the carcass. He collected an armload of wood from a nearby deadfall and started a small fire, hanging strips of meat over the flames to roast. Tango hadn't bothered to wait for cooked met; he'd already devoured the less desirable remains of the first coyote.

Sam ate his fill and settled in to skin the rest of the coyotes before the meat turned rancid. By noon, he'd processed the animals. With the hardest part behind him, Sam took on the task of building racks to jerk the meat on. It didn't take long. When he was satisfied with his handiwork, Sam set the racks near the smoky fire, which he kept burning all afternoon to cure the meat. Determined to make the best of things, he hung the hides from tree limbs just beyond the jerky racks, allowing the furs to cure in the smoke as well. Every so often, when he had a burst of energy, he fetched wood from the area's many deadfalls to gradually cover Patton. He placed the saddle and tack on a low-hanging tree limb, along with the rest of the gear left by the assassins.

Tango had spent the day lying in the sun, raising his head now and then to watch Sam work. After retrieving his blanket and supplies from the shelter below, he turned his attention to gathering firewood. By nightfall, he'd amassed enough to keep the meat curing through the dark hours. He knew the smell of death was likely to bring more predators and scavengers; a good fire would be essential to keeping them at bay.

Bears began to emerge from their mountain dens in spring, Sam knew well. The abundance of meat in his general vicinity was worrisome. In the best of circumstances, a hungry grizzly was far more formidable than pack of coyotes; injured and slow, Sam didn't stand a chance against a hungry bear. His only chance for survival would be to relinquish his spoils of war in a hasty retreat.

He would not allow Patton's carcass to be torn apart and gnawed by scavengers of the wild. Sam shoved one of his quick fuel discs beneath the dead timber he'd stacked over Patton's remains; with the wood up off the ground, it hadn't taken long for it to dry in the high-mountain sun. A few strikes from his fire starter ignited the quick fuel. With a practiced hand, Sam laid green spruce boughs on the fire; soon the flames had worked their way up the old wood, swirling around the limbs to the top of the pile. Thick plumes of smoke twisted into the afternoon sky and bent north as if it herded by the southwest wind. Into the night, Sam added wood to keep the fire burning. He watched his old friend turn to bone and ash.

When Patton's fire finally died down, Sam rose and waited reverently for the last flame to flicker out.

"So long my friend," he croaked with his heart in his throat. "I pray

God lets horses in heaven so that one day we'll ride a trail of gold."

Sam rubbed his eyes dry with his thumb and forefinger, wiping the rest of his face with a sleeve. "Smoke's killing me," he muttered to no. Tango whined knowingly. He'd miss the old horse, too, though his grief was easier to hide.

Sam was tired and sore, but he quickly returned to the other fire. He checked the coals and meat strips, turned each carefully. Tango rested nearby, hoping for one of the tasty morsels to hit the ground. Sam smiled at him for a second and let a chunk of meat slip deliberately through his fingers.

"Oops," he complained with a chuckle.

Tango rose gingerly in slow, deliberate movements. The dog was sore, but he still had a healthy appetite.

Sam ate a few more strips of meat as well. They'd both require an abundance of protein to heal. Likewise, if they had any hope of climbing out of the high country on foot, every bit of sustenance helped.

The night sky was clear. Sam made a bed under a large spruce tree close to the fire; the tree sheltered him from above while a bed of dried needles provided comfort and warmth on the ground. He rolled the saddle blanket into a pillow and covered himself with a wool blanket discarded by the assassins.

Damn Jackals. What were they even doing here?

Sam thought about the last few years, the events that had led him to this moment. As big as the country was, he doubted his encounter with evildoers was mere happenstance; he'd been a fool to let his guard down. A chilly wind gusted over the fire, blowing out the flames.

With a groan, Sam stoked the fire again, agitating the coals to flame and crawled back into bed under the spruce tree. Tango squeezed into the space to curl up at Sam's side. Sam gave his friend an affectionate pat and gazed half-lidded into the fire.

Visions of Jennifer flashed through his mind. So beautiful, so fierce and intelligent. She'd been through so much, as had the girls. Realizing that evil was once again emerging from the shadows to haunt the ones he loved, Sam felt awash with despair. With a heavy heart, he fell into deep slumber.

Sunrise was burning dew from the mountainside when Sam finally woke and tried to stretch, realizing immediately just how old and sore he really was. He chewed on a piece of jerky and packed the remaining strips in his saddlebag. With both sides full, he felt confident that—with careful rationing—he could make the meat last for a couple of weeks. The hides were still curing in the smoke. The repetitive chore of collecting wood was becoming more difficult; Sam had to range farther out each day to find fuel for the fire. Days passed. As a veteran of the high country, Sam knew this Indian summer wouldn't last much longer. More storms and even snow were inevitable. He'd soon need warmer clothing and more substantial shelter.

Sam gathered the coyote remains and stripped sinew from their legs, followed by anything else that could be used as cordage. He laid it all across the jerky racks and stoked the fire back to life. He used his knifepoint to puncture a series of holes down one side of each hide and then stitched them together with strips of dried sinew, fashioning a square from six hides. Satisfied with his stitching, he cut a slit in the center of the square to poke his head through. Using similar techniques, the remaining hides were sewn into a makeshift blanket that could double as a pack.

After seven days, Sam felt healthy enough to travel. His wound was healing well with no sign of infection. Tango moved around as if he'd never been injured.

Over the last week, the temperature had steadily risen during the day but dipped into the twenties at night. Sam stood over Patton's ashes one more time and bade farewell to his old friend. He thought about Jennifer and the girls again and prayed they were safe. If there was a team of Jackals about, something big was stirring. With the staff he'd used against the coyotes, Sam started down the trail with Tango at his side. Though he longed to be reunited with Jennifer and the girls, the trail he took did not lead home.

CHAPTER 9

A chilled north wind stirred the spring aspen leaves, rustling them at its touch. The trees swayed gently as if dancing to an old, romantic, love song. Sam's couldn't help but dwell on Jennifer and their life together. God, how he wished that he'd stayed home. Yet he knew in his heart that everything happens for a reason. If what he feared was true, staying wouldn't have changed a thing; the Jackals would've found him there, eventually.

A sound caught his attention. He looked to his backtrail, hoping against common sense to see Jennifer running toward him, but found only a chipmunk scurrying by with a pinecone in its mouth.

Sam had blazed his trail vigilantly so that Kuruk would know where to follow. As he looked to the mountains on either side of the valley, he took note of various landmarks in case he needed to return this way. The sky was blue with few clouds, the heat of the day fading in surrender to the approach of darkness.

A week had passed since Sam left the scene of the ambush; the rigorous toll of hiking the high country in search of the villains who'd killed his horse was rapidly wearing him down. His feet were tired and bruised from navigating trail after trail, looking for any sign that would lead him to the Jackals. The snowstorm and rapid melt had washed away any footprints, leaving Sam to the whims of guesswork. He'd finally decided to follow the path of least resistance down the valley in hopes of intersecting a fresh trail. His wound was healing but a dull ache was a constant reminder that he was a long way from healthy. Worse, his stores of coyote jerky hadn't lasted anywhere as long as hoped, despite rationing. Berries weren't ripe yet on the mountain, and the many streams were too swollen from snowmelt for Sam to even consider fishing.

The valley dipped through a basin that was still soft from the previous storm. Something caught Sam's eye; he crouched to confirm what he already knew. Preserved in the wet soil was the unmistakable imprint of an unshod horse hoof. Actually, there were several, and they appeared to be headed in the same direction.

Motioning for Tango to stay behind, Sam scrambled noiselessly up the bank and peered over a downed log. Beyond was a meadow where a dozen horses grazed. As he watched, he felt something beside him and realized that Tango had moved up the bank to lay down beside him. The wind began to gust, whipping Sam's shaggy hair; suddenly, the horses lifted their heads and looked directly at Sam and Tango. Sam glanced down at his wolf and wagged a finger at the big yellow eyes.

"Stay!" he grumbled. "I mean it this time."

The big dog rested his head on his paws in reluctant acceptance. Sam turned his attention to the herd. He stepped over the log and took a seat on it as the horses grazed indifferently, not at all disturbed by his presence. Occasionally, one in particular lifted his head to check the wind. Sam figured he was the lead stallion. The horse was a pale blue roan with a black mane and tail. All four feet were black as well, giving him the comical appearance of wearing socks. Sam stood with careful movements and took a tentative step forward. Again the horses alerted to his movement, yet once they saw it was only him, they returned to feeding.

These horses aren't afraid. Sam inched forward and waited for a reaction.

Nothing.

He took several more steps, winning little more than a bored glance or two. He laid his pack and staff against a tree and walked slowly into the meadow. The horses met his gaze and watched him for a few seconds; realizing he wasn't a threat, they returned to grazing. Sam moved within a few feet of a large black mare; nearby, the big male lifted his head with a snort, as if to say, "*I'm watching you...*"

Emboldened, Sam turned back to the mare. Chewing on a mouthful of grass, she casually pressed her nose against Sam's chest and inhaled deeply. As the stallion approached from behind, Sam remained still. The roan seemed to be assessing Sam's potential as a threat, though it was hard to be sure. Threat assessment was something Sam was familiar with; under the circumstances, he had to think like a horse or risk spooking the herd.

Sam lowered his head and turned partially away from the herd, keeping a watchful eye on the big male all the while. Sam's body language—he hoped—would communicate no intent to harm the horses.

To his relief, the stallion appeared satisfied, dismissing Sam with a flick of his tail. Sam watched the horse take up his post at the edge of the clearing, where he maintained vigilant watch over the herd.

Sam touched the mare lightly and watched her skin twitch as if bitten by a horsefly. Though wary, she remained unconcerned by the human standing next to her. Sam began to stroke the horse's neck as she grazed; she lifted her head again, nuzzling the middle of Sam's chest. With a surge of emotion, Sam remembered Patton doing the same thing. He started to pull away but hesitated and leaned in instead. As he used to do with Patton, Sam rested his nose on the mare's velvety forehead.

What's your story, old girl?

The mare was jet black with a bit of silver in her mane and tail. She was almost as tall as Patton, but not as thick. Sam bent over at her side and asked for her left foot. The mare hesitated but lifted it. Sam held it across his knee to examine the hoof. Once satisfied, he gently released her foot and thanked her with a rub to her forehead. She had excellent confirmation and her hooves looked remarkably solid for being unshod in the Rocky Mountains.

Sam backed away to watch the mare, chewing the inside of his cheek thoughtfully. She glanced at the herd for a moment and then back at Sam. Abruptly, her gaze shifted past him; her head lifted, ears hinging toward the woods behind him. Sam stole a glance over his shoulder, where Tango sat dutifully at the edge of the trees.

Now for the real test, Sam thought.

With a click of his tongue, Sam called the dog in; Tango trotted to his side without hesitation. The mare took a step forward and bent her head, exchanging sniffs with the wolf. Satisfied that Tango was friendly, she strode back to the herd. Sam smiled. She had accepted them as one of her own, he realized.

"Tango, there just might be hope for my sore feet, after all."

Sam returned to the edge of the trees to rest on the fallen log. He rummaged through his pack for a bag of leather straps and remnants. As cordage was a survival necessity, Sam always kept a bag of leather strips and paracord in his pack. He began to weave strands together, fashioning a makeshift halter. Without a proper bit, his only option was to design the halter as a side pull. He braided lengths of paracord together to create the nose band and used leather strips for cheek pieces and a crown piece. Once the halter was complete, Sam braided leftover bits of coyote hide to serve as reins. The sun had passed behind the mountains by the time he finished. Exhausted, he prepared to camp for the night.

The log Sam was sitting on was one of two trees that had fallen—one on top of the other—creating a v-shaped barrier on two sides. Between the logs, the ground was covered in thick meadow grass that would be comfortable to sleep on. He cleared a place for a small fire and gathered wood. The horses seemed content to remain in the meadow as Sam prepared his bedding. The stars were out when he finally laid down, using his pack as a pillow. He watched the pinpoints of light wink between the leaves of the swaying limbs. He listened carefully to the music of the mountain night, smiling at the once-familiar sound of horses bickering. It was comforting, soothing even. Soon, he couldn't hold back the lids of his eyes.

As the horses continued to move about the meadow and graze beneath the stars, Samson Crow slept.

He woke at dawn. Sleep had been unkind to Sam lately, yet he felt rested this morning as he faced the eastern sky, where morning light was rushing over the mountains. Darkness was quickly becoming gray; soon the landscape began to take more discernible shape. Sam stretched and glanced around.

Tango?

The wolf had wandered off, which was far from unusual.

Probably chasing down a morning morsel.

Sam regarded the meadow and watched a young colt struggle to his feet. Most of the horses were up already, filling their bellies with rich green grass. The colt looked at Sam, his nostrils flaring with curiosity. In a display of youthful hormones, the colt pranced over to the man with his head held high as if to issue a challenge. Sam chuckled and took a step toward the playful colt. The animal darted to one side, kicked his rear hooves into the air and bolted back to the safety of his mother's side.

"I'll catch you later," Sam called after him. "Right now, I need to have a talk with the big guy over there."

As Sam moseyed in the stallion's direction, the roan raised his head and took an inviting step forward. Sam strode slowly to the big horse's side and spoke in soft, comforting tones, assuring the herd's protector that he meant no harm. He stroked the stallion's thick neck, and when the horse predictably lowered his head, Sam held the homemade halter to its nose. The stallion sniffed the leather and raised his head to look Sam in the eye. He held Sam's gaze for a second, shifting his weight uneasily.

Sam prepared for the worst. If the horse made a run for it, Sam had no way to hold him. Sam had placed all his cards on the table by showing him the halter. The stallion had clearly been trained at one time. He might well be too wild now to want any part of that lifestyle again.

As Sam held his breath, the stallion appeared to consider a future under the saddle again. With a nod and a snort, the roan delivered his verdict. The big gray horse turned abruptly and walked back toward the herd.

"Damn," Sam groaned. "Just like high school. Friend zoned again."

He returned to the deadfall where he'd spent the night and tossed his makeshift halter across the log. He reached into his pack for the last of his jerky and examined the shriveled piece of dried coyote meat. With aching feet and a sore body, Sam remembered something Kuruk had told him long ago, at a time when they'd seemed to be on the edge of defeat.

"Be thankful for what you have," the Apache chief had told him. *"Things can always get worse. But most of all, have faith."*

Pondering Kuruk's sage words, Sam was reminded of the seriousness of his situation. He had work to do, with or without a horse. He turned his gaze skyward and smiled. "Father, thank you for this food. May you bless it for my nourishment. Guide and direct me by your will. Amen."

Sam chewed slowly on the last of his jerky and prepared his pack for travel. He neatly folded the halter and laid it across the contents of his pack. With the flap tied closed, he slung the pack across his shoulders, took up his wooden staff and turned to bid farewell to the meadow and the herd of horses.

Much to his surprise, the stallion was waiting no more than five yards away.

Sam grinned. "Well, I guess we'll have to find you a name, now."

CHAPTER 10

Jennifer woke with a shiver. She and Sara had hidden in thick brush at the river's edge, snuggled against each other for warmth under the willows. The night had left a heavy frost on the ground; the cold was almost unbearable. Morning had broken, lightening the eastern sky in ashen tones. Gray blotted out the stars with splashes of yellow and orange in pursuit. Jennifer stole a look at the house and waited, looking for any indication that it was safe to approach.

Sara rolled to one side and stretched, stifling a yawn. "I'm so cold," she muttered through chattering teeth.

Jennifer weighed her options for a moment. They wouldn't last long out here; that much was clear. They needed to warm up, one way or another.

"Wait here," she said to Sara. Rising cautiously, she crept toward the house.

Just as she emerged from the brush, a man donning a cowboy hat rounded the corner of the house. He carried two buckets, heading straight for them.

Jennifer caught her breath. "Quick," she hissed over her shoulder. "Hide!" She crawled back under the brush next to Sara and piled leaves on top of them. "Be very still," she warned. "Don't even breath."

The crunching of footsteps on frozen grass approached the trail leading to the river. Jennifer admonished herself for hunkering down so close to the trail. The crunch of grass transitioned to the grind of gravel as the man neared the river. The hollow slosh of buckets dipping into water was close.

Too close.

Moments later, the footsteps headed back up the trail but came to an abrupt halt. "You ladies ought to come on up to the house; you're welcome to warm up and grab some grub."

Jennifer rolled to one side and tried to catch a glimpse of the man, but the brush was too thick. She stood awkwardly, pulling Sara to her feet and trying to hide her embarrassment. The ladies brushed leaves from their clothes and hair, stalling to think.

The cowboy put down the buckets and tipped his hat with a smile. "Name's Tim. I saw you this morning from the house and thought you might need some help."

Jennifer scrutinized him for a long moment, skeptical but hopeful. Tim grinned at Sara. Blushing, she stepped past Jennifer to offer a hand. "I'm Sara," she said. "And this is Jennifer."

"Pleasure, ladies. Why don't you follow me up to the house, and we'll see if we can get you a little more comfortable."

Tim retrieved the buckets and headed off. Jennifer and Sara slung their rifles over their shoulders. With a discerning look, Jennifer shook her head almost imperceptibly. The young lady smiled knowingly in response. With a wink, she fell into stride behind Tim.

Across the house, two more ranch hands were seated at the kitchen table. Both rose with a start and removed their hats, nodding politely at their pretty visitors.

"Morning, Tim," one said. "Where'd you find these two?"

"They were sleeping in the willows down by the river. Thought they could use some coffee and some food." Tim stepped toward Jennifer. "Ma'am, can I put your things in the corner for you? Y'all step over by the stove and get warm. It'll knock the chill off real fast."

Jennifer hesitated, but surrendered with a smile. "Sure, that would be great. Sara, hand me your AR and I'll put them by the door." Jennifer leaned their rifles against the wall and made her way around a coffee table near the wood burning stove.

They seem nice enough, she told herself.

Jennifer couldn't bring herself to trust strangers, not after all that she'd been through. The strain of torture, of mental and emotional abuse—the assassins had put her through three years of hell, and hell had left scars that would never heal. She stood by the stove next to Sara, keeping her back to the wall so that she could see everyone in the room. Her gaze followed Tim through the den and into the kitchen.

There. A back door. Two visible exits.

Sam had taught her to establish a secondary exit whenever she entered an unfamiliar building. It was a lesson that had paid off more than once.

The house seemed well maintained and nicely furnished. Perhaps too nicely for a group of ranch hands.

Tim returned from the kitchen with a pot of coffee and two cups. He filled them generously. "Enjoy. It's as black as I could get it; not much cream or sugar around here, I'm afraid."

The other men abandoned the kitchen to join Tim and the ladies, refilling their own cups in the den. Tim nodded toward the men.

"Jennifer and Sara, this is Randy and Seven."

The men nodded and slurped their coffee.

"Pleased to meet you," Seven said, wiping his mouth dry with a shirtsleeve. "Where y'all from?"

"Nowhere, really," Jennifer replied before Sara had a chance to give them any real information. Her stomach was in knots. With every passing second, Jennifer felt more assured that she and Sara had been lured into a trap.

Sara sipped her coffee and gave Jennifer a sidelong glance, realizing that her stepmother was in a defensive mode. With no prompting needed, Sara followed her lead. Both women scanned the room curiously, assessing the space for potential threats and resources. Jennifer left the stove behind to casually walk around the coffee table. Pretending to peer outside, she appraised the men from the corner of her eye, noting sidearms beneath their jackets. Sara made her way into the kitchen for a glass of water.

"Seven," Jennifer said with a casual smile. "That your real name?"

"No, ma'am. My real name's Steven. I just met these guys a few weeks ago. There were six of them, and my name is Steven. For some reason, Tim here started calling me Seven. You know—six plus one?"

"Is that right?" Jennifer chuckled.

"Close enough," Tim snickered. "Why don't you ladies have a seat and relax. We've got some friends gonna be here soon, and they're supposed to bring some food."

Sara returned from the kitchen without a cup of water or coffee. Her wide eyes sought out Jennifer's. From one trembling hand, Theresa's scarf dangled like a pendulum.

Tim and Randy had their backs to Sara, so they couldn't see her expression. Seven, however, saw exactly what Jennifer was seeing and reached beneath his coat. Jennifer took a long step back, moving directly behind Seven. In one swift motion, she drew a 9mm Glock from the small of her back and pressed the barrel against Seven's head.

"Hey, hey. Now, wait just a minute," Tim chided as he rose, pushing his chair back from the table. "No need for that."

Jennifer drove the cold barrel harder against his head. "Let me see your hands!" she barked. "Let me see 'em!"

Sara stood nearby, frozen in fear; but then her mind seemed to whirl into motion. Sam's insistent training began to flow through her, awakening muscle memory she'd developed through repetitive drills—drills she and her sisters had performed over and over, day after day until they'd all begged Sam for a break. As everything slowed in her mind's eye, Sara stepped behind the doorjamb for cover and reached into her jacket for her own handgun.

"Don't make me say it again," Jennifer was saying. "Hands on the table. Now!"

As instructed, Seven withdrew the hand from his coat and splayed both hands on the coffee table.

Jennifer gestured for Tim and Randy to do the same. "Go on," she growled. "You, too."

The men placed their hands on the table, watching as she plucked a sidearm from Seven's waistline.

She pointed the pistol at the other two men. "Sara, holster your gun and search those two."

Sara removed two handguns from the cowboys and disabled each by removing its magazine and slide, throwing the loose components across the room.

Jennifer glared at Tim, who no longer wore the innocent smile of a young cowboy. "Where are the others?" she demanded.

Tim answered her question with silence, returning her glare defiantly.

Jennifer removed her gun from Seven's head and drove the barrel into his hand. "How about you, Seven? You have anything to say?"

"Wait, wait," he sputtered. "We can't tell you. He… he—"

The shot surprised everyone but Jennifer. Even Sara hadn't expected her to pull the trigger. The smell of gunpowder was sharp; the sound of screams, overwhelming against the ringing in their ears.

"Seven, get ahold of yourself. Calm down. I'm a doctor, and I can assure you that as much as that hurts like hell, you'll survive that wound. But I can promise you this: you won't survive the next one. Now, where are my girls?"

She moved the barrel an inch above Seven's ear just as he began to cry.

"I'm sorry. I'm so damn sorry, lady," he moaned. "They're upstairs. All of 'em."

Jennifer nodded to Sara, who bolted up the stairs without hesitation.

Tim stared coldly across the table at Seven, shaking his head in disgust. "Coward. Man, if I had a gun right now, I'd shoot you myself."

Jennifer's eyes flashed across the table at Tim, who retained that defiant glare. *How in God's name did I fall for this*?

"Are you assassins?" she asked. "Survivors from the war?"

Tim smirked. "The assassins you speak of no longer exist."

"Okay, then. *Were* you assassins?"

Tim continued to glare openly. It was obvious that the only thing keeping him from killing her was a 9mm advantage. She remembered another lesson Sam had taught her: silence in the face of an accusation is an admission of guilt.

"Mom!" cried Sara from the top of the stairs. Jennifer cast a worried glance toward the stairwell as Sara appeared with an arm around Theresa. She tried to guide her down the stairs, but her older stepsister wasn't much help; she was clearly drunk, or more likely, drugged. Sara was in tears, yet as much as Jennifer wanted to run to her side, she was forced to hold her gun on the men. Sara helped Theresa to the sofa and tried to seat her in an upright position, but Theresa couldn't hold her head up. Her eyes rolled once as she attempted to look around the room, and then she passed out.

"Where are Elise and Tiffany?" Jennifer asked.

Sara just stared blankly ahead, swaying her head from side to side.

A flush of sickening worry overtook the older woman. "Sara, look at me. Where are they?"

No response, which said it all.

Turning to Tim and Randy, Jennifer fought down the urge to blow their heads clean off their shoulders. While Tim's grin revealed a soul of pure evil, Randy's eyes were wide and afraid. One eye twitched, and then something seemed to click behind his gaze, as if a switch had been thrown. His lips formed a wicked smile, ogling the woman holding a gun.

Jennifer met his gaze with unmasked confusion; something was wrong with his eyes, she realized. His pupils were noticeably dilated; his movements had become jerky and erratic.

"That Push is kickin' in, ain't it?" Tim snickered. His own eyes had grown wild too, and from nowhere he started to laugh.

With lightning speed, Randy drew a knife from his belt and leapt onto the coffee table, advancing on Jennifer.

"Yeah, man. Do it," Tim urged. "Kill the bitch!"

Jennifer staggered back against the wall and raised her gun. She fired two shots and paused. She couldn't believe his reaction. Randy looked down curiously at his chest, where two red spots had begun to bloom. He raised his head skyward and unleashed a howl.

Jennifer adjusted her aim and squeezed the trigger again. Randy's head recoiled under the impact of a 148-grain semi-jacketed hollow point; the message center was now disconnected from the body. All watched as the lifeless body crumpled onto the coffee table in a pile.

Jennifer turned to Tim, whose abiding grin revealed no concern whatsoever for his friend's death. "Oh, my God!" he cackled. "You're one evil woman, and I love it."

Jennifer trained her gun directly at him. Seven had all but crawled beneath the table, crying over his mangled hand.

Tim glanced casually at his watch. "Where are our buds?" he asked no one in particular. "They went out to rustle up some chow, and I'm starting to get hungry. "

Jennifer knew she had to end this quickly in case Tim wasn't lying. She fired two more rounds, catching Tim in the shoulder. The heavy pieces of lead spun him around, where he stumbled against the wall.

He slid down the wallpaper and began to laugh again. "Man, you are one mean bi—"

Jennifer finished his sentence with a shot to the head. The den became eerily quiet, except for the whimpers coming from under the table. Smoke from Jennifer's discharged weapons hung low in the air; the acrid smell of burnt gunpowder was strong.

"P-please don't kill me," Seven stammered. "I d-did nothing to your friends. I'm not like these guys, I swear!"

"Get out of there," Jennifer snapped.

The wounded man crawled from under the coffee table, leaving a trail of blood on the carpet. "P-please," he said. "I didn't do anything."

"What were your buddies on?" Jennifer demanded.

Dropping warily into a chair, he swallowed hard. "I-I don't know, some kind of souped-up meth mixed with something. They call it *Push*. Never seen anything like it. Th-they go nuts. I wouldn't take it."

Jennifer's lips clamped shut. "Don't move, or I'll kill you."

"I b-believe it!"

"When are the others due back?"

"Not until tomorrow morning. They went to Pagosa. I-I think Tim was just trying to throw you off."

Jennifer retrieved their rifles from the wall beside the door and laid them on the couch next to Sara, along with the handguns they'd liberated from the wannabe ranch hands. To Sara, she hissed, "If he moves, kill him."

The young woman nodded faintly, still in shock.

"Sara, look at me. I need you to focus."

The girl blinked hard.

"Sam trained us to survive," Jennifer said. "And now we've got to do just that. Are you hearing me?"

Sara wiped her eyes and nodded more confidently. "Yeah, okay. I got this."

"Good. Now, where are Elise and Tiff?"

The younger woman stifled a sob and tried to regain her composure. "Upstairs. Last room on the right."

Sara picked up her rifle and shuffled to where Seven sat. She sat on the coffee table and thumbed off the safety on her AR-15. She let the rifle rest across her legs with the barrel leveled evenly on Seven. Her fingers wrapped expertly around the pistol grip, her index finger brushing the trigger eagerly. "See what I've done here?" she glowered with pained eyes.

"Yeah," Seven replied quietly. "I get the picture."

Jennifer made her way upstairs and down the hallway. She paused at the last door to gather her wits. With a deep breath, she pushed it open.

Once upon a time, children had laughed and played inside—little girls, based on the decor. A pair of twin beds divided the room, along with matching chests of drawers positioned across from each other. Girlish drawings and family photos still hung from the walls.

Jennifer didn't look at her girls directly. Instead, she approached the window and pushed the drape aside; she had a clear view from here across the field to the willow thicket where she and Sara had spent the night. Three candles had burned down on one of the chests, which explained the flicker of light they'd seen the evening before.

Anguish rushed over Jennifer, shaking her to the core. Then anger and rage took over, consuming her with the realization that she'd been less than a hundred yards from these sweet girls while they were raped and tortured to death.

Shaking, she approached the beds, where the inanimate bodies of Elise and Tiffany were tied. Jennifer recognized the method of torment, based on Kuruk's description. *Death by a thousand cuts*. The lacerations themselves weren't fatal—not individually, that is—but they were painful. Performed by a master, the ritual could last for days. Her only consolation was that her girls hadn't been gone long enough; the ritual had to have been performed in haste.

Jennifer pulled a knife from her pocket and cut the girls' restraints. She wrapped their bodies in blankets from the beds and half-carried, half-slid them down the stairs. She stood at the foot of the stairs for a moment, staring blankly into space. She couldn't yet find the tears; she was too angry to cry.

In a burst of rage, Jennifer stormed across the room and kicked the chair from underneath Seven. "What the hell are you even doing here?" she barked. "Where's the family that used to live here?"

Seven crawled into a sitting position with his wounded hand cradled against his chest. Tears streaked down his scruffy face. "We killed them," he whispered, choking back a sob. "Ma'am, I'm so sorry. I'm not like this—l-like them. I was j-just trying to survive. When I realized what these guys were, I wanted to leave. But I… they swore they'd kill me if I tried."

Jennifer dropped to the couch across from Seven. "Who are these guys?"

"They're assassins. They bragged about all the stuff they did during the war, how they escaped before they could be executed. They've been playing the part of cowboys to fit it in."

"Are there more?"

"Yes, ma'am. There's a bunch. But they don't fight like they used to. They've returned to the old ways, from a thousand years ago. They talked about dressing like locals and moving to their towns, making friends with everyone—you know, to win their trust. And then, when folks least expect it, the assassins cut their throats in the night."

Seven swallowed visibly, his pallor a sickly green.

"These guys? Well, they're messed up. They've been talking about finding kids—little ones, like babies and toddlers."

Jennifer leaned forward. "So you're telling me there's an army infiltrating our communities, pretending to be nice guys so they can kill us and take our children?"

"Yeah, that's exactly what I'm tellin' you. It worked on you, didn't it? If Tim would've worn a rag on his head instead of a cowboy hat, would you have followed him in here?"

Jennifer closed her eyes, trying to wrap her head around this new information. One thing was for sure: things had just gotten that much more dangerous.

What in God's name are they doing with small children? she thought. "Why didn't they kill her?" Jennifer wanted to know, nodding in Theresa's direction.

"They were just saving her for the guys coming tomorrow."

Jennifer nodded. "What did they give her?"

"I don't know, but it knocked her out pretty quickly. They didn't touch her. I think she was supposed to be a gift for the Captain."

"The Captain?"

"An arrogant bastard, way more evil than these guys could ever hope to be. I'd rather die than face him tomorrow, when he sees all this."

"Are there any horses here?"

"Yeah. Four in the stable, probably still saddled from earlier. They don't treat their horses good, either."

"Steven, If I let you live, will you help me with my girls? Help me secure them to a horse so we can get away? I can't stand the idea of leaving them here."

"Yes, ma'am. I'll do my best, but what can I ride? They'll catch me on foot. The Captain's like an Indian scout—he can track anything. I swear, he sees stuff that ain't there."

"You can have our canoe down by the river. It's covered with branches not far from where Tim found us."

Jennifer took a few minutes to dress the wound on Steven's hand. It had begun to swell, but at least the bleeding had subsided. Sara brought the horses up from the barn. With Steven's help, Jennifer and Sara draped the bodies over the back of a horse and tied them in place. Jennifer passed the reins of another horse to Steven.

"What? No, I'll be okay in the canoe."

"Look, your hand is a problem. It's hard enough paddling with two hands, believe me. Just take the horse."

Steven nodded gratefully. "Where will y'all go?"

"Don't take it personally, but I'd rather not tell you. Now, go on before I change my mind."

"You know they'll be coming after you," Steven said.

Jennifer smiled flatly. "Let 'em come."

The path along the riverbank was well-defined, a veritable highway for those traveling on horseback. Jennifer pushed the group hard for the first hour, determined to cover as much ground as possible with the little light remaining. The distant rumble of thunder made Jennifer slow her horse and look over her shoulder. She examined the terrain for familiar landmarks. With her bearings established, she spurred her horse onward.

"What's the plan?" Theresa shouted.

"Let's try to reach Chimney Rock before the storm hits."

"Why push so hard?" Theresa asked just ahead of a distant lightning strike.

"Well, there's that," Jennifer replied, indicating the storm. "More importantly, I don't think we're done with those men back there. I have a feeling they'll be coming soon, assuming they aren't already on our tail. We need to put as much of this world between us and them as possible."

"We can't outrun the storm," Sara argued.

"No, but we can gain some time and maybe find some shelter." Jennifer dug her heels in and urged her horse into a trot.

With daylight quickly dwindling and a menacing storm at their backs, Jennifer guided the girls away from the river; within minutes, they intersected the road to Chimney Rock.

The road had been paved once, but hot summers and frigid winters had taken their toll over time. The wind had filled the cracks with dust while grass and rain did the rest. The once-smooth lane was now little more than a weedy trail of asphalt and rocks. The horses had little trouble with the trail, which was nice; more to the point, numerous stretches of crumbled asphalt would make it difficult for anyone to track the riders.

The weary group rode on in silence, following Jennifer's lead. The sky darkened with cloud cover, as well as the setting sun. Lost somewhere in the memory of the last few days, Jennifer was suddenly startled back to the present by a clap of thunder; it seemed to come from nowhere, yet the intensity of its percussion rattled her teeth. Stinging rain followed, pelting them with water droplets that felt as cold as winter, despite the season.

"Hurry!" Jennifer shouted above the storm. "Follow me, and stay close."

The darkness had deepened with nightfall; the trail was now only visible by the occasional lightning strike. An old road peeled to the right; Jennifer tugged her horse's reins in that direction. She trusted the horse to stay on the trail, and therefore let him have his head. Lightning struck close by again. Jennifer jerked hard on the reins, startled by how close they'd come to an old farm without even realizing it. She dropped to the ground and led her horse around the corner of a barn and opened the door. Cautiously, she peered into the darkened interior.

"In here," she called to the girls.

They followed her inside. Jennifer secured the doors to keep the horses from bolting. She fumbled through her saddlebag for a flashlight and thumbed the switch on and off several times. When it finally came to life, she turned her attention to starting a fire in the middle of the barn floor.

Theresa began to untie the girth on her horse, but Jennifer stopped her.

"Leave them saddled," the older woman advised. "We may need to leave in a hurry." She turned to Sara. "Put the horses in a stall and check the bindings on… on your sisters."

For the first time since Jennifer had seen the bodies of her adopted daughters, she dared to let her emotions catch up to her. She tried to keep moving, to work through the pain. She gathered some wood and busied herself with laying out kindling. When Sara stifled a sob nearby, Jennifer took her in her arms. Theresa piled on and the three embraced for a long time, almost afraid to let go.

"What are we going to do?" Sara whispered.

Jennifer forced a smile. "We're going to survive." She returned to the task of building her fire.

"But what's our plan?" Theresa persisted. "Are we going to carry Elise and Tiff with us? Where will we go?"

Jennifer lit the fire and fed tinder to the flames. "Here," she said, patting the earth beside her. "Sit down with me."

Her blue-green eyes reflected the firelight like gemstones, accenting the ferocity of her words.

"The three of us have faced a lot. For most of our lives, evil men have hurt us over and over. You were raised in the thick of it. I wish things were different, but we have to accept that evil will always be there trying to find a way to beat us down." She wiped a tear from Theresa's cheek. "Come morning, I fear those men will be chasing us and we can't afford for Elise and Tiff to slow us down. We'll hide them in the loft for now. Once this all blows over, we'll come back for them. They deserve a proper burial."

"But where are we supposed to go?" Sara pleaded.

"We can't go back home. They'll expect that; they probably have guys watching for us in Pagosa. I think we need to get lost in the mountains and find Sam."

"That'll be like finding a needle in a haystack," Theresa muttered.

"Okay, let's get everything situated so we can leave before sunup. Sleep if you can. Tomorrow's sure to be a long day."

The younger women stretched out close to the fire on the barn floor while Jennifer rested against a post that supported the loft above. She gazed up at the loft, hoping it would be a safe resting place for Elise and Tiffany until more permanent arrangements could be made. Emotion overwhelmed her again, blotting her vision with bitter tears.

Not now, she told herself, wiping her cheeks dry. She was tired but knew she wouldn't be able to sleep. Her mind was restless with scattered thoughts as she watched the girls try in vain to sleep. She gazed into the fire for a long time. When the flames finally withered and died, she had found a form of peace within. It wasn't pretty, but blueprints for revenge rarely were. Her anger and wit were her greatest weapons; she'd squeeze them for everything they were worth.

The enemy would not go unpunished.

CHAPTER 11

The hidden room had a dry, dusty smell mixed with a hint of gun oil. The space was the size of a small walk-in closet. Zack sat on the floor with legs crossed, shoulders hitching. The only people he'd ever loved or trusted were gone. His dad was dead, his mother held captive. He had to do something to save his mother and baby sister from that horrible group of men.

What can I do?

Zack's thoughts drifted to a story his father had been fond of telling—a tale in which a small, seemingly vulnerable porcupine learned to defend itself with its sharp quills. Even the most ferocious of woodland predators gave the porcupine wide berth because of its defenses.

Zack couldn't hide in this closet forever; if he was to help his mother and sister escape, he needed an equalizer. Porcupines had quills. What did he have?

He turned his attention to the wall of guns.

On one wall was a shelf with a built-in rifle rack. A few of the guns Zack recognized; others, he did not. Beneath the gun rack were stacks of ammunition, along with corresponding magazines. The guns in there were more complicated than the shotguns and rifles he'd learned to shoot on. He would've preferred his own gun over these. The one his dad had given him.

On the opposing wall was a similar setup but with various handguns hanging by their trigger guards on a pegboard. Beneath the shelf were several cases of liquor. Eddie's family had scavenged as much liquor as they could find to store for the future. Whiskey and Vodka were always good for cleaning and disinfecting wounds. Certain varieties were also useful when it came to barter and trade.

Zack returned his attention to the guns. Whiskey was useless at the moment, but the handguns were a different story.

Zack had turned eight just after the Battle of Washington ended. His family had been in Georgia at the time, close enough to the war for his father to volunteer. The involvement of the military coupled with tales of the heroes from Colorado had opened his dad's eyes to opportunities for land and potential wealth to the west. Homes and businesses full of resources had been abandoned. Entire towns were now empty.

The day Zack's family left Macon, his father had met him in front of the house with a sentimental grin. The man dropped to one knee and presented a rifle to Zack, one he would come to cherish.

"This was my grandpa's rifle," his dad explained. "He gave it to me when I was about your age. He died not long after."

The gun was a little rough with scratches on the stock and some wear on the bluing, but it was his. The Winchester model 100, chambered for .243, was the perfect size for Zack. He'd brought it all the way across the country in a scabbard his father had made. Riding his horse with the Winchester hanging from his saddle had made him feel like a real cowboy.

At every stop, they'd bartered and traded services for ammunition. Once they arrived in Creede, the group had begun a systematic pillaging of empty homes in the area. Their ammunition stores grew, as had their supply of canned goods. Yet his parents realized that to sustain a healthy life, they needed to plant gardens and hunt game. More than anything, life after the war had taught Zack that someday, the burden would be his to protect what was theirs.

Zack looked on the shelf and found a handgun he liked. It was olive drab in color, like something a soldier would carry. It was a little big for his hand, but he chose to look at it like his mom looked at clothes and shoes. He could almost hear her voice.

Don't worry, hun. You'll grow into it.

He read the characters engraved on the slide. PMR 30. The pistol had four magazines in a pouch, each loaded to capacity. He drew the handgun from its holster and checked the safety. He leveled it at an empty spot on the wall and racked the slide, locking it to the rear as his dad had taught him. He ejected the magazine and let the slide close on an empty chamber. The gun felt good in his hand.

Satisfied, he unbuckled his belt and threaded it through a pair of corresponding slots on the holster. Returning the handgun to its nylon holster, Zack practiced his draw for several minutes. The nomenclature of the handgun was similar to the one he'd trained on with his dad.

Since arriving in Creede the previous summer, Zack and his father had practiced shooting whenever time and weather permitted. He'd been working with a Ruger Mark IV .22, which he'd learned to shoot very well. The PMR-30 was slightly larger, mostly to accommodate a high-capacity magazine of thirty .22 magnum rounds. With four additional magazines, Zack could keep the enemy ducking for quite a while. Feeling determined, he slid the magazine back into the grip well and chambered a round before holstering it at his side.

He turned to the rifle rack. He needed something with the ability to hit a target farther off than a handgun could hit with any accuracy. A rifle caught his eye. With a wooden stock, it resembled his Winchester. He removed it from the rack and took a few minutes to get familiar with how the action worked. The Ruger .223 Mini-14 Ranch Rifle was a little smaller than his Winchester, but the Ruger had larger magazines, and would therefore hold more rounds.

Like the handgun, the rifle felt good, like it was meant for him. Comfortable with the rifle, he inserted a magazine and charged the weapon to make it combat-ready. As he turned to leave, something else caught his eye; hanging from a hook next to the handguns was a fixed-blade hunting knife. He unsheathed the knife and rubbed his thumb against the edge; it was sharp and tidy. Satisfied, he returned the blade to its sheath and looped it onto his belt behind the handgun.

Zack left the weapons closet and slipped noiselessly through his friend's home to make sure the cowboy was truly gone. At a downstairs window, he parted a set of drapes to peer down the block; from his vantage, he could easily make out two men sitting in lawn chairs outside his front door. His little sister was crying on the ground next to them, bound with ropes.

"Shut up," barked one of the men. "Shut up, you little brat!"

Evening was approaching. He needed a plan to save his sister. A distraction—something to lure them away from Emily. Zack was pretty sure they'd be looking for something to eat soon. His thoughts shot back to the cases of liquor upstairs; if he could somehow get a bottle of booze into their hands…

Zack knew Jimmy had really bad allergies, especially during late spring and summer. The kid's poor mom used to give him some kind of liquid medicine that stopped his sneezing, but also made him too drowsy to play. Zack had taken something similar from his own mother once, when he'd gotten poison ivy all over his arm. He remembered falling asleep fifteen minutes later and sleeping for three hours.

Zack ran upstairs and returned to the war closet. He snatched two whiskey bottles from a case under the handgun rack. He went into the master bathroom, which had been ransacked by the cowboy earlier. In the cabinet beneath the sink, he found three boxes of liquid Benadryl. He opened a bottle of whiskey and poured a bit of its contents down the drain and replaced the brown liquid with the hay fever medicine. He gave the bottle a few shakes and held it up to the light.

Perfect. Can't tell the difference.

He repeated the process for the second whiskey bottle and returned downstairs. In a coat closet, Zack found a familiar backpack—Jimmy's mother had used it to gather berries, if he wasn't mistaken—and filled it with as many canned goods from the kitchen cupboards as he could carry. He grabbed one of Jimmy's coats for Emily and stashed his plunder behind some bushes on the side of the house.

Leaving Georgia to live off-grid had taught his group how to be self-reliant. It required ingenuity and the ability to develop unconventional materials into useful resources. With the help of the other men, Jimmy's dad had moved an old iron wood-burning cooktop beneath a covered patio in his backyard. The man had also stockpiled an enormous amount of kindling from dried-out pine trees. Lighter wood was easy to ignite and burned hot enough to catch even the greenest fuel on fire. The families used an integrated system of solar panels and windmills to power freezers for meat storage. Jimmy's freezer was heavily barricaded in a storage shed next to the house. Winter temperatures kept meat cool enough without much electricity, but the heavily-clad shed prevented bears from raiding their food stores.

The town of Creede had a perpetual crosswind that traveled from Jimmy's house down the block; Zack always knew what Jimmy was having for supper because he could smell his buddy's mother cooking on the old wood stove.

Zack unpacked some elk steaks from the storage shed and laid them in a bowl next to the cook stove. He placed the two Benadryl-spiked whiskey bottles next to the steaks. He struck a match and held it in the belly of the stove until a pile of kindling caught fire. In seconds, the flames had begun to engulf the seasoned wood. When he was sure the fire had taken, Zack returned to the forest trail behind Jimmy's house.

He jogged through the woods for a hundred yards until he reached the back of his own house. There, he dropped to the ground and belly-crawled to the group of rocks he'd hidden behind earlier. He unslung the rifle and laid it on the ground beside him, settling in to watch and wait.

A breeze brushed against his face, tickling his nose with a hint of smoke. Emily was no longer crying, he realized; she lay quietly in the grass, worn out from struggling against her restraints. One man was snoring loudly with his chin resting against his chest. The other was cleaning his fingernails with a pocketknife. A third man approached from down the road with a bag slung over his shoulder, whistling a tune Zack didn't recognize. When he reached the other two men, he dropped his bag at their feet. Full of canned goods, the bag hit the ground with a loud *thunk*, waking the sleeping man with a start.

"As-salaam 'alaykum," the man said in greeting. "Brought some grub."

"Cut it out, Mark. You know we can't talk like that."

The man crossed his arms defiantly. "And who's supposed to hear us way out here?"

"I wouldn't let Rowdy hear you. We've got to put all that behind us, now. You heard what the Captain said: there's no place for religion in our future."

"Look, I don't mind this business of pretending to be a cowboy if it gets us what we want," Luke grumbled. "But why bother with the charade when no one's watching?"

Mark leaned forward in his chair. "Listen, you fool. If one person realizes who we are and what we're doing, you might as well go back to living off scraps in the shadows and wearing assassin gear. Or how about a stinkin' swastika on your forehead? You keep talking like a friggin' cowboy until Rowdy says different, hear?"

Matt scowled for a second. Abruptly, he lifted his nose to the wind. "You guys smell smoke?"

Luke rose from his chair; he and Mark tested the wind for themselves.

"It's out of the north," Matt said.

Luke gave Mark a chin nod. "Hey, go check it out."

Mark, who had crouched to rummage through the cans of food, dropped the bag and followed his nose across the yard.

Zack watched the cowboy pass the end of his house, and then the next one, stopping a house down from Jimmy's to test the wind again. Eyes narrowing, he took a few steps into Jimmy's yard. He glanced back to Matt and Luke with a shrug. Drawing his gun, he disappeared around the house. Minutes passed in silence. Luke and Matt grew nervous. Luke had just resolved to check things out for himself when Mark reappeared from the side of the house, jogging excitedly toward them with something in his hand.

"You guys aren't going to believe this. Steaks and booze!"

The cowboy presented the whiskey reverently, like a cherished treasure. The bottle was old, but it was real.

Old Classic Tennessee Whiskey. 10 years old, 90 proof.

Luke gaped. "Jackpot! Where'd you find that?"

"There's a little cook shack behind one of the houses. It's got a wood stove burning hot with a platter full of steaks beside it. Looks like one of them ladies was about to grill some meat."

Rowdy stepped from the front door, buckling his pants. "Did I hear someone say *steak*?"

"Yeah," Mark replied with a giddy grin. "I guess they were fixin' to have a cookout. The grill's hot, and we found some whiskey."

Rowdy smirked. "Well, why the hell ain't one of you back there cooking?"

Luke thumbed the air in Emily's direction. "What about her?"

Rowdy frowned at his second in command, shaking his head. "Bring her with you, fool."

Luke rolled his eyes at Matt and flicked a hand toward the girl.

Matt scooped the girl up and draped her diminutive body her over his shoulder. The cowboys walked in a hurried procession, two by two, into Jimmy's back yard. The smell of smoke was thick and inviting. One side of the stove had had a smokebox that could be used to grill or slow-smoke a roast. Rowdy opened the box and lowered the grate closer to the embers inside. With a practiced hand, he laid the steaks on the grate and seared each side. Then, he raised the grate to let the meat cure in the fragrant smoke.

"Smells good, boss," Luke said.

"Damn right, it does."

The cowboy closed the smokebox door. Glancing at his watch, he reached for the whiskey bottle and plucked the cork free. Rowdy closed his eyes and passed the opening under his nose, inhaling deeply. "Ahh, the sweet scent of fine, golden corn juice." He lifted the bottle to his lips and took a long pull, swallowing hard.

"Hard bite at the end, fellas," he coughed. "But it's good stuff."

Rowdy passed the bottle on to Luke, who took a swig and handed it off to Mark. They took turns nipping from Zack's knockout hooch until both bottles were empty. Rowdy opened the smoker to check the steaks. They were done. He retrieved each with a pair of tongs and piled them in a cake pan. In the meantime, Matt laid out plates and silverware from the kitchen.

Daylight was beginning to fade. Rowdy noticed a string hanging from a light fixture above the table. He gave it a yank and the light came on. Rowdy delivered the platter of elk steaks to the table with a clatter. Wavering on his feet, he leaned on the table and took a deep breath.

"Whew," he laughed. "Kinda sneaks up on you, don't it?"

The men plowed into the delicious meat, shoving their mouths full with gusto. But as the drink began to take effect, the movements of each cowboy became more deliberate, clumsier. Before long, they struggled to stay awake.

Zack slipped through the woods and let himself into his house, where he bounded upstairs. With his whole body trembling, he crept into his parents' bedroom. His mom was on her back with a sheet draped over her body. Her face was blanketed in thick dark hair, each of her ankles tied to a corner post. Zack noticed that her ankles were bloody where the ropes had torn into her skin.

"Mom?" he whispered, his voice quivering.

There was no response.

He strode to her bedside. "Mom?"

Still no response.

Zack stepped to the window and looked toward Jimmy's back yard. Rowdy was trying to stand with obvious difficulty. Zack returned to his mother's side, brushing her hair back from her face. It was then that he realized something was wrong; her head was resting awkwardly to one side. Worse, she wasn't breathing.

Oh, God. She's...

At once, Zack's knees buckled. Racked by uncontrollable sobs, he held his mother's hair in his hands, burying his face in the covers beside her. It was too much. In a matter of hours, Zack had seen everyone he cared about slaughtered like sheep. Except for his sister, his entire world was gone. No, not merely gone...

Dead.

"I'm only ten years old!" he cried. "You're not supposed to leave me yet, Mom." He let the tears flow for a full minute.

Emily.

She was all he had left. The thought propelled him into motion. He yanked the knife from his belt and cut the ropes from his mother's ankles. He closed her lifeless eyes and kissed her cheek, whispering goodbye through tears that kept coming and coming.

Mercifully, the young boy's sadness turned to anger. He lingered over his mother, wiping away bitter tears that seemed to geyser from within. He wrapped her in a blanket, knowing that he had only a short window of opportunity to save his sister. Whispering a prayer, Zack ran from the bedroom and headed down the stairs.

Outside, he ran back to Jimmy's and opened the gate to his backyard, where he'd stowed his gear. He slipped a hand into the backpack and grabbed the winter coat. From there, he stomped deliberately to the cook shack, almost hoping for an excuse to start blasting. He found Rowdy and his men lazing with their heads on the picnic table. They'd left the oven door open; from within, hot coals radiated enough heat to warm the cold night air.

Unlike her captors, Emily was awake. She looked at Zack through long brown bangs and tried to talk through her gag.

Zack held a finger to his lips. Gingerly, he removed her gag and cut away her bindings. His heart almost stopped as Rowdy twitched and raised his head, one eye looking directly at him. Zack nervously drew his handgun and pointed it like his dad had taught him.

Rowdy closed his eye and let his head drop back to the table.

"Thank you, Jesus," Zack muttered. He holstered his pistol and disappeared into the night with his little sister cradled in his arms.

CHAPTER 12

The Rocky Mountains has a way of speaking to a man's soul. One could get lost in a single breath of morning air, crisp and full of promise, even before the sun had a chance to rise. Samson Crow was far from immune.

He rolled to one side and gazed through the canopy budding above. Despite the rising sun, the moon still shone. Sam blinked several times and cringed at the gnawing in his gut. It had been two days since he last ate. His store of coyote jerky was long gone, leaving him to slowly starve to death. With much effort, he pulled his legs beneath him and got to his feet, stretching achy limbs. Tango trotted over and nuzzled Sam's hand, apparently as starved for attention as Sam was starved for food.

The wolf had returned the day before, and Sam was glad for the company. For several days, he'd busied himself with the task of working the stallion. The horse had once been well trained, but years in the wild with no human interaction had eroded his memory of ground skills. Sam was counting on the horse to regain what he'd forgotten quickly; Sam needed a place to heal, after all, and he needed help getting there.

His wound was healing with no sign of infection, but it was a slow process. The last three weeks had been endured with very few calories; as a result, his health was now at risk.

In his weakened state, Sam walked the horse to a fallen log that could be used as step. Sam had never ridden bareback before; this was likely to be a painful learning experience. He draped his hand-sewn coyote poncho across the horse's back and climbed on. He was uncomfortable, and based on the stallion's whinnies, the poor thing wasn't doing much better. Sam did his best to keep the horse still by gripping tightly with his legs. The horse calmed. Sam held the reins firmly, praying the horse wouldn't buck.

He clicked his tongue and gave the horse a gentle nudge with the heel of his boots. The horse took one step forward, then stopped. Sam nudged him again. The horse took another step, hesitated and then settled into a steady stride. Sam tested his makeshift side-pull rein system with a tug to the right and the horse responded by turning appropriately. Sam urged the horse into a trot, running him in a circle. He then repeated the drill in the other direction. It didn't take long for Sam to realize the horse was special; it responded to the lightest touch. He'd obviously been trained by a master horseman.

Sam slid to the ground and gathered his pack. He slipped his arms through the straps and held his staff in one hand as he stepped onto the log once more. He settled onto the coyote hide; with a click of the tongue and a nudge of his heel, he urged the horse down the mountain. Tango trotted beside him as the sun crested over the peaks to the east. The trio soon reached the valley below, and as the golden orb sent forth its warmth, the heavy frost began to melt. A dense fog stretched across the valley.

Riding bareback was going to take some getting used to. Sam's legs and backside were already getting tender. When the trail widened and opened into a meadow, Sam halted the horse and surveyed the opening. Tango moved farther right, letting his instincts keep him in cover at the edge of the meadow. Sam saw no danger ahead, yet he felt uneasy as if a shadow had been following him. Glancing over his shoulder, he looked from left to right, scanning the woods around him with care.

Nothing. But something just doesn't feel right...

Sam had felt this before—a sense of impending danger that began with a chill. A warning that stemmed from a lifetime of chasing evil, of hunting those who embraced darkness in one form or another. Sam couldn't help but worry that he had little or no defense. He trusted

Tango with his life, but a dog and a stick didn't stand a chance against what he feared was stalking him. Hunting him. He knew inherently that whatever it was, it had to be evil.

An evil he would face soon enough, one way or another.

Sam shuddered at the memory of dreams from days past, visions that had come true. He set his jaw and concentrated his resolve. He needed to focus on the here and now, not demons from his past. He gazed into the meadow and beyond, urging the horse forward with confidence he didn't truly feel. Shaking off the chill, he peeked over his shoulder, convinced that someone or something was lurking just outside his view. He shook his head with worry and urged the horse into a trot.

Something's wrong, he thought.

At the edge of the meadow, Sam slipped into the cover of forest again. Cautiously, he slowed the pale stallion to a walk and ventured through the dense woods. Old-growth pines and spruce blocked most of the sun, leaving the forest floor devoid of plant growth, completely barren, except for deadfalls and pine needles. The trail was poorly defined, yet the soft ground muffled the sounds of his horse's hooves.

Sam kept an eye on Tango, whose instincts held him to cover. The big wolf trotted from one tree to another, constantly testing the air. He alerted to the slightest scent or sound in a spectacular display of the wild animal he truly was.

A brook trickled across the trail ahead. Sam let the horse stop to drink. Tango joined them but kept a cautious watch, eyes flicking to and fro even as his tongue lapped mechanically at the water. Sam was getting weaker by the minute with no relief in sight. The gurgle of water was relaxing; adding to his fatigue, it nearly drove him to dismount and take a nap. But he resisted. He had to move on.

The afternoon sun crept across the sky while clouds gathered in the west. Sam crested a ridge and gazed over the meadow below. His eyelids drooped; his chin slowly dipped to his chest. The stallion continued down the trail into the field with Sam's head bobbing in rhythm with the horse's gait; as the trail veered left, Sam slid from the horse and landed in the tender spring grass. He tried to roll to his side but was too weak. The weeks of rationing jerked meat, of healing from a gunshot wound, had taken its toll. His body couldn't heal without proper nourishment. That, coupled with the stress of constant activity, was gradually shutting his body down.

He closed his eyes for a moment, enjoying the smell and feel of new grass. "Rest," he muttered to no one. "Just let me rest, and I'll be okay. Just need a minute."

Tango nuzzled Sam on the forehead. He licked the man once on the cheek, then sat facing the meadow, surveying the trail in both directions like a trained sentry. The horse remained close by, grazing on the high country's abundant grasses. Sam twitched as a raindrop slapped against his neck.

At once, cold water began to pelt his body, shocking him awake like a swarm of bees. Leaning on his staff, Sam pulled himself up and stumbled to the horse, who grazed on without a care. Sam relieved the animal of his pack and coyote fur and dragged them to the biggest spruce in the meadow. Exhausted, he crawled beneath the branches closest to the ground. He rested his head on his pack and curled under the warm fur blanket. Within the warm embrace of the tree, Sam felt pleasantly safe and secure. He barely felt the rain. The sound of the storm was strangely comforting.

He was asleep in seconds.

The storm rampaged for most of the night, with Sam none the wiser. He woke with a start in the early morning hours as lightning struck nearby. His head snapped up and leaned into the darkness. The complete absence of light was unnerving. Beyond the limbs of the spruce tree, a pair of glowing red eyes returned his gaze. A chill ran through the old marshal, raising the hairs on his arms.

"Come with me, Sam," a familiar voice said.

Sam was immediately reminded of his previous encounter with the fallen angel. He recalled how the Father of Deceit had offered him and his friends the world if they would only join him. Such a small concession.

Sam was very weak, yet he mustered the strength to whisper, "No."

"Aw, c'mon, Sam. Look at yourself. You're knocking on death's door as we speak. You don't have to suffer like this—I can give you anything that you want. If you can imagine it, I can give it to you."

Sam retreated deeper into the safety of the spruce limbs, hoping to somehow escape the nightmare. "Leave me alone," he pleaded, barely louder than a whisper.

"You're dying, Sam. Jennifer's in trouble, and you can't help her in your pathetic condition."

The mention of Jennifer's name triggered a surge of adrenaline. Sam faced the red eyes with ferocity. With fear reduced to a gnat in his periphery, Sam crawled back to the edge of the tree limbs, inches from the glowing eyes.

"Jennifer? What have you done to her?"

"Me? I've done nothing, but the assassins… you remember those guys, don't you? They're hunting her, and they're close to catching her."

"Don't take me for a fool," Sam replied in anger. "Everything that is evil in this world is under your command. Don't pretend to have nothing to do with those who do your bidding."

The eyes flickered, transforming into something almost human. Suddenly a face resolved around the eyes; it was a face Sam remembered from three years earlier. His weakened state forgotten, he crawled from beneath the tree to face the evil one.

"If I'm such a threat to your cause, why not kill me now?" Sam demanded.

"I don't wish you dead, my friend. You might be even more dangerous to me as a martyr."

"Then why do you torment me and my people?"

A condescending laugh. "It's my job! That's kind of what I'm here for. I don't intend to make things easy for anyone, much less you. I have one mission, and that is to destroy as many souls as I can. We both know I have a deadline. One day, all this will end, and Father will bring his wrath down on me. You've already caused me a great deal of grief, you know. Your mere presence on this lovely little planet has given people hope that America—or at least the dream that is America, is still a *thing*. If I could somehow turn you to my side? Oh, that would be my greatest accomplishment."

"Why are you so candid?" Sam asked warily.

"Because I don't need to lie. I can give you everything you want, including Jennifer's safety."

"You're trying to negotiate? What exactly do you want from me?"

"Your allegiance, that's all. One mission."

Sam shook his head. "No, I can't. That would compromise everything I am." The adrenaline had run its course by now; Sam swayed and lost his balance, falling to his knees. Shaking, weak from starvation and exposure, Sam whispered, "No, no. I can't… I won't."

"Well, my friend, you haven't hit rock bottom yet. Think it over. And remember—you have a deadline, too."

At once, Sam was alone. His body still shook as he crawled back under the spruce limbs. Weak and cold, he curled into a shivering ball beneath the coyote blanket and fell fast asleep.

The storm soon found new life and began to rage, yet the shelter beneath the spruce tree held. Tango returned from his nightly rounds, shook the rain from his thick fur and crept into the space beneath the spruce limbs. He found a place close to Sam, circled his chosen spot and squeezed against his friend. He rested his head across Sam's shoulder, then tested the air with his nose. His lips withdrew, flashing gleaming fangs toward the very spot where glowing eyes had lit the night only moments ago. Tango resituated his head onto his paws, but glared ominously into the darkness, sensing the lingering stench of evil in the night air.

The rain persisted into the early hours of morning while Sam slept like the dead. When the storm finally passed, the clouds parted and lifted high above the mountains. Occasionally, the moon peeked through the thick cloud cover. Even diffused by clouds, the crescent shape of Earth's only natural satellite still managed to cast strong shadows. Eventually, the clouds withered and wandered from sight. The sky became a dazzling display of lights that drew the attention of all who were awake to appreciate it, even the black wolf.

Tango gazed across the meadow, where his new brother grazed; by the light of moon and stars, the pale horse seemed to shine. Sensing that he was being watched, he turned to face the black wolf. He met Tango's yellow eyes and nickered.

Sam stirred in response to the horse's voice and tried to raise his head. He felt warm fur next to him, smelled the comforting scent of his wolf companion. All was well. He almost let his eyes close once more.

So tired, he thought. *I need something to eat.*

Sam's survival instinct prodded him awake, driving him to scan his surroundings. He peered from under the spruce limbs and glimpsed his horse in the meadow, looking in his direction. The roan whinnied and moseyed across the field in search of greener grass. Sam smiled as starlight highlighted the stallion's flawless conformation. The elegance and grace of the animal set against the Rocky mountain meadow seemed unnaturally beautiful for an animal whose stature implied so much power.

The beautiful blue roan moved about the meadow, oblivious of the light dancing on his pale coat. When clouds passed overhead, the horse all but disappeared, reappearing at another spot in the meadow after the clouds had moved on.

He's a ghost, Sam thought as the strain of the day drove him back to his bed. He eased back under the fur blanket and closed his eyes. Within seconds, he was asleep again. Tango settled into a comfortable yet alert position, accepting the role of guarding his pack.

Sam stirred and rolled to his side, mumbling in his sleep.

"Shadow..."

CHAPTER 13

As was common for spring in the Rockies, a storm appeared on the horizon and moved quickly across the land. Thick gray clouds gathered in the southwest, blotting out the midday sun and sending the temperature into a dive. A chilling wind hit the ranch house on the leading edge of the storm.

Steven waited patiently on the front porch in an old rocking chair with his feet resting comfortably on the porch rail. He gazed expectantly down the road to the east. Rain began to fall, puddling the dirt road. It didn't take long for the tracks left by Jennifer and her girls to turn to mush.

Steven laughed and hinged his head skyward. "I see what you did there, Father. Nice move, but I'll find them. And sooner or later, they'll lead me to Crow."

Steven flexed his injured hand and removed the bandage. He balled a fist and then stretched his fingers, revealing unblemished skin without the faintest trace of a scar, much less an open wound.

"Malphus, what are you doing here?"

At the invocation of his real name, Steven turned to regard a bearded old man in a white bathrobe. "Logos! So good to see you, my friend. Where have you been keeping yourself?"

The old man retrieved his pipe and packed it for a smoke. "You know where I've been, Malphus. I've been where you should be. The eons haven't been kind to you, my brother of old. You've aged poorly."

"Is that right?"

"Sadly, the evil you've come to embrace has made you quite ugly. But still, I do miss you. Home hasn't been the same since you fled with your master."

The fallen angel sat quietly for a long moment, appraising the old man as he lit his pipe.

"You've never been one to mince words, Logos. Thank you for your candor. In a way, I still miss walking the corridors of the ancients with my brothers. But I had to follow my destiny."

"You had a choice, Malphus. No one made it for you—it was yours, and yours alone."

"You're no different than I am, Logos. The fact that you sit here indulging in earthly pleasures proves that. I accepted my choice long ago, and I'll embrace eternal fire one day. But when I do, I'll have enjoyed pleasures you cannot imagine."

Logos settled in next to Malphus and puffed his pipe.

"I agree—we aren't much different, old friend. A single decision is all that separates us. I chose to follow our creator. You chose to follow one of his creations. One is good, the other evil. Father never thought too highly of rebellion."

The angel and demon sat in silence for a time. Long ago, the two had been close friends but mountains of time and contrary choices had risen between them. They were enemies now, though neither could deny a persistent fondness for the other.

Malphus watched the rain while Logos savored his pipe until there was nothing left to smoke.

"Logos, why are you here?"

The older man leaned forward in his chair to hold his pipe over the railing. He slapped the bowl against an open palm, dislodging a shower of ashes. With a burdened sigh, he returned the pipe to his pocket and turned to face his old friend.

"What do you mean to do with the girls, Malphus? You've already taken two."

"I didn't touch either of them. I never intended to bring them harm.

The deviance of some humans never ceases to amaze me. It truly has limitless possibilities. A little taste of depravity goes a long way. Killing is highly addictive, like a drug to these animals. They build a tolerance quickly, and as with any addiction, they need more. They'll do anything to satisfy their cravings. All they need is a little *Push*, if you'll pardon the pun."

"Is that what you call the drug you've been feeding them?"

Malphus smiled. "You always did catch on quick, Logos. We have them convinced they're unique to this world. Elite warriors trained to be assassins, just as we did in Persia a thousand years ago."

"Why make addicts of your warriors?"

"I'm afraid that's out of my control, brother. My plan was to give *Push* to the people and let the evil nature of addiction destroy families, towns and communities. It was forbidden to our assassins until Lucifer saw how much more destructive the drug made them. Once, they were addicted to their religion, which made them the most feared warriors in history. Now that their religion has failed them, they've been reduced to little more than common thugs."

"Tell me about the girls."

Malphus smiled. "I can only tell you this: I won't let any harm come to them until Samson Crow is destroyed. The man has become a thorn in Master's side; he must be turned or slayed."

Logos nodded thoughtfully as the rain changed to a drizzle. "Crow will not be turned. You must know that." He rose and ambled to the edge of the porch, where he leaned against a corner bannister. He smiled at the puddled muck that had been a road only minutes earlier. "I guess I'm done. I've had my smoke and a good conversation with an old friend. I don't suppose I can convince you to return home with me?"

Malphus smirked. "Not for all the souls in this world," he said, but Logos was already gone, leaving the demon's words to fall on an empty porch. He leaned back in his chair and lost himself in memories from long ago, memories of a time when his friend mattered, when his father still looked upon him with affection.

The clouds soon passed, and the sky became clear. The demon beheld the sunset and shook his head.

Father's creation, he thought with tears in his eyes, *the beauty of it never gets old.*

He watched the golden orb fall behind the western peaks and thought again of Logos, of good times long past. His gaze fell to his reflection in a nearby puddle. The horrific visage of evil peered back at him. Wrinkled and scarred from a thousand centuries of peddling misery and torment had defiled the beauty of Father's perfection. The demon cradled his head in long, spindly fingers and considered the inescapable gravity of his past, of the future. The eternity of it all was overwhelming.

There was no way to justify his decision to follow Master, he knew. Unlike humans, fallen angels could not be forgiven. Logos was right—Father did not favor rebellion, even if the mission wasn't based on defeating Father. Malphus was fully aware of his destiny, yet he blindly followed Master down this path of destruction. Their mission was to destroy lives and capture souls. Malphus had initially followed Lucifer because, like his brother, he was envious of humans; he wanted God's perfect creation for himself. He had hoped this paradise would eventually be theirs and, as the fallen had done after Heaven's Civil War, he hoped to make slaves of the humans.

Master had devised a plan that would surely overcome Father's power; it had been put in motion over a thousand years ago by convincing an arrogant trade merchant that he was a chosen prophet. From there, it was a simple matter of exploiting the man's greed. He would serve as a conduit for the greatest deception in all of Father's creation. He and his followers were a cult of lies; one way or another, the deception would eventually consume every human who turned his back on the Christ to follow the false prophet.

The sound of horses approaching from the east broke his train of thought. He cleared his mind of all distractions and took on human form again. He stood and leaned against the railing as three riders came into view. They dismounted at the front of the house and tied their horses to a hitching post near the porch.

"Where the hell have you been?"

"Sorry, Captain. We got tied up in Pagosa trying to get info on that

Crow fella'."

"Yeah, Cap. Seems he's gone missing, along with his wife and kids."

Malphus scowled. "You idiots. I had the girls here. If you'd gotten back in time, we could've had his wife."

The men knocked mud from their boots before mounting the porch steps. The first rider was tall and lean with a full beard. He eyed the Captain and tried to hide a smile. "So, how'd they get away, Cap?"

"Rob, don't even start. The girls were typical—they trusted us from the beginning because we smiled, wore cowboy hats and said 'howdy y'all.' But that woman—Crow's wife—she was different. She knew from the second Timmy opened his mouth that something wasn't right. She's been tested by fire, that one. There was no fear in her eyes. Only vengeance. That woman took out Tim and Randy singlehandedly—killed them without batting an eye. We can't underestimate her again."

A short, pear-shaped cowboy stepped from behind Rob. A thick mustache plunged from the corners of his mouth and stopped at his jaw line. When he'd finished knocking the mud from his boots, he gave the Captain his undivided attention. "What's the plan now, boss?"

"We'll eat and get some rest."

"But what about the girls?"

"You let me worry about them. You just do what I tell you."

The third rider was barely a man. At eighteen, he had dark hair and a baby face that had invited much ridicule in his teens. Raised at an early age alongside the assassins, the young man never smiled. He possessed a heart as dark and sinister as any demon. Of the three, he was the only one Malphus really liked—probably because he kept his mouth shut. And when the kid did speak, his words were few, his tone cool and sober.

The Captain gazed at the young man knowingly, his mouth curling into a wry grin. "Don't worry, Poe. You'll get to draw some blood soon enough."

The kid had earned the nickname because of his resemblance to the macabre author of short stories and poetry. The young man acknowledged the Captain with empty and soulless eyes, offering a faint nod.

Malphus returned a fond smile. "We'll ride at first light."

CHAPTER 14

The leaf twisted and turned, pulled along by the ice-cold stream toward a small but inescapable cascade. Sam watched as the current manipulated the leaf and launched it over the edge with brutal efficiency. The leaf churned in the falls until the current caught it again and hurried on downstream.

Sam watched in dazed fascination, feeling much like the leaf, with his own life tumbling out of control. It took him a moment to realize that he wasn't weak or hungry anymore, that his wound was gone. No scar or scab. Just… gone.

Sam closed his eyes. Peace and comfort swept over him like a wave of pure joy. The day was picturesque, the temperature perfect. He listened to the wind caress the leaves of budding aspens. He watched a bear drink from the stream, not at all concerned by Sam's presence.

The soft fall of footsteps caught his attention. Sam opened his eyes to find an old man with a head and beard of gray hair, dressed in a white bathrobe and flip flops. Sam chuckled to himself and scooted down the log to give the man room to sit. But the man didn't sit. Rather, he smiled and sauntered by and sloshed into the glacial water, kicking off his flip flops along the way. He sat at the edge of the stream with his feet submerged.

Sam watched with curiosity as the old man embraced the frigid water of the Rocky Mountains with a cringe. Once the initial shock subsided, he flashed Sam a wide grin.

"Come. Join me, old man. You have no idea how invigorating this is. Old age needs a little help every now and then."

Sam laughed. "Old man? Isn't that the pot calling the kettle black?"

"Yes, I suppose it is. I'm much older, but you, my friend, are certainly no spring chicken."

"Don't remind me."

The old man chuckled and teased a pipe from his pocket, along with a small pouch. Loosening the pouch string, he packed the pipe with fine tobacco. When he was satisfied, he tied off the pouch and returned it to his pocket. He planted the pipe between his teeth and produced a match from a hidden pocket in his robe. Deft fingers snapped the match once, then twice. It burst into flame. Sam watched with amusement as the stranger put the flame to his pipe and puffed billows of fragrant smoke until the tobacco was lit. The old man sighed and closed his eyes, savoring the flavor.

Sam rose and sat down beside his guest, plunging his own feet into the stream. Once the shock wore off, he dared to speak. "What's your name?" he wanted to know.

"You may call me Logos."

"Okay, then. So who are you, Logos?"

"Merely a messenger."

"A messenger," Sam parroted. "From who?"

Logos withdrew his feet from the stream and laid them on a rock above the water to warm in the sun. He gave Sam a patronizing smirk.

"Who sent you, Logos?"

"Isn't it obvious? I'm not here to negotiate your surrender, nor will I hold your loved ones hostage. But neither have I come to tell you anything you'll want to hear. You will see my heart and intentions; you'll know me by my actions."

"Then why are you here?"

Logos smiled. "To soak my feet and to sneak a smoke," the old man chuckled. "Some of your human habits are quite irresistible, I'm afraid."

Logos put the pipe to his lips and breathed in deeply. He closed his eyes reverently and exhaled a plume of rich-smelling smoke that closely matched the gray of his thick beard.

"Scotch is another," he confessed. "I've never sipped more than a small taste at a time, but a single-malt highland has an essence that could persuade even the likes of me to falter. I avoid it like a plague. Not that a plague would affect me in the least. It's just a saying, you know."

Sam nodded thoughtfully and slipped into silence, enjoying the peace of the day.

Logos remained reclined with his feet propped on the rock as if napping on a chaise lounge. "I absolutely love this place," the old man crooned.

"Yes, it is nice. But this is nothing compared to other places I've seen."

"No, I mean Earth. This whole planet. Father's creation is so wonderful. I don't get to see it very often, as you might imagine. I'm normally home with Him. I know I shouldn't, but sometimes I envy you humans."

"You still haven't told me why you're here."

"I know. The longer I procrastinate, the longer I get to stay. I'm hoping to return often as this ordeal progresses."

Sam's eyes furrowed. "Ordeal?"

"Yeah, well, I guess it's time I told you. A great trial awaits you, Sam. One unlike anything you've ever seen. The enemy is here, and I'm sure he'll try to get to you."

"I saw him in a dream last night."

"No, Sam. That was more than a dream. He was being nice, trying to take advantage of your weakened condition. Because of your physical state, your mental state is slipping. Your guard is down, making you easily manipulated. I won't lie to you—things are going to get very ugly. Today is just the beginning. I can only give you one piece of advice: keep Tango very close. He can smell the enemy coming, and evil has no power over him."

"Tango is special?"

"Yes. And no. All dogs see and smell evil. They just adapt to their surroundings. Those raised by evil lean toward evil ways—they simply don't know any better. Tango was raised to be good and has learned to be at war with evil, just like his master. Do you not know the story of Muhammed and the black dogs?"

"I know he had them all killed."

"That's true, but there's so much more to the story. Muhammed was to meet with his spiritual guide one day to receive what he was told would be God's word. The messenger missed the appointment and Muhammed was beside himself. Fearing that he had failed his god somehow, he walked outside and lifted his hands to the sky and pleaded for forgiveness. The advisor appeared and told Muhammed that an unclean beast was in his home, and that he couldn't reenter until the animal was removed. Muhammed returned to his home and searched the rooms frantically. He found his young wife Aisha cradling a black puppy. Enraged that a dog had prevented his advisor from delivering the message, he ordered every dog to be killed."

"That's insane. I'm assuming he killed the pup as well?"

"All dogs," Logos replied solemnly. "You must remember that neither God nor any true messenger of God would ever fear one of God's creations. The messenger of Muhammed was fearful of the beast because the messenger himself was not from God."

"So, who was Muhammed's advisor?"

Logos took one last puff from his pipe and blew smoke into the sky. When he looked at Sam again, his expression had hardened. "If the messenger was not of God, there's only one other who could've sent him. God is infinite and omnipotent; He created everything, and everything He created is complete and without flaw. Likewise, His word is complete, without flaw from beginning to end. It stands alone with no need for supplement or clarification. God makes no mistakes."

Sam nodded nervously and started to ask another question, but Logos cut him off with an upraised hand.

"I'm out of time, for now. Despite your weakness, you must get up and move. Follow your instincts and keep Tango close. The enemy is after him as much as you; they've already taken your war horse. I must be going, but I do expect to return soon. Hopefully we can finish this talk later. I wish you well, Samson. Heed my words."

Suddenly, the space next to Sam was empty. He leaned back and rested against the log, considering Logos's words as a light breeze stirred the trees around him. He yawned and rested his eyes. The stream gurgled across the rocks and hissed over the small cascades.

"Move!"

Sam woke with a start. Eyes darting around, he realized that he was still beneath the spruce tree. A perfect guardian on watch, Tango lay next to him with his head up and alert, facing the meadow.

Shadow was still grazing; he turned to glance at Sam as the man crawled from beneath the protection of the evergreen branches and rose to stretch his limbs. Sam caught a familiar scent in the wind and looked around to make sure he was alone. Recognizing the lingering aroma of pipe tobacco, he couldn't help but smile as he bent to pick up his staff and blanket.

Probably my imagination.

Sam waded through the tall grass of the meadow and fitted the makeshift headstall and reins on Shadow, followed by the fur blanket across his back. Grabbing a handful of mane, Sam managed a modest jump, swinging his leg over Shadow's back. The movement was quick to remind him of the bullet wound on his side.

Reality.

He winced and favored that side as Shadow followed Tango down the trail. The pain numbed eventually, allowing Sam some much-needed relief. The rest had been good for Sam, but the rain had all but washed his tracks from the trail since his arrival. He could only hope that Kuruk was somewhere behind him. Either way, Sam continued to blaze a trail for him, leaving three slashes on the occasional tree at head level. Most would mistake it for the hallmark of a bear marking his territory, but a seasoned tracker would easily differentiate the cut of a blade from the slash of claws.

The trail paralleled the stream for most of the way down the mountain. Gradually, the spruce and pine gave way to aspen. The path finally came to an end in a large valley, where the stream connected to a larger creek. Sam peered up the valley and glimpsed a herd of elk grazing. They paid little attention to the motley trio crossing the field.

They've never been hunted, Sam realized. *They don't know to be afraid.*

Sam's stomach began to growl at the thought of a tender elk steak cooking over an open fire.

Yeah, you tell me to move, and this is the thanks I get?

Grudgingly, Sam turned the horse away from the elk to follow the larger creek down the valley. At the other end of the valley, Sam found an old logging road. His hopes rose that he might soon find something more substantial than a spruce tree to sleep under. The sun kissed the mountain horizon; it would be dark before long, he knew.

Tango continued to be diligent on the trail; Sam found himself wondering if Logos had spoken to the wolf as well. Nothing would surprise him lately. Normally, the wolf was off chasing game and scent trails, yet he stayed close by now.

The road turned to gravel, and soon they were climbing again. When they rounded a curve, Tango stopped abruptly and sat, eying Sam with pleading eyes. Just ahead was a driveway with a gated entrance.

Sam raised an eyebrow at his big black wolf. "I'm guessing this is where you want to go?"

CHAPTER 15

Just as Sam turned his horse to face the gate, he heard a loud click. Somewhere out of sight, an electric motor had been remotely activated, opening the gate in a mechanical hum. With a quick glance skyward, Sam realized he was out of time; the sun had all but set. There wasn't much time for a Plan B. Abruptly, a voice broke the stillness of the early evening.

"Don't just sit there gawkin'. Gate won't stay open long. Oh, and if you don't want to blow up, stay on the driveway."

Sam took a moment to blaze a tree for Kuruk, chuckling when he spied a well-hidden speaker in its branches. With a shrug, he urged Shadow through the gate just as it started to close.

I sure hope you're back there somewhere, Kuruk.

The speaker came to life again. "Follow the drive for about a mile and you'll see me."

With dark closing in fast, Sam chewed his lip thoughtfully. If these were bad guys, they would've just killed him on the road. He glanced down at Tango and smiled as the wolf broke into a trot. "I guess we're okay then, huh?"

The gravel drive wound past old-growth ponderosa pines and through the very creek they had followed down the mountain. It continued up a gradual incline across several acres of aspen, and then wound behind a ridge. Eventually, they emerged into to a meadow overlooking the ponderosa treetops they'd passed through earlier.

Sam stopped to take in the view over the trees. He could see most of the drive from here, the creek and the gated entry at the road. Nearby, a small platform spanned the limbs of two trees, supporting two chairs and a spotting scope on a tripod. The tree limbs had been pruned over the years to maintain a natural blind, concealing the platform and any occupants.

"What do you think of our little Eagle's Nest, here?" a voice asked from behind.

Sam stiffened, but kept his cool. "Very defendable. A rock wall at your back and a wide field of fire in front."

"We have a hidden advantage, as well. Mother Nature made this with us in mind. We can stand here unseen and observe everything down there. Because of the slope and the trees between here and the creek, no one can see us; but we can see them. We've got that spotting scope, binoculars and night vision with FLIR technology, as well."

Sam turned to get a look at the man. He was old and willowy. "That's pretty amazing," Sam said. "But I have to ask: why'd you let me in? And why are you spilling your secrets to a stranger?"

"You're no stranger, Mr. Crow. I know who you are. I'd be a fool not to. There aren't many mountain men running around with a black wolf, and you two are practically legendary in this part of the world. Name's TJ, by the way."

"Legendary?" Sam laughed. "No sir, not me. I'm just a man trying to make things right." Sam offered his hand. "Nevertheless, it's nice to meet you, TJ."

"Well, from the looks of things, you've had a rough go of it lately. Let's get you some food and a shower." TJ sniffed and rolled his lips. "Maybe a shower first, from the smell of things."

Sam smiled. A click of his tongue got Shadow moving. The old man led his guests to the back of the meadow. Hidden within the tree line, Sam could see several log homes. To the west, a spring-fed water wheel rolled almost noiselessly in the creek.

Sam slid from the blue roan, took a step and began to stagger. Grimacing, he planted his staff into the ground to steady himself; unfortunately, balance was only part of his problem.

"TJ, I'm afraid I'm going to need some help."

Weak and malnourished, Sam fell to one knee. He caught himself and tried to stand with the aid of the staff, but try as he might, he couldn't muster the strength. TJ bent down, pulled Sam's arm over his shoulder and helped his visitor over to a campfire that was burning outside the nearest home. The old man helped Sam to a chair that looked to have been hand carved from a huge stump. Sam eased into the chair and leaned back. Resting his head against the smooth, sanded surface of the chairback, he felt relief for the first time in more than a week. He watched the fire for a moment, lost in the haze of his weakened state. TJ headed for the house in the old-man equivalent of a jog.

For the first time since dreaming of Logos, Sam noticed Tango leave his side. The wolf darted from tree to tree with his head close to the ground as if looking for something. He circled the entire perimeter of the Eagle's Nest, pausing every so often to give the air a careful sniff. Seemingly satisfied, he returned to Sam's side and rested beside his chair.

As tired as Sam was, he instinctively took time to assess his surroundings. He looked to his left at the houses; they were built close enough to the mountain to enjoy protection from the north wind, yet far enough away for falling rocks to pose no threat. The homes were constructed from logs, rock and mortar; the rooves, sod. But for smoke from the fire, this little community was invisible to the outside world.

TJ returned with a bowl and a cup fashioned from the spiral horn of a bighorn sheep. He handed the bowl to Sam and set the cup on a nearby stump that appeared to be designated for this specific purpose.

Sam smiled at TJ. "Thank you."

He stirred the bowl's contents for a few seconds before glancing up at TJ; the man seemed to be anxiously waiting for a response.

"Smells good. What is it?"

"Oh, it's elk stew. Mostly broth, though. You don't look ready for the hard stuff yet."

Sam nodded and spooned a mouthful of the rich liquid. After weeks of smoked coyote jerky, followed by days with an empty stomach,

Sam's senses all but exploded. The flavor and aroma overwhelmed him as the hearty broth hit his throat. He began to cough. He cleared his throat apologetically, gathered himself and began to shovel the broth down greedily.

Abruptly, TJ snatched the bowl away to stop his guest from eating so quickly. "I'd think a man of your experience would know better, Sam. Take a breather and have some water."

Sam didn't reply. He knew TJ was right, after all. He nodded like a chastened child and sipped his water. By now, the veil of darkness had covered the Rockies. The night was cool and clear with a half moon rising in the east.

"You're not concerned about this fire being spotted?" Sam wanted to know, trading the water for broth. TJ didn't stop him.

"The only way this fire can be spotted is from the air. We have a guard watching the front twenty-four seven. We rotate the position every eight hours.

"We?"

TJ's eyebrows rose. "Oh, yeah. You might not see anyone, but we have quite the little community here. We're very isolated, though, and most of us don't take well to strangers. At all. Matter of fact, you're the first we've let through the gate in ten years."

Sam took his time spooning the broth and sipping water. He was already feeling invigorated by the reintroduction of food and water to his system. "Ten years is a long time to be isolated with the same group of people," he pointed out.

"Yeah, but we like it that way. Some of these people prefer isolation. In fact, most of us would have trouble in populated communities."

Sam turned the bowl up and drained the remaining broth and then set it on the stump. "Why is that?"

TJ moved a chair closer to Sam and sat down. "Sam, I was an investment broker back in the nineties. It seemed everything I touched turned to gold, and I made one hell of a lot of money. I set aside enough to carry me and my family comfortably for the rest of our lives. Early in 2008, I saw the writing on the wall. The economy was on the verge of tanking. Everybody in the business knew it was inevitable; we were in for a long fight for financial survival. But I was tired. Didn't have it in me anymore.

"One day, I went to work and called my finance manager. I sold out. Some of it was for pennies on the dollar, but I didn't care. I had more than I needed. I spent the next year looking for that perfect piece of property. Once I found it, I started a search for some very special people. Eventually, I found them. We disappeared from society and moved here on July 4th, 2010."

Sam considered this. "What do you mean by 'special people'?"

"It took a while, but I finally found a group of warriors who had sacrificed everything—people who had given damn near all they had for the sake of their country. Some were superficially wounded; others lost a limb. Or two. A couple lost something inside that might never be replaced. Today, they're all living wonderfully productive lives at the Nest. Most are down on the backside of this mountain, by the way, hunting or preparing the gardens. But they'll mosey on back soon enough."

As the sun dropped, so did the temperature. From nowhere, the evening air had turned frigid. Light from the campfire danced and flickered against the trees. Women and children approached the fire in small droves and found a place to sit nearby. Sam struggled to rise but managed to remain standing once he got upright, keeping a tight grip on his chair for support. He removed his hat and held it against his chest. With the arrival of each lady, he nodded and offered a polite, "Ma'am."

Shortly after the women and children were settled around the campfire, the men began to arrive from their daily activities. Several took their places with families or friends. The children were well behaved, perfectly content in this primitive setting.

Sam caught a little girl looking at him and smiled. "Hello, young lady. My name is Sam."

She returned the smile. "Hello, sir. My name is Allie." She approached Sam and presented her tiny hand. It all but disappeared in Sam's as he gave it a gentle shake.

"Nice to meet you," he replied with a warm smile.

"May I play with your dog?"

"Well, of course. But only if you scratch his ears. If you do it long enough, he might fall asleep."

Allie knelt beside Tango and began petting the large wolf. Sam glanced around the circle and found the gazes of other kids who were envious, but too timid to follow Allie's lead. Sam waved them over.

"C'mon, guys. It's okay. Tango likes this kind of attention."

The children trickled forward, surrounding the wolf with wide eyes. Sam watched in amusement, fascinated that one of the most ferocious beasts on the planet could be gentle as a lamb with children. He felt enormous pride, watching them interact.

"How was your day, Allie?" Sam asked.

With a little drama—and a hint of embellishment—she responded like a typical ten-year-old. "Oh, I guess it was okay," she said with a drawn-out sigh, which was coupled with a well-practiced rolling of the eyes. "Chores in the morning, school all day, more chores in the evening."

Sam whistled. "Wow, that sounds busy. What did you learn in school?"

"History, math. You know—boring stuff."

"You know what's so cool about history?"

"No, sir. I can't think of anything cool about history."

This drew a smattering of snickers from the group.

With a chuckle, Sam leaned forward, gesturing to the entire group with arms outstretched. "We—you and I—we're living it right now."

Allie's eyebrows bunched with confusion.

The old marshal smiled at the sincerity of her youthful expression. "History is more than words in a book about a bunch of dead people. It was real life for folks just like you and me who lived it. The Revolutionary War, the Civil War, World Wars I and II—each depended on people just like you and me, sitting around a campfire, talking. Who knows—maybe in a hundred years, they'll be teaching kids about *you*."

Allie looked into the fire, her lips parting as if she was seeing the future. "Do you really think I could make history?"

"You may have already."

Sam looked around the fire, its flames illuminating placid faces. Several of the men and women wore prosthetics; every one of them carried a rifle or handgun. All eyes were on Sam as TJ stepped into the ring to address their visitor.

"We meet here every evening for a short time to discuss the day and plan for tomorrow. I know you're tired and aching and would like to get to that shower, but would you kindly tell us what brought you here?"

Sam nodded and crossed his arms, taking a few seconds to gather his thoughts. So much had happened, it was hard to summarize. "Well, to make a long story short, I was ambushed by a group of men. I never got a good look at them, but I believe they were fragments of the enemy assassins we fought in D.C. and Salida."

A wave of gasps and whispers passed over the group.

"Where did this happen?" TJ asked.

"Several days, maybe a week's ride from here. South over the top, close to Turkey Creek Lake. I tracked them for a while on foot, but they left me with nothing and had a pretty good head start. It didn't take long for the weather to take care of their sign."

TJ looked around the fire at the former soldiers, male and female alike. They exchanged glances between themselves with darkened expressions, betraying their own recent encounters with the assassins.

"You've seen them, too," Sam surmised. "What happened?"

TJ cleared his throat. "A week ago, a group of riders passed through the valley behind this mountain. It's a very isolated valley, basically a wilderness area. The very fact that it bordered this property was one of the reasons I chose it. In over a decade, we've never seen evidence of outsiders in the valley. These guys came over the mountain from the south, just as you did. Only, they were one ridge over."

"You seem troubled by this. If they were just passing through, what's the big deal?"

TJ frowned deeply, his eyes flashing in the firelight. "They didn't just pass through, Sam. They took one of our children."

One of the ladies bit off a sob. She got to her feet and took a few steps away from her people. All was quiet for a moment as her husband rose to follow; she waved him off but turned to face him.

"I'll be okay," she whispered. "Stay. Stay and help."

Sam watched the man return to the fire, looking worried and exhausted. The guy probably hadn't slept in days, Sam realized. He returned his attention to TJ.

"What happened?"

"After years of isolation, I suppose we grew complacent. Living like we do, untouched for so long? We thought we were untouchable." He shook his head, swallowing audibly. "Three days ago, Tanner took his wife and daughter to the valley alone. He went hunting while they worked the garden near the creek. The water was higher than usual, so the noise of the roaring water masked the sound of horses approaching from upstream. Jamie—our tracker—believes they used the stream to hide their tracks while they snuck up on Daphne and her little girl, Chasity. They fled the same way they came—following the creek."

From across the fire, Tanner met Sam's gaze. The man was visibly upset throughout the exchange. With tears in his eyes, he added, "When I got back from hunting, I found Daphne beaten, and… and raped. She was unconscious. Chasity was… she was just gone. They took her."

Sam acknowledging Tanner's pain with a sympathetic shake of his head. He tried to rise from the chair. TJ and one of the female warriors stepped to his aid; Sam noticed her prosthetic leg as she grasped his arm. He staggered for a second but managed to stay upright. Sam planted his staff firmly into the ground to steady himself, giving the woman a nod of appreciation. Glancing around the campfire, Sam peered into the faces of men and women who had already sacrificed so much.

His gaze traveled back to TJ, then to Tanner. "If you can help me recover over the next few days, I'll try to get your little girl back. I'll need weapons and supplies."

TJ grinned. "Right now, you need food and rest, Sam. And a shower. Probably a shower more than anything, actually."

This drew a few chuckles, the onlookers relieved for a break from the serious tone.

"Okay, everyone, let's give Sam a breather. Jan, could you bring him some more stew and maybe a roll or two? Sam, you sit back down and enjoy our hospitality. We'll leave you alone for a bit."

"I'm actually enjoying talking to people for a change."

Tango sat up with his ears alerted toward the north. He tested the air with his nose and bounded past the group around the fire, disappearing into the darkness.

TJ regarded Sam with curiosity, and a little concern. "Uh, is that normal?"

"Depends on what's normal for a wolf," Sam quipped with a laugh. "He probably heard or smelled a rabbit. Who knows?"

TJ eased Sam back into the chair as Jan returned with more stew, along with two rolls. Sam was no longer hungry—however small, the serving earlier had filled his shrunken stomach—but he knew he needed every calorie he could get to heal rapidly. His time by the fire was relaxing, driving away the night chill. He turned to TJ, who sat quietly next to him.

"Is that shower still available?"

"Yes, of course. I'll show you another attraction that led me to buy this property."

Now that his food had been given an opportunity to settle, the fat and calories were energizing Sam. He stood without help from anyone, though TJ was ready to catch him at the slightest falter. Sam leaned on his staff and followed TJ to the closest of the log homes.

"Let me get you a towel and some soap. Then I'll show you the bathhouse. I've asked one of our guys to loan you some clothes while we clean and repair yours. He's about your size, so they should fit."

Sam followed TJ through the house, taking in the craftsmanship of the abode's log construction, as well as the homemade furniture. "Did you build all of this yourself?

"Oh, no. Back when the world was still normal, I had a contractor build these homes in preparation for my plan to escape the rat race." He laughed bitterly. "I never imagined that just a short time later, I'd be escaping a danger far worse than a monotonous lifestyle."

Sam tailed TJ out the back door. The old man turned on a flashlight to guide them down a stone path toward the rock wall. Sam gained confidence with each step, and as they got closer to the wall, he noticed that the same stream turning the water wheel disappeared into a large crevice in the side of the mountain. Mist drifted from the opening, thinning and then disappearing altogether downstream.

"The entrance is kind of tight, but it widens just inside."

TJ turned sideways to squeeze through the opening. Sam followed. The narrow entry opened into a large cavern that was lit by strands of LED lights. The space was warm and humid, which surprised Sam; he'd never seen a thermal spring inside a mountain. The lights gave the room a mystical appearance. Sam was mesmerized.

"I don't hear generators," he pointed out. "Should I assume you have solar power?"

TJ nodded. "We have several sources of power. Solar is one. We also have windmills near the summit of our mountain. Plus two water wheels—one that you probably noticed near our homes, another on the creek you crossed earlier. We have more energy than we need. The truth is, we don't need much." He crossed his arms thoughtfully. "Now, I assumed you might want to shave or trim your beard, so I brought scissors and a razor. You'll have to use soap to shave with, though. It's homemade."

Sam nodded, still admiring the bath cave. "How does all this work?"

"Our shower system uses the natural force of the water and gravity to turn a mechanical pump. It pulls the water through a system of pipes to provide a warm shower, or waterfall. Once you've showered, I'd highly recommend a long soak in the pool; it'll definitely make you feel better."

Sam walked to a mirror that hung from the rock wall next to the shower. He scrutinized the man staring back at him but didn't recognize the face. Gaunt with hollowed eyes, his face was that of a haunted soul. He remembered the words of Logos.

A great trial awaits you, Sam. One unlike anything you've ever seen.

"And this is just the beginning," Sam muttered to himself.

TJ turned quickly. "Excuse me? I'm sorry, I'm half deaf."

"Oh, nothing. I was talking to myself. I've been doing way too much of that lately."

TJ chuckled and headed for the cave opening. "I'll be back shortly with some clothes."

Freshly showered and shaved, Sam had been relaxing in the hot spring for several minutes when TJ returned with a shirt, pants and a jacket. He picked up Sam's soiled clothes in one hand and his sweat-stained hat in the other; with a grimace, he looked back at his guest. "I'm not sure we can save these, Sam. I think they're totaled."

Damn. "I'll miss the hat. I've had it for years. It's been everywhere with me."

"Well, you can keep these," TJ said, nodding to the stack of clean clothes. "I'll see if anyone has a hat to throw in the pot."

Sam almost regretted getting out of the spring, but it wasn't long before he was stretched out comfortably on a homemade bed. It was an enormous improvement over sleeping on the ground with nothing more than coyote fur and a small fire to stay warm.

He thought of Jennifer and his girls, praying for their safety. From there, his thoughts bounced from one topic to the next, his mind fighting the urge to sleep.

Where was Tango?

Why hadn't Kuruk found him yet?

Why had the Jackals taken the little girl?

Fatigue finally consumed him, drawing him into a deep, hard sleep.

It seemed he'd only just closed his eyes when TJ shook him awake. "Sam, Sam. Wake up, my friend."

With a groan, Sam rolled over to face TJ. He blinked a few times to clear away the fog and grumbled a response. "Okay, okay. I'm up. How long was I asleep?"

"Almost a whole day. Of course, you needed it. I'd let you sleep to your heart's content, but we have a problem. Our watchman glassed a party on horseback not far up the valley."

Sam slowly rolled out of the bunk and planted bare feet on the cold floor. Stiff and weak, he forced himself into motion. Tango hadn't returned while he was asleep, he learned. That coupled with the news of trespassers in the valley had Sam worried.

"Which way are they headed?" he wanted to know.

"This way, I'm afraid. It looks they're tracking you!"

CHAPTER 16

The sun peeked over the mountains to the east and began to thaw the frost-covered ground. As morning light crawled across the canyon floor, a dense fog gathered in the valley below the Eagle's Nest, preventing the watchman from tracking the men on horseback. Without a word, Sam gathered what little gear he had left and prepared to leave.

"What are you doing?" TJ asked.

"I have to leave. I can't jeopardize the security of your community."

"We'll be happy to help, Sam. What can we do?"

"Stay here and defend your home, brother. Keep your people safe. I'm betting the Jackals already know you're here; they just don't have the guts to mess with an outfit like yours."

"You plan to take these guys on alone?"

"Yeah, I guess. I think that's why I'm here."

TJ chewed his lower lip, eyebrows narrowing. "Uh, why you're here?"

Sam sighed knowingly. "It's hard to explain, and you'd probably think I was insane if I tried."

TJ wasn't satisfied but recognized there was no sense in pursuing it further. "Hold on, then. Go back inside and eat your fill. You're still too weak to do much on an empty stomach. I'll get some supplies while you eat and have one of the guys saddle your horse." The old man headed down the side of his cabin in a brisk stride.

"I don't have a saddle!" Sam called after him.

TJ slowed and glanced over his shoulder. "You do now!"

With a full belly, Sam prepared to leave. As he stepped onto the porch, TJ approached from one of the cabins with Shadow trailing behind him. He carried a ballistic nylon bag in one hand, and from the look of his quavering lips, the load was fairly heavy. For the first time, Sam noticed the door of TJ's cabin was clad in thick metal; it had the appearance of an old bank vault, right down to a combination lock and a five-pronged handle.

TJ dropped the bag at Sam's feet on the porch steps and grinned. "You won't do much damage out there without a little firepower."

Sam went to his knees and unzipped the bag. His eyes widened as he withdrew a rifle.

TJ smiled knowingly. "I thought you'd like that one. I have two armorers here; I think they built that with someone like you in mind. It's a .300 Winchester Magnum, built on an a slightly modified AR-10 platform. The barrel was shortened to twenty-two inches for tactical reasons, but it still has a lot of boom at long ranges. It's a bit heavy for most, but you strike me as a man who can handle such a weapon.

"I'm sending you with ten magazines, twenty-round capacity. There's a load-bearing vest that will carry them all. The scope is a three-to-nine power with a range-finding reticle; it's been calibrated for the exact trajectory of that rifle, along with the custom ammunition we've supplied you with. You've got a laser rangefinder in the bag, too—just in case you need to reach out and touch someone. Also, you'll find two 10mm Glock 40s with six additional magazines. There's a backpack in there loaded with a week's supply of MREs. Oh, and a canteen with a built-in water purifier."

"God Almighty," Sam mumbled. He holstered the Glocks, one on each hip, and loaded the vest with all six Glock magazines, along with two of the .300 magazines. The rest he kept in the backpack. He unsheathed his Bianchi Night Hawk to check its edge. Using the whetstone from the knife's sheath, he quickly honed the blade. Once satisfied with his handiwork, he stropped the blade against the leather on the back of his sheath. He tested the edge on the hair of his forearm; with little effort, the blade left a patch of bare skin in its wake. Sam sheathed the knife and turned to TJ with an outreached hand.

"Thank you, my friend."

"Come back when you don't have so much to do," TJ replied, giving Sam's hand a vigorous shake.

Sam smiled and nodded. "Will do." He slung the rifle across his back, took Shadow's reins and climbed onto the blue roan.

A shrill voice brought him to a halt. "Wait!"

Glancing back, Sam found little Allie running toward him with something in her hand. She skidded to a stop in front of Shadow. With dainty hands, she handed Sam a hat.

Allie's mom arrived a few seconds behind her daughter and smiled at Sam. "My husband's never been much for cowboy hats," she explained. "He'll probably never wear it, anyway. He left early this morning to hunt, but he made a point to tell Allie she could give that to you before he left. We didn't know you were leaving so soon."

"Yes, ma'am. I've got some things I have to take care of."

"Where's Tango?" Allie wanted to know.

"Good question. He wanders off from time to time, but I tell you what: if he comes back here, you hold on to him until I get back. I think he'd like it here with you."

Allie beamed, as did her mother. "Thank you, Mr. Crow. I'll treat him like he was my own."

Sam gave the hat a quick appraisal. It was a tan Stetson; dated, but hardly worn and in very good condition. Sam placed it on his head and adjusted it for a moment. To his surprise, it fit.

He settled into the saddle and tipped the hat to Allie's mother. Without another word, he turned the pale steed around and urged him down the same road he'd followed into the Nest only two days earlier.

Sam worked his way up the canyon toward the last known sighting of the horsemen.

He had to stop them from finding the Nest. With a little luck, he'd lead them away from his newfound friends. The food and rest over the last few days had given Sam a much-needed boost, but he was still only functioning at a fraction of his usual strength and ability. He focused on covering ground quickly, knowing a face-to-face confrontation on the road wouldn't end in his favor.

The fog had all but vanished when he reached the meadow. He stopped just short of the clearing and secured Shadow behind a group of spruce trees.

Sam moved between the trees, using them for cover as he reconnoitered the meadow. Unslinging his rifle, he eased into the tall grass on the eastern edge of the clearing. According to the watchman, the men had been traveling southeast across the open field. Given that Sam had followed this very route, it stood to reason the men were tracking Sam. Yet, the only tracks Sam had seen so far were his own.

A game trail skirted the meadow twenty yards inside the edge of the trees. Sam followed it, moving stealthily from tree to tree. Within minutes, he'd cut the tracks of the horsemen and begun to put their story together. The watchman had spotted them in the meadow just after sunrise. There were four, traveling east, moving slow. Like they were tracking someone. Or something.

Sam followed the trail another fifty yards; analyzing every detail, he learned as much as he could about the men ahead of him. Abruptly, he stopped to kneel beside a track. It appeared to be the partial footprint of a small running shoe. A few yards down the trail, Sam found another print, this one considerably smaller than the first.

They're tracking kids.

Sam recovered Shadow from the meadow and gave chase down the trail after the horsemen. He guessed the men were about three hours ahead of him; if he was right, it would take a miracle to overtake them before they caught the children.

Sam was unsure how well Shadow would perform under saddle in these conditions but there wasn't exactly time for a test drive. With the heels of his boots, he urged the horse into a trot. He leaned forward in the saddle, shifting the bulk of his weight onto the stirrups. Sam was surprised by how well the stallion behaved. His responses were precise and without hesitation, as if he'd been under a saddle for years.

The two maintained speed until they reached a point where the trail sloped into a deep valley. Cut centuries before by the shift of glacial ice, the canyon walls were steep. The trail descended in a series of precarious switchbacks, yet Shadow never faltered. As they approached the valley floor, the sound of rushing water became deafening. A creek swollen from spring melt cut through the valley. They had to be getting close, and since they couldn't hear over the creek, Sam slowed Shadow to a walk.

Horse tracks still trailed ahead of them, boosting Sam's confidence that he was catching up. He dismounted and followed the tracks to the edge of the creek. The bank was still wet where horses had exited the icy water. Sam couldn't imagine the kids crossing that creek; the water was too deep and far too swift.

The Jackals have lost the trail, he realized with a stab of hope.

Sam knew he had a chance now to find the children first, but he also realized there was only a brief window of opportunity. The horsemen might well double back once they realized their mistake.

Returning to Shadow, Sam led the pale horse back up the trail. His eyes darted from side to side, scanning the ground for any hint of where the kids might've gone. Once he reached the base of the switchback, he started to climb. From nowhere, Shadow planted his feet and refused to continue.

Sam tried urging the horse with his heel; Shadow turned his head and cocked his ears up the ridge they were about to climb.

"What's got you spooked, friend?"

Sam examined the ground carefully and let Shadow lead him into the brush. Several blades of freshly-broken grass caught his attention, but any animal could've caused them. Children were small and light; they didn't leave much sign.

The farther he went into the brush, however, the more promising the sign became. He continued to let Shadow weave through the many willow bushes until he finally found what he was looking for. On a bare spot of sandy ground near an old creek channel, Sam found another partial track of a child's shoe.

Suddenly, the splashing of horses entering the stream back at the crossing caused Sam to jump. They were much closer than he'd expected, and all he could do was hold Shadow firmly and pray the stallion would remain quiet. Stallions were territorial by nature, Sam knew; quick to voice disapproval should another horse dare to violate his space. Sam laid a soothing hand over the bridge of Shadow's nose and held the horse's head down, hoping the animal wouldn't object to the passing horses.

Once across the creek, the men came to a halt. Sam heard their voices, but the rushing water of the creek drowned out their words. Minutes later, they spurred their horses up the switchback and disappeared over the ridge.

Sam exhaled a sigh of relief, unaware that he'd been holding his breath to begin with. He scanned the ground again. The ridge was too steep to climb, the creek too deep to ford. The only option for the kids was to follow the creek and hope for a deadfall bridge or a shallow crossing.

As Sam paralleled the flooded creek, the water level began to rise. The last few days in the high country had been unseasonably warm; with ice melting steadily up top, the creek was rapidly breaching its banks. The area funneled into a chokepoint, where two ridges came closer together. He needed to find the children quickly; it wouldn't be long before the creek became a roaring river.

When the willows began to thin, Sam stepped into the saddle again. The tracks were becoming more obvious in the open area; worse were the poor attempts to cover them. In one spot, void of limbs and debris, he found a track left in mud. A stick had been used to distort the track; then, leaves from a nearby bush had been neatly distributed over the track.

Sam smiled.

They're trying, he thought. *Too bad that attracts more attention than the track itself.*

The floodplain of the creek opened into a valley as the ridge on his right faded to the south. The creek sloped gradually toward the center of the valley, spreading along the plain and losing velocity. The sun was high overhead; Sam hoped to reach the kids before dark. They couldn't be very far ahead now, and he knew the riders weren't going to give up.

Sam guided Shadow farther down the creek, moving through a large cottonwood grove. The trees were enormous, their leaves mesmerizing as they twisted and fluttered in the light breeze. Sam brought Shadow to a halt for a moment and peered ahead through the trees.

He thought he might've heard something, and a flash of movement caught his eye. Shadow inched forward, and Sam let him return to a walk. But Sam had learned long ago to trust his instincts.

Something was wrong.

Sam slid the rifle to his chest on its single-point sling and checked the Glock on his right hip. Warily, he pushed Shadow into a gallop, keeping close to the willow thickets along the creek. Again, he saw movement ahead. He sighted through the rifle scope and caught glimpses of color—perhaps clothing?—moving amidst the trees. Try as he might, though, he couldn't identify who or what he was looking at.

He dismounted and tied Shadow to a sapling. With eyes darting about, he removed his backpack and tied it to the saddle rings behind the seat. He crept forward with his AR seated neatly against his shoulder. At over a hundred yards, Sam stopped next to a ponderosa pine and peered through the scope again. The image that filled his view was the face of a sweet, innocent child smiling at her brother. The boy was collecting firewood and struggling to carry it all.

Suddenly, from a ridge off to Sam's left, the horsemen came barreling down the steep embankment, charging directly at the children.

Sam leveled his rifle and tried to pick a shot through the trees, but the riders were moving far too quickly. He let the rifle dangle on its sling and made a run for the children. Blessed adrenaline came to his rescue, fueling him to surprising speeds through the woods. Still, the horsemen were almost on the kids, and Sam was more than fifty yards away. He skidded to a stop and peered through the scope again. He couldn't believe his eyes.

Standing between the oncoming horsemen and the children was a large black wolf with his head low, hackles up and fangs bared.

Tango! So that's where you've been.

Sam scanned the trees for a target to put in his crosshairs. He selected a rider and followed him with the scope, holding the weapon with a steadiness that—given the adrenaline pumping through his veins, and the heaving of his chest—came from experience alone.

Breathe.

Squeeze.

Surprise shot.

A deafening crack of thunder shook the countryside as the rifle launched its projectile downrange. The round splintered wood and scattered bark from a tree, catching Rowdy by surprise. The man jerked his reins to one side with the sudden realization that he and his posse were no longer alone. In that moment of hesitation, the boy stepped defiantly in front of the little girl and drew his own handgun from a holster, firing rounds in the general direction of the riders. Sam's rifle roared once more. The .300 magnum cartridge blasting from a short barrel felt more like artillery munitions than the round of a hunting rifle. He missed again but hit another tree, close enough to turn the rider. The others followed, ducking low as they retreated up the creek. Tango pursued them with an occasional nip at the back legs of the nearest horse.

Sam slung the rifle over his shoulder and walked toward the children.

CHAPTER 17

Explosions rang like thunder as an unknown intruder fired upon them. The two children huddled on the ground, holding their hands over their ears. The horses plunged into the forest, darting left and right to avoid trees as their riders urgently made their retreat.

Rowdy winced as bark exploded from a tree and pelted his face in passing. He ducked low against the neck of his horse and followed his men to safety. Within seconds, they had moved through the dense forest out of range; still, they didn't dare look back. Rowdy slowed his horse to a trot but maintained his heading; he and his men needed to distance themselves from their deadly pursuers as much as possible.

"Who the hell was that?" one of his men demanded.

"It's gotta be Crow," Rowdy replied. "I'm sure of it. I saw that black dog, too."

"We should've finished him at the ambush," added another.

Rowdy scowled. "We didn't know it was him until the dog showed up, you idiot. Besides, would you face that demon wolf without a plan or some kind of tactical advantage?"

Without another word, he headed up a ridge. His men followed dutifully. Once they reached level ground, Rowdy stopped to check their backtrail. No one appeared to be in pursuit. He regarded Matt and Luke.

"You two, ride on to Pagosa and see if you can find another team.

Don't stop for anything. Get a message to the Captain; tell him that Crow is headed toward Creede. We'll wait for y'all at Wagon Wheel Gap, east of town. Follow this creek. It'll take you to the highway east of Pagosa. See you in a couple of days."

The two men headed southeast down the West Fork of the San Juan River without question. The river had long ago cut a valley through the Rockies; it wound around the majestic range and eventually surged into Pagosa Springs. Rowdy watched his men ride down the ridge to a trail beside the creek. Satisfied with his plan, he turned his horse northwest to follow the ridge back toward Sam and the children, unaware that eyes followed him and his remaining companion up the trail.

*****

"Hold it right there, mister," the boy said, raising his handgun.

Sam froze and held his hands in front of him. "Hey, buddy, I'm on your side. I'm here to help."

"We're doing just fine without any help."

Smart kid.

Sam whistled and Tango leapt into the clearing, trotting to Sam's side and running circles around him. The wolf greeted Sam with a series of playful yips and barks, followed by a giddy howl. The enormous animal eventually settled in front of Sam and reared on his hind legs, planting his front paws on Sam's shoulders. Sam's hands remained up throughout Tango's antics, lest he be shot. He stole a glance toward the boy. Unsure if Sam was a threat or not, but swayed by Tango's display of affection, the boy lowered his gun.

"You're Samson Crow?"

"Yes, sir. That'd be me. Looks like you've already met Tango. What's your name?"

The boy swallowed hard. "Zack."

Sam nodded toward the little girl, who hadn't moved a muscle since the first gunshot. "She okay?"

"Yeah. That's my sister, Emily. She's been like this since… since those men killed everybody."

Sam let his hands drop slowly. "What happened?"

Zack's head hinged toward the ground. When he closed his eyes, the nightmare of the last few days all but overwhelmed him. His chin quivered when he finally spoke.

"Our dads were out looking for new places to hunt. While they were gone, these guys showed up. I didn't trust them, so I hid in the woods. They… they killed everybody. Everyone but Emily." He wiped a rogue tear from his cheek. "I got her out of there, and we've been on the run ever since."

His mouth pressed into a thin line, Sam sighed with empathy for the boy. "And your dad?"

"That's how they found us. I heard them talking. They killed him and followed his backtrail to us."

"Where were you living?"

"Creede."

Sam nodded and turned to little Emily. "Emily, you're safe now. You want to go with me and get something to eat?"

She peeked at Sam from under the edge of the blanket. Without expression, she stood and shuffled to her brother's side. Sam called Shadow in with a click of his tongue and helped the children into his saddle. Sam led them up the switchback he'd followed into the valley. Spent, he dug deep for the strength to climb the steep trail. They stopped to rest at the top of the ridge. Sam pilfered an MRE from his pack and shared it with the children.

"These aren't the greatest," he warned, "but they're better than nothing."

Sam kept a vigilant eye on his surroundings, wary of the horsemen's return. He thought about the other child—Chasity, wasn't it?—and wondered where the Jackals had taken her. Tango had stretched out below the trees on a shady spot in the dirt.

"Zack, how did you come across Tango?"

"An old man with a pipe brought him to us. He told us not to be afraid, that the wolf would help us."

Sam smiled at the thought of Logos helping the kids.

He knew I was safe at the Nest and wouldn't need Tango's protec-

tion for a while.

"Zack, did the men do or say anything that might give us a clue who they are?"

Zack thought for a moment. Through a mouthful of military-issued brownie, he replied, "Yeah, I heard one of them say something like, 'aslum alcum' but his buddy got him in trouble for it."

"You mean 'As-salaam 'alaykum'?"

Zack nodded. "Yeah, that's it. What's it mean?"

"It's an Arabic greeting. It means 'Peace be unto you.'"

"What?" Zack balked. "But those guys aren't peaceful!"

"I know, I know. They're probably Islamic assassins. Listen, I know this is tough and it probably feels unfair. But to survive this, we've got to become numb to their evil deeds. Don't let their actions shock you into inaction."

Zack swallowed and gave Emily a sidelong glance.

"In other words, don't let what they do intimidate you into doing nothing. We have to fight back."

The boy's face hardened. "Yes, sir."

"Good. Now think—is there anything else?"

Sam watched Zack try and fail to focus. A million thoughts—images that would never fade—got in the way.

Poor kid. He'd been through so much.

Sam glanced at Emily and found that she was staring at him. "Emily, can you think of anything?"

"The Captain."

Sam barely heard her whispered reply. "What was that? Captain? Who is he?"

Emily's gaze fell to her lap. Sam turned back to Zack.

"What about you?"

The boy shrugged. "I don't know. I heard them talking about meeting up with him soon, but that's all."

"He's coming for me," Emily interjected with a detached quality.

Sam frowned. "Coming for you… what makes you say that?"

"He said they needed me for something special."

"Who told you?"

"The old man."

Sam rose and ventured to the edge of the woods; he looked across the vast meadow of swaying grass, sprinkled here and there with beautiful spring flowers. He could only imagine what the enemy had planned for such an innocent child. He turned back to the children but froze when movement caught his eye.

Across the clearing at the far edge of the woods stood a lone horseman. He blended almost seamlessly with the trees. He'd only been spotted at all, in fact, because he'd moved. The stranger peered over his shoulder as another rider emerged from the tree line, followed by another. Sam bolted back to the children.

"Zack, take your sister and hide in those rocks. Looks like I've got some work to do." Sam unslung his rifle and let it rest comfortably against his chest. It was easily accessible on the sling, freeing his hands for a tactical transition to his handguns if needed.

"What's going on, Mr. Crow?"

"We have some company, and they might not be friendly. Now, get behind those rocks and hide like I told you."

"Let me help," Zack pleaded.

"No. If they get through me, Zack, it'll be up to you to protect your sister. Now hide. I mean it!"

Feeling fatigued all over again, Sam stepped into the saddle and steered Shadow toward the meadow. Just inside the edge of the trees, he slowed to a stop and let the shade of the woods conceal him. He watched the men cross the clearing; they rode casually, as if on a trail ride rather than a hunt. Their horses ambled along, and none of the riders brandished a weapon. As they drew closer, Sam guided his gray stallion into the clearing, where the sun shone bright and warm against his back. He held the reins in his left hand, the rifle firmly in his right. Leaning forward in the saddle, he dug his heels into Shadow's side and urged him into a gallop.

If a fight was what they wanted, he was ready to take it to them.

CHAPTER 18

The storm passed just after midnight. Jennifer was restless. She'd watched Sara and Theresa drift into deep sleep yet failed to follow suit. She quietly gathered her bedroll and checked the rigging on her horse.

She returned to her girls, still sleeping soundly by the glowing remnants of their small fire. She lingered long enough to say a silent prayer for the two and rushed back to her horse. She opened the barn door with care, yet there was no helping the gritty protest of rusted hinges. Her gaze snapped over her shoulder; neither girl moved. Both seemed content. Lost in a dream, perhaps; a happier place or time.

It wouldn't take much, Jennifer thought with an inward scoff.

She walked her horse down the long drive, waiting until she was on the road to Chimney Rock before stepping into the saddle. The night was cold and crisp; the partial moon, added to a wide expanse of stars, provided plenty of light for her to see. She clicked her tongue, urging her horse to pick up the pace. She took the old road back to the highway that paralleled the Piedra River. There, she followed the highway until she came across the trail they'd used for their escape.

Her mind was numb. She felt as if her heart had been torn from her body, leaving her with nothing but hate. She no longer cared about herself, and she knew that Theresa and Sara would survive on their own.

She slowed her horse to a walk, finally coming to rest a quarter mile from the house. She could barely see the clearing and the barn through the trees. Jennifer dismounted and tied her horse to a tree. The ground was still wet from the rain. Without an ounce of fear, or even excitement, she retrieved her rifle and extra magazines. Crouching low, she darted from tree to tree as she drew closer to the house. The lights were off; all was quiet.

Jennifer slipped through the back door of the barn. The horses stirred inside, one snorting in protest of the early-morning interruption. One side of the barn was more like a shop or tool shed. Jennifer cupped a small flashlight with her hand to conceal the beam as much as possible. She let the subdued glow illuminate the barn's interior and moved from shelf to shelf, looking for something useful. In the farthest corner, she hit pay dirt. Two gas cans filled with dirty gasoline.

It probably won't start a car, but it'll burn down a house.

On a bench next to a storage room, she found a collection of nails and screws in mason jars. She emptied the jars onto the soft ground and filled them with the old gasoline. The workbench was littered with filthy shop rags, which Jennifer used as fuses for her Molotov Cocktails. With her rifle slung over her shoulder, she carried the jars from the barn and lined the them up in front of the house. She crept around to the rear of the house and barricaded the back door with a four-by-four post, securing one end against the door and the other against a metal handrail next to the steps.

The house was over a hundred years old, built at a time when windows were a luxury. Not only were they expensive, they made a house harder to heat. The first floor's only back window opened into the bathroom; it was far too small for a grown man to crawl through. Satisfied that no one would be escaping behind the scenes, Jennifer returned to the front yard. The second-floor windows here were high enough to injure anyone desperate enough to jump from them. It was a chance she was willing to take.

Six jars, six windows. The shop rags, old and greasy from years of wiping dipsticks and tractor hoses, lit with little effort. She picked up a jar and hurled it through the lower right window of the house. The shatter of glass was punctuated by an eruption of flames. The farmhouse was old, its timber frame dry and weak; it ignited like paper.

Jennifer worked her way down the line of windows until each had flames bellowing from within. A voice pierced the night.

"Fire!"

Footsteps thumped down the hall, followed by pounding down the stairs. Jennifer stepped behind the old cottonwood tree in the front yard and unslung her AR-15. At once, the front door flew open, slamming against the house; a tall, slender man tripped down the porch stairs with an arm on fire.

At this range, Jennifer didn't have to aim. She instinctively put a round in his head, ending any need to extinguish his arm. Before the crack of her rifle had a chance to fade, another body bounded through the front door. This one a short, pudgy man wrapped in a blanket; he tripped over his fallen friend and took a bullet to the chest before he even hit the ground.

The remaining occupants of the house had become wary now, after two of their own had fallen under Jennifer's trigger. Undoubtedly, they were trying to escape at the back of the house by now. Suddenly, a body crashed through a first-floor window at the farthest end of the house, wrapped in a flaming blanket. He hit the ground and rolled from the blanket as Jennifer fired three shots. The last one knocked him to the ground, where he lay motionless. Jennifer waited to see if anyone else dared to face her wrath. As fire consumed the home, the heat battered her face. It felt good.

It felt like justice.

The roof began to buckle as the fire reached its peak; soon, the flames became too hot for Jennifer to remain close. She was about to retreat when movement in the doorway caught her attention. There stood Steven, just inside the door, seemingly unaffected by the fire. His clothes were engulfed in flames, yet he didn't so much as flinch. Rather, he glared at Jennifer. She couldn't believe her eyes. The fire was too hot, too violent to bear now, forcing Jennifer to back away.

Steven stepped through the doorway, his clothes falling away in smoldering tatters. His skin melted away. What remained was a hell-ish-looking beast, a horribly scarred face that spoke of pain and destruction without a single word.

Jennifer's feet were frozen to the ground, her mind unable to process what she was seeing. Though afraid, she took a step forward and raised her rifle. The beast began to laugh. The sound became a roar that swelled until it drowned out the noise of the burning home.

Jennifer's fear finally took over, compelling her to flee into the woods. There, she hid behind a tree to see if she was being followed. The beast watched her even as he stepped off the porch and lifted the body of the last man she'd shot. He carried the body past the house and into the field, beyond the flames.

Jennifer found her horse and dashed for the road to Chimney Rock. As she rode, the sun began to rise. The light made her feel better, but she couldn't shake the images in her head. She looked over her shoulder constantly, fearing the beast was following her.

More confident as the sun sent the shadows scurrying, she slowed her horse into a comfortable gallop. Finally, she reached the road to Chimney Rock; soon after, she turned down the drive to the barn. Jennifer dismounted and opened the barn door, leading the winded horse inside. The girls were awake now, sitting anxiously around the fire. They had collected more wood after daybreak.

"Where did you go?" Theresa demanded.

Jennifer tried and failed to summon the words. She shook her head and moved close to the fire to warm up. "Oh, nowhere," she finally managed. "Just for a ride. Checked our backtrail to make sure no one followed us."

Sara appraised Jennifer for several seconds. The older woman was clearly agitated. Sara flashed a wry grin. "What did you do?"

Jennifer's game face slipped into a guilty expression, as if she'd just been caught with her hand in the cookie jar. "What?" she argued lamely. "Nothing, not a thing."

Theresa cut her eyes at Jennifer and shook her head. "You're a horrible liar."

Jennifer's gaze shifted to the ground, and then to the fire. She didn't dare look into the eyes of either girl, knowing her fear would be plain to see. "I-I went back to the house."

"Why?" Theresa wanted to know, her eyes wide with dismay. "What were you thinking?"

Suddenly, there was a knock on the barn door. All three women stiffened. Jennifer drew her sidearm and rose, looking around the barn for somewhere to hide.

Sara started toward the door. "Mom, you're kind of messed up right now," she insisted in a hiss. "Just sit down and I'll talk to whoever's at the door."

When her mother failed to yield to Sara, Theresa stopped Jennifer with a hand on her shoulder. "Relax, Mom. We got this."

Sara was nearly at the door, now; Jennifer pushed past Theresa to stop her. "No!" she insisted. "I'll get it."

Sara rolled her eyes but dogged off at the last second.

Jennifer cracked the door open, still holding her weapon. She was surprised to find an older gentleman in a bathrobe at the door. He regarded Jennifer with a comforting smile and packed a pipe with tobacco from a pouch.

"I'm sorry to trouble you, ladies, but may I come in?"

Still visibly unsettled by earlier events, Jennifer couldn't help but question her sanity. She blinked a few times, half expecting the man in the bathrobe to disappear. He didn't. Her gaze fell to his feet.

Flip flops?

After all that had happened over the last few days, an old man wearing a bathrobe in the middle of nowhere might've been the closest thing to normal she he'd seen in a while. She shook her head to focus on the moment.

"Why not?" she said, surprising herself. "Come on in."

Jennifer made a grand gesture of opening the door and showing him to the fire. The girls gaped with bugged eyes. While Sara stifled a giggle, Theresa dragged a hay bale over for the old man to sit on and then took a seat next to Sara, who still wore a goofy grin.

Jennifer gestured for the man to sit. "It's not every day you run into The Big Lebowski in the high country."

The old man smiled and cocked his head. "The big *who*?"

"Never mind."

He shrugged and bit down on his pipe. With a flick of his thumb, a match flared to life and disappeared into the nest of tobacco.

Jennifer cleared her throat. "I'm sorry. It's just strange to see a man your age strolling through the Rocky Mountains this time of year, especially in flip flops and a bathrobe—like it's Pensacola Beach in mid-July. Do you live close by?"

"Oh, no. I'm not from around here. I suppose I should explain the purpose for my visit. There isn't much time, after all."

Jennifer frowned. "Uh, not much time?"

"Yes, well, your little visit to the Captain's house this morning has set some things into motion. It's very important that you listen now. And as hard as it might be, you really must trust me."

Theresa's eyes narrowed, burning a hole through her mother. "Mom, what did you do?"

The old man held up a hand. "Please, there isn't time. I need you to listen," he said firmly with a stern expression. "Right now."

The women fell silent, snickering at the unexpected chiding.

"You aren't dealing with typical men of flesh and bone," the old man said. "The Captain is not human. He's a fallen angel—a demon, if you will."

Sara's grin fell away.

Theresa watched Jennifer with pursed lips. Her mother had cradled her head in her hands, turning her back to the group.

"A demon," Theresa muttered incredulously. "So, what exactly does that make you?"

"Well, I should think the answer is obvious." He waved this off with a pipe-laden hand. "Nevertheless, my name is Logos. I am a messenger from our Father. Most of the time, you refer to Him as God. Under normal circumstances, I wouldn't be quite so forthcoming. But as I have tried to emphasize, time is of the essence. What you three need to know is that the Captain's real name is Malphus; he's Satan's right hand and is responsible for everything that is happening."

Sara swallowed audibly and stole a glance at Theresa.

"At this very moment," Logos continued, "there are many assassin teams in and around Pagosa. They're actively hunting you and Sam, among others. Their endgame is to take over the Rocky Mountains; they view Sam and his friends as their only major obstacle."

Logos paused to draw on his pipe for a moment. For the sake of time, he emptied the pipe bowl of coals, even before his smoke was done. "I hate being in a hurry."

Theresa drilled the old man with a cynical frown. "Why should we believe you? An old man running around in flip flops in this weather? You might just be a Silver Alert out of the next little town."

Logos turned a sour gaze on Jennifer and tucked his pipe into his robe pocket.

"I believe him," she replied in his stead. "He knows about the house. I saw him… the demon. I burned the house down, but he just… he walked right through the flames." She swallowed and shook the image from her head. "I was twenty-five yards from the house; the heat was so unbearable, but… the flames—it's like they didn't touch him."

"Oh, they touched him," Logos assured her. "I've seen him for myself. The fire hurt him plenty. But it's hard to kill a demon. He'll recover in a few hours, but you can bet he was hurt. That's why he didn't come after you right away."

"So, what do you want us to do?"

"The first thing I want you to do is take care of those you've lost. I'll go talk to Malphus and buy you some time. We were friends, once—before he left Heaven, that is. He still listens to me." Logos chuckled. "Well, sometimes. As for Sam, he's fine and will soon have his friends to aid him."

"You've spoken to Sam?"

"Yes. He's near Creede trying to help others. Soon, though, he'll face his biggest challenge."

"We'll go to Pagosa for supplies, and then travel to Creede," Jennifer said.

Logos flashed a stern frown at Jennifer. "No. Look at me, and let me make this very clear, Jennifer. You're being hunted by men with hearts of pure darkness. The worst thing you can do is get caught. If you do, rest assured they'll use you against Sam and his divine mission."

The girls exchanged a worried glance.

"Pagosa is a very dangerous place right now," Logos was saying. "Assassin teams have been gathering there for several days, and the three of you are well known. Find a place to hide. They've already taken the lives of your two daughters. I don't want that number to grow."

Jennifer opened her mouth to say something, but the hay bale was suddenly vacant.

CHAPTER 19

Malphus no longer wore the skin of Steven; the damage caused by the housefire had left the demon with too little to work with. The only living human in the vicinity now was the young man he'd nicknamed Poe. The demon rested in the woods beyond the smoldering farmhouse and watched Poe. The young man had leapt from the flaming structure wrapped in a blanket. As a result of his quick thinking, the fire had done very little physical damage to his exterior. Yet the smoke had all but singed his lungs. Poe tried time and time again to fill his chest with air, but his lungs were too weak and damaged, leaving him well short of breath.

The demon had come to admire the young man and his callous deviance. Since leaving paradise with his master, Poe was the first human he'd met who seemed as naturally evil as himself.

Naturally evil? Malphus contemplated. *How could God's child—a creation of Father himself—be naturally evil?*

Yet the boy was inarguably deviant, as evil as any demon Malphus had ever met. It would be a waste to take such a prize as a skin; but if the boy died from his injuries, the demon would have nothing. For all his power, there were limits; Malphus could not possess a dead skin.

"Let him die," a voice advised from beyond the darkness.

Malphus smiled. "Logos, my friend. Come, chat. This subject is very deep, indeed."

Logos stepped into the flickering light of the farmhouse's remaining flames. "This battle tires me, Malphus. I'm so weary of seeing innocents suffer. Even this young man could have been something else. Something better, had evil not stolen his future."

"I agree, Logos. But our past has determined our future; we have but one destiny."

"Do we? Have you lost your ability to choose a different path?"

"I can and will choose what I want, but I have an undeniable predisposition for self over benevolence."

"But that wasn't always the case. I remember a time when—"

"I know," Malphus interjected. "Believe me, I know. How can I possibly forget when you remind me every time we meet?" He sighed. "I remember those days all too well. We walked the halls with Father, and everything was *perfect.*" His voice had taken on a cynical edge that was hard to ignore. "Logos, why do you continually try to win me back? We both know that my choice was final. There's no forgiveness for the fallen."

"Would repentance be worth it if you could make Father smile one more time?"

Malphus thought for a moment, looking into the eyes of his old friend, and for a fleeting second Logos could swear he saw something that resembled regret. But it was gone in an instant.

Malphus looked away and rose. "No, that cannot happen. Father will never smile on me again. I'm lost, forever condemned." He paced the forest floor, eyes bouncing from Logos to Poe. "What are you here for, Logos? Buying time for the girls to get away?"

"Well, yeah. That's part of it, I suppose. But I'm here to offer you more than that."

"What more could you possibly offer? Did you not see what that woman did to my men?"

"Yes, and I saw what your men did to her children."

"Those were not *her* children. She didn't give birth to them."

"That's a subject beyond your comprehension, Malphus. No, she didn't bear them as her own, but she possessed them in her heart. The bond created by their love was as real as that of any biological family."

"You're right, Logos, I can't comprehend that. Compassion is beyond me now. Which is why I will follow the women to Crow and kill the lot of them."

"Forget the girls, Malphus. I'll give you Crow if you leave them alone."

The demon blinked, a wide grin splitting his face. "What? You'll *give* me Crow?"

"Well, in a manner of speaking. I'll tell you where he will be; taking him will remain up to you. But you must promise to leave the girls alone."

"A promise?" Malphus laughed. "From a demon?"

"I'll take you at your word, my friend. Crow for the girls."

"So shall it be then, Logos. Crow for the girls."

Logos took one last look at the young man, who was barely breathing. "Let him die," the angel pleaded again.

"You have all you'll get from me this night, Logos. Now tell me where Crow is."

Logos sighed. "Very well. He will soon be in Creede."

Malphus watched Logos fade into the darkness and stared into the splendor of the night sky.

What are you up to old friend? he thought. *Crow for the girls... Why?*

The demon strode to the tree, where the young man lay. His chest barely rose and fell; with each labored breath, his time grew shorter. Malphus lifted him up, holding the human by the shoulders.

"Poe? Can you hear me?

The man's eyes flickered. "Yes," he wheezed.

"Do you have faith in me, son?"

"Yes."

"Will you serve me?"

The young man was very weak; his head fell forward to rest on his chest. Fearing the worst, Malphus gave the man a shake. "Will you serve me?" he shouted.

"Yes."

Malphus smiled as the barely audible whisper escaped the young man's lips. He held the young man close, absorbing flesh against flesh. As they became one, the demon's mind swallowed that of his human counterpart. He saw inside that depraved, human mind and nearly shuddered as the memories became his own. And for the first time since he'd become one of the fallen, the demon remembered compassion.

*****

Three riders continued to bear down on Sam with no reaction to his charge. Tango's long legs stretched out to a full run, carrying him ahead of the gray stallion. Sensing competition, Shadow seemed to find another gear; within a few strides, he'd pulled even with the wolf.

Sam had covered just over a hundred yards with as much left to go. The lead rider pulled up and halted his horse. He leaned forward and crossed his arms, resting them casually on his saddle horn. The other two riders took positions on either side, unconcerned with the threat charging at them. As Sam approached the trio, he recognized something familiar about the rider in the middle. A grin split his face as he gave the reins a tap to slow Shadow to a trot. Chuckling to himself, he reined the gray horse to a stop.

The rider in the middle pushed back his hat and smiled. Tango ran circles around the group, stopping next to Kuruk's horse. Rising on his hind legs, he planted his huge paws on Kuruk's thigh to beg for scratches behind the ears.

"Your old eyes getting too tired to recognize your friends?" Kuruk jibed.

"Sorry, brother. Haven't seen many friends lately."

Kuruk offered his hand and Sam welcomed it with a firm shake. He nodded at Eli and Bendigo.

"These two are no longer the bean poles I remember."

"Amazing what a couple of years and a whole lot of good cooking can do," Kuruk retorted, giving Tango an affectionate scratch. "Can't say the same for you, though; you look like hell."

Sam took the gaffe on the chin and shrugged. "Life happens, I reckon." He turned his horse toward the two children watching from a safe distance.

"I'll fill you in later, but these two lost their family to a pack Jackals pretending to be cowboys."

"That's pretty much why we've been trailing you for the past few weeks. Seems they've developed some new tactics. They came after you at the Moon Dog, you know."

Sam's eyebrows rose. "What? No, I didn't know. Is Jennifer…"

"She's okay, Sam. She and the girls were fine when we left them. They took canoes down the Piedra River to the Chimney Rock farm. Hopefully they've reached the reservation by now."

Sam spurred Shadow into a trot with the three men in tow. They slowed and came to rest just short of Zack and Emily. Zack stood bravely in front of his sister, clutching his rifle with every intention of using it. Kuruk removed his hat and smiled.

"How are you, young man?"

Zack took in the size of the man, his long silver and black hair; it blended with his bearskin coat, which made him look twice his actual size.

The boy gave Kuruk a suspicious nod. "I'm okay, I guess," he replied, his finger easing off the trigger. He looked to Sam for reassurance.

"Zack, these are very good friends of mine. I've known them long enough to trust them with my life. They've come to help us."

The Apaches dismounted and greeted the young warrior still clutching his rifle. He tensed as the three large men approached him but held his ground.

Kuruk took a knee, looking the young man at eye level. He presented an open hand. "I'm on your side, little brother."

Cautiously, Zack accepted Kuruk's hand and watched his own disappear within the fold of the Apache's mighty grasp. They shook hands, Kuruk peering deep into the boy's eyes.

"There is much fire in you, little warrior. I pray we can help you put out that fire."

Eli and Bendigo approached the young man and shook his hand almost ceremoniously.

Zack seemed to relax, loosening his grip on the rifle. "This is my sister, Emily." He stepped to one side, presenting his little sister to his new friends. The Apaches greeted Emily with a warm smile.

Kuruk nodded toward Sam's new horse. "We found were you left Patton. What happened there?"

Sam grimaced at the memory, the pain still raw and unhealed. "It's a pretty long story, and I'd rather not spend much time out here in the open."

Kuruk nodded and then turned to Zack, extending his hand. "Would you like to ride with me?"

Zack mustered a grin and slung his rifle over his shoulder. He accepted Kuruk's hand and pulled himself into the saddle behind the Indian. He positioned himself on Kuruk's soft saddle pack and settled in for the ride.

"Let's find a place to camp so I can get some grub," Sam suggested. "I could use a rest, too. I've been running on empty for way too long."

Kuruk glanced at Sam from the corner of his eye and grinned. "Yeah, and I'm looking forward to hearing the story behind that pile of coyote bones, not to mention why they were so close to Patton's final resting place."

Sam groaned, knowing they would ride him long and weary because he ate the coyotes. "Hey, I'm alive. That's all you need to know." He situated Emily on the pack behind his own saddle and turned the gray horse north.

"I figure we're about halfway to Creede, and I'm guessing that peak over there must be Piedra Peak. Let's drop into that canyon, get out of the wind to rest for the night. We can take Piedra Pass and be in Creede by sundown, tomorrow."

"Why Creede?" Kuruk wanted to know.

"It's where these two ran into a team of Jackals, and they have some family that may need tending to."

The afternoon crept along as Sam led the group into the valley and up through the Pass. Snow still lingered up high, and as the sun began to set, the mountain chill of late spring settled in. Feeling Emily shiver behind him, Sam suggested they camp soon. Kuruk sent Bendigo and Eli ahead to find a suitable campsite. Bendigo returned in minutes with good news.

"We found a large pond on the southeast side of Piedra Peak. Good water, and not much wind. Eli stayed back to collect wood and get a fire going."

Sam nodded and urged Shadow into motion.

Soon, the horses were watered and hobbled to graze in a small meadow near the pond. Emily and Zack sat close to a fire, each poking the flames with sticks. Sam rested his back against a log, rummaging his pack for MREs that he'd acquired from TJ at the Eagle's Nest. He selected two of the meals and tore the bags open. Using the heating elements that came with the meals, he warmed the main courses. The heating elements were designed from a mixture of Magnesium metal alloyed with a small amount of iron. Adding one to water brought it to boiling temperature in seconds. Sam motioned to Zack and Emily. They threw their sticks in the fire and trotted to Sam.

"Do you guys like spaghetti?" He presented a bag of warm pasta and two sporks.

Zack sniffed his spaghetti and beamed as if Sam had pulled a rabbit out of his hat. "Smells pretty good."

Sam laughed. "It's a lot better than coyote jerky, for sure."

"I guess that explains the pile of bones," Kuruk muttered nearby.

Eli and Bendigo chuckled as Sam tossed them their own MREs.

"You guys get the tuna casserole," Sam said. Kuruk accepted a meal of beef and noodles and dug in while Sam returned to his log to dive into a pouch of stroganoff. All were content for a while; the only sounds among them were an occasional burp, followed by a childish giggle—not necessarily produced by a child.

Tango appeared across the water and stopped to drink his fill. Sam smiled as the huge wolf trotted around the pond and curled up next to Sam's bedroll.

The sun set too early for Sam's liking. The day had been better than most in recent history, ending on a happy note. The few clouds in the sky turned from white to yellow, and then seemed to bloom into brilliant orange. As the sun disappeared, orange deepened to crimson and finally faded to gray.

Eli and Bendigo had collected enough wood to stay warm through the night. Sam let Zack and Emily have his bedroll. The children were drained; with the rare luxury of a full stomach, they fell asleep almost instantly.

As the stars began to pierce the darkness, Sam skirted the fire to sit next to Kuruk. The bear of a man was almost snoring, his head hinged against his chest.

Sam nudged him awake. "Kuruk, what were you going to tell me about the Jackals?"

Kuruk took a moment to clear his mind. He started slow, explaining how he and the boys had come across a trail that led to the young scout who'd been tortured.

"It was horrible, Sam," he whispered. "They'd peeled his skin back and cut him to the bone while he was still alive. It was worse than anything I've ever seen."

"What exactly did the Jackal tell you?"

"He was stronger than I thought. Getting the information from him was almost more than I could stand." The Apache closed his eyes, clenching his jaw. "Turns out my heart isn't dark enough to equal his cruelty. He finally broke, though. Eventually, he begged me to kill him. I was happy to oblige."

Kuruk took a shaky breath, cringing against the terrible memory in his mind's eye.

"He said they're coming. Coming from the north. Many retreated to Canada after the battle in Washington. They have teams here already, pretending to live normal lives. They've infiltrated small towns throughout the Midwest and the Rocky Mountains. He believed they would control the Dakotas very soon."

Sam frowned deeply.

"They move into communities," Kuruk continued, "pretending to be normal, decent folks. And once the community lets its guard down? Those Jackals slit their throats without batting an eye. They've learned from us, how easily we forget. And how generously we forgive."

Kuruk went silent again to take a sip from his canteen.

"What exactly is their mission?" Sam wanted to know. "Why are they doing this?"

"Why?" Kuruk laughed bitterly. "It's the way things have always been. Ultimately, they want world domination by theocracy. They saw the strength in our old buddy Mahannad years ago, when he infiltrated the United States with ISIS camps and stole our children. They watched passively as the United States flexed its muscle and became energy independent. They realized they'd lost any leverage they ever had on us. Later, we withdrew our troops and financial aid, and that's when their world began to crumble. Different factions warred with each other, which kept them broken until they saw Mahannad's dream come alive."

"What dream are we talking about?"

"The damn Pandemic."

Sam's eyebrows scrunched. "But, the oil…"

"Yeah, I know, Sam. That's what it always comes back to. If they cut off our energy by controlling the west, they'll eventually succeed in their goal."

Sam contemplated Kuruk's words in silence for a long moment.

"It's madness," he finally grumbled. "If we tell the communities what's going on, people will die in the hysteria that follows. Anyone who looks or acts suspiciously could end up on the wrong end of a lynch mob. It would be like the Salem witch trials all over again."

"And," Kuruk added, "we don't have the military here to lean on anymore. There's only a small contingency close by. Most were ordered to the east coast to help rebuild infrastructure and keep it secure."

"There's no way to contact them, anyway," Eli pointed out.

Sam flashed a sober frown. "This really has become the wild west again."

Kuruk gave his old friend a wry grin. "Glad we're on the same side, this time around."

Sam and Kuruk reclined against the log and gazed into the fire, neither seeing the flames. Its hypnotic pulse flickered until the decaying firewood was reduced to glowing embers. Soon, all were asleep. The live coals burned down to dim cinders.

Tango raised his head as a figure approached the circle of weary travelers, all huddled around the dying fire.

The old man smiled at the wolf, covering his lips in a silent plea for silence. Tango rested his head on paws the size of dinner plates and granted the old man his wish.

The visitor added several sticks to the dying fire and retrieved a match from his bathrobe, striking it with his thumb and forefinger. Flicking it into the firepit, he watched the fire awaken to a glorious blaze.

Sam stirred. Through one exhausted eye, he saw a familiar figure sit on a log near the fire and begin to pack his pipe.

"Evening, Logos," Sam mumbled.

"Good night, Sam. Pleasant dreams."

CHAPTER 20

Sam's eyes fluttered and opened wide. He looked to the empty log next to the fire and felt an immediate stab of regret for missing another conversation with Logos.

"I'm here," came the old man's voice from behind him.

Sam jumped at the sound. He sat up and twisted for a better view. "Logos? I thought—"

"No, I'm still here." Logos shuffled into view, meandered around to the dying coals in the firepit and laid a handful of sticks across the embers. "I tried to keep the fire burning all night," he explained. "As it turns out, pulling an all-nighter at my age is quite exhausting."

Sam smile, his eyes tired. "We usually don't bother."

"Well, you needed rest, and I wanted to keep the kids comfortable."

Sam closed his eyes for a moment more then returned his gaze to Logos. "Every time you appear, you give me something. A clue, a message—always something. I appreciate your friendship, Logos, but I have to wonder why you're here now."

Logos gave Sam his back and stoked the fire. He fed several more sticks to the flames before turning back to Sam. "What you must understand is that God has had a plan for you since the beginning of time. He has prepared you for this moment all your life. You must trust Him. I can't tell you how many times I've seen His work, His will. Each and every time, I'm amazed at how perfectly His will manages to fit. I can't explain it any other way; His will *always* fits."

"So I don't have a choice?"

"You always have a choice, Sam. You could run away and never be seen again. But you won't. That isn't who you are."

"Then what do you mean by 'His will fits?'"

"Only that Father finds ways to make things work out. It's hard to explain. Things just come together. It might not seem like it from your perspective, and it might not align with what you want or when you want it. But never forget: God's will always fits!"

A gust of wind threw smoke and ash from the fire into Sam's eyes. He turned his head instinctively, covering his face. When his gaze returned to face the angel, the old man was gone.

As usual, the message seemed vague, though Sam assumed the messenger had told him all that he could. Sam stood on groaning knees and kicked one of Kuruk's boots. The big Indian's eyes fluttered, then squinted against the morning light. Sam left him to check on the kids, who were still bundled in his bedroll. Sam peeled the bedroll back a smidge; beneath, Zack had an arm across Emily, protecting her even as he slept. Sam nudged the young boy and, as expected, Zack bolted upright, ready for a fight.

Sam gave him a warm smile. "Hold on, fella. It's okay. Time to get up, though. We need to get moving."

Kuruk ambled over and yawned.

"Sorry to spoil your beauty sleep," Sam said. "But we need to leave quickly and be ready for action. I have a feeling they're close."

He passed Zack and Emily one of the MRE food bars and let them eat while he saddled the horses.

Kuruk readied his own horse, then gave Zack a nod. "You ready to ride, cowboy?" he asked cheerfully, trying to get the boy in better spirits. Zack rose from the log beside his sister and approached. The Apache chief handed over the horse's reins.

"Hold what you got for a minute," he said. "I'll be right back." Scattering what remained of the fire, he made sure there was nothing left burning.

Sam tightened the cinch on Shadow and glanced up to find Kuruk looking intently up the ridge, southeast of the pond. Turning back to his horse, Sam spoke just loud enough for Kuruk to hear. "Yeah, I know. Someone's up there. Let's put Emily with Eli and Zack on Shadow, and then ride across the meadow through those dense trees. I'll drop from my horse and stay in the trees with Tango. With any luck, I'll catch a glimpse of whoever's trailing us."

"How will you catch us?"

"Ride slow, then take a break in an hour or two. I'll catch up."

Soon the horses were ready, and everyone was in the saddle. As planned, they cut through the thicket of dense trees. In the obscurity of underbrush, Sam slipped from his horse and let Zack take the reins. Sam placed his hat on the boy's head. "Pretend you're me, now," Sam whispered with a wink.

He removed the .300 magnum from its scabbard and slung it across his back. He packed three extra magazines in a pocket on his load-bearing vest. With both Glocks checked, he disappeared into the woods with Tango at his side.

Kuruk nodded to Zack. "Lead on, little brother. We'll be right behind you."

The Indian gave Zack a lead of several horse lengths, hoping the distance between them might diminish the disparity in their sizes. With Eli and Bendigo taking up the rear, the group headed north toward the Piedra Pass in a slow-moving line. The Pass was little more than a series of washes and animal trails, which led the group down to Red Mountain Creek. At the base of the Pass, the trail opened into a vast meadow that followed the creek for well over a mile.

Kuruk stopped his horse and dismounted by the creek to let his horse water for a few minutes while Eli and Bendigo kept watch; afterward, the chief took on the task of keeping watch so the younger men could water their animals.

"We'll wait here," Kuruk said.

Back in the forest, Sam moved quickly to the tree line, watching the ridge above their campsite for any sign of movement. Tango waited patiently at his side; the wolf seemed to understand the nature of their mission. Sam had developed an uncanny bond with the wolf over the last four years. At times, they truly seemed to know what the other was thinking.

Especially when it came to the hunt.

Sam snuck south just inside the tree line for half a mile to avoid being seen from above. At what appeared to be the headwaters of the East Fork of the Piedra River, a small thicket of scrub gave him an opportunity to cross the meadow undetected.

Sam felt good for a change. Although still recovering, his body was responding well to more consistent food and filtered water. Tango's head darted in every direction, occasionally fixing on some movement or sound. Sam made it a habit to watch the wary animal because its senses were so much keener than his own.

They found a fairly well-used game trail leading up the ridge. Game trails of this sort were usually free of debris and obstacles, making travel more efficient than bushwhacking through the dark timber on either side. The trail opened onto a shelf about four hundred feet above the pond where they'd camped. The view was still obstructed because of the dense trees, so Sam and Tango continued to climb. On top of the ridge at the tree line, the trail forked into multiple paths. While various animals shared the trail, each traveled in its own direction, once in the open.

Sam came to rest at the edge of the trees, concerned that his watchers were still close. The ridge rose slightly as it followed the Pass, and then shot toward the valley that led to Creede.

As Sam moved into the open at the edge of the woods, he positioned his .300 magnum to hang at his chest, his right hand resting on the grip with a thumb on the safety. Sam gave Tango a glance; the wolf stared back at him anxiously, trying to anticipate his next move. Sam made a fist with his right hand and bumped his chest. This was a silent command for *passive hunt*, which signaled Tango to sit when he found something, rather than swoop in or attack.

The wolf trotted forward cautiously. With ears swiveling independently, he seemed attuned to movement in all directions at once. He lowered his nose close to the ground, zigzagging across the meadow. After about seventy yards, he froze, turned in a circle and lay down. Tango hadn't actively alerted to anything else in the clearing, giving

Sam confidence that no danger awaited him in the open.

Tango's keen senses had always amazed Sam, even when the wolf was a cub. Sam had taken advantage of an opportunity to hone the dog's abilities several years earlier in a military K9 training course. In preparation for the battle at Washington, Sam had taught the wolf his own set of silent commands so that no one else could tell Tango what to do. Even after the fighting was over in D.C. and Sam had put down roots at the Moon Dog, he'd continued to work with the wolf regularly.

Sam slipped beside Tango with an eye on the trail the wolf had crossed. The terrain was mostly rocky at this elevation, but Tango had managed to find a stretch of game trail with enough soft earth to imprint under the hoof of a shod horse. Foraging in the direction of the track, Sam found more evidence that they were being followed. Two horses, both shod—mostly, that is. One had lost a shoe from his right back hoof. At some point, the horses had stood side by side on the slope above the trees, facing down the mountain with a perfect view of Sam's camp. Sam was just about to return to the cover of the woods when he noticed a different track.

On a flat piece of soft earth was a smooth indentation. He almost missed it; if the early color of a nearby mountain paintbrush hadn't caught his attention, he probably would have. Left in the soil was the partial track of a human clad in a moccasin. Sam knelt beside the track and glanced around. Tango stood at his side, waiting for another command. Sam rubbed the dog's big head and scratched his ears.

"Seems someone is spying on the spies," he whispered to his faithful friend.

They followed the moccasin tracks to the edge of the woods, where the tracks stopped and appeared to retreat in the direction from which they had just come.

Checking the sun, Sam realized they'd spent almost three hours on this expedition. The two worked their way back down the canyon. Downhill travel was much easier on his tired bones, so they made better time. It only took an hour to cut the horse trail of his friends, and another hour to catch up with them in the meadow. Zack and Emily were finishing lunch upon his arrival. Kuruk tossed Sam a sack of jerked venison and the remnants of their last MRE.

"I saved you the dehydrated fruit bar and an oatmeal cookie," Kuruk said. "You can thank Zack for scarfing down your last bag of skittles."

Sam skewered the boy with an exaggerated frown. "Don't ever mess with a man's Skittles, boy. It might just be the last thing you do."

The boy giggled from his perch on a log next to his sister, with whom he'd happily shared his candy.

Sam turned back to Kuruk. "Well, looks like we have two nosy birds somewhere up on that ridge. But what's more interesting is that someone else is watching *them*."

Kuruk's eyebrows shot up. "Did you see them?"

"No, I didn't want to call them out too early. I found three sets of tracks: two men on horses, one set of moccasins."

"Moccasins?" Kuruk parroted with surprise.

"Yeah, I almost missed them."

Kuruk chewed his lip for a moment, contemplating the identity of the lone scout shadowing their pursuers. "It seems we may have more friends in these woods than we knew," the Apache muttered thoughtfully.

"Yes," Sam added. "That, or a stranger with a common enemy."

CHAPTER 21

Nestled away in the Rocky Mountains, the tiny town of Pagosa Springs once treaded a fine line between modern escape and the stereotypical persona of the wild west. Before the Pandemic and subsequent Fall, those seeking high adventure or solitude could find both in Pagosa. After, the town withered to a ghost town as the townsfolk sought out the security of larger cities, seeking safety in numbers. A few remained, however. Following the Battle of Washington and the arrival of Samson Crow, the town had begun to prosper again.

In recent months, the streets had become busy with steady horse traffic. Occasionally, the surprise arrival of an automobile drew smiles and applause, proof of the gradual return of technology. Being a great distance from the controls of the government had its benefits, at times; but the wellbeing of the new west was out of sight, and therefore out of mind for those on the east coast. The residents of Pagosa Springs were truly on their own, for better or worse.

Jennifer pulled her hat down low as she turned the corner and ducked inside Linda's General Store and Mercantile on Pagosa Street. Once inside, she made a beeline for the back of the store, where she rapped lightly on the stockroom door. It opened a crack, revealing an older woman in a red flannel shirt. Slender and tall, the woman widened the opening and pulled Jennifer inside, closing the door hurriedly behind them. Inside, Theresa and Sara were waiting in chairs against the far wall when Jennifer arrived with a bag of food and supplies she'd just bought from the drug store.

The woman in the flannel pointed a long, skinny finger at Jennifer, as if admonishing an insolent child. "Listen to me. You're too well known to be running around this town like a damn fool."

"Linda, there are things I have to do. I can't sit on my thumbs while those Jackals plot my husband's death."

"Well, they'll be plotting yours if you don't lay low. Mark my words."

Jennifer deposited the bag of goods on the table and strode to the window. Pulling back the curtains, she peered into the alley behind the store. "I feel like I'm in a prison," she grumbled.

The stockroom doubled as a breakroom, complete with a bathroom and shower. Plenty of room for the girls to work, if they could keep from turning on each other.

Linda planted her hands on her hips and leaned toward Jennifer with her head slightly tilted. "Lady, you're alive, and right now survival is your only job. Out there, you'd be one more thing for Sam to worry about, and he doesn't need that. Y'all can stay with me at the ranch. These Jackals, or whatever you call them, won't have a clue. Now, let's see about making y'all a little less recognizable."

Jennifer emptied her bag. Among other things, it contained three boxes of hair coloring. "You have no idea how hard this stuff is to find," she said. "Surprised I found any at all. You'd think vanity would be a thing of the past, but I guess some women will always put a high price on their appearance."

Sara giggled.

The younger ladies sifted through the pile of accessories. Linda laughed, thinking, *girls will be girls*. "I have plenty of clothes to work with, too, so help yourself."

Jennifer had met Linda on her first day shopping in Pagosa, back when Jennifer and Sam first settled in the area. The two women had become fast friends.

Linda left the girls to their work and returned to the front of the store to man the register. Time passed as patrons came and went. Out the front window, she watched foot traffic with curiosity, intrigued by the growing number of tourists enjoying the spring waters across the river.

Well, that's new. Where'd they all come from?

Linda opened the front door and walked out to the sidewalk. Across the river, the resort was packed for the first time in years. People were milling around, shopping and soaking in the spas as if on vacation. She crossed the street to lean against the rail overlooking the river. Squinting for a better view, it suddenly dawned on her.

They're all men...

She returned to the store just as Jennifer closed the stockroom door and approached the register. The younger woman's salt-and-pepper hair was now blonde, accentuated by an old Stetson cowboy hat. She'd traded her tattered clothes for a comfortable pair of jeans and a western shirt.

Linda took a moment to admire the transformation before closing the front door behind her. She shook her head with a sigh. "Well, they might not recognize you as Jennifer Crow, but every man on this side of Wolf Creek Pass is going to be watching you."

"I really didn't intend to call attention to myself."

"Girl, I don't think that's something that can be helped. It's pretty much who you are."

"Well, fix it then! I can't be seen."

Linda chuckled. "Okay. The hat is a nice touch—it hides your face, so we'll stay with that. But let's try a hoodie to soften those curves." She plucked a small barn coat from the men's rack and handed it to Jennifer. "Gotta take care of the curves on the bottom, too."

"So, pretty much, I have to dress like a guy."

"Well, yeah," Linda replied with a laugh. "Can't go around flaunting a body like that with all these men around. They're dangerous!"

Jennifer crossed her arms. "What men?"

Linda's smile dimmed. "Oh, I don't know. I looked outside a little bit ago and noticed the resort was full of men."

"Any idea where they came from?"

Linda shrugged. "Hun, I haven't a clue. But if what you told me is true, they're probably up to no good."

Jennifer peered through the front window. Across the river, the resort was indeed crawling with men who appeared to be relaxing and enjoying the sunny day. Her jaw tightened; the soft features of her beautiful face hardened. She stole a glance at her dear friend with tears in her eyes, pointing across the river. "Linda, I have to go. I have to help Sam."

"Not a chance, child. You don't even know where he is."

"I have to do something."

"So what's your plan, then? Walk across that bridge and see how many you can take out before they get you? Sam's been through this before. Anyone standing against that man is in for a rude awakening. I honestly feel sorry for the men over there, because if they're stupid enough to take on Samson Crow, they'll be dead soon enough. That or they'll wish they were."

Jennifer and Linda watched another group of strangers ride by. Several turned right to cross the bridge, yet as the last man passed the store, his horse faltered. The man's head swiveled to the store window; somehow, Jennifer knew he was looking straight into her soul. A smile tugged at the corners of his mouth. A moment later, he followed the other men across the bridge toward the resort.

"That's him," Jennifer whispered.

"Who?"

"*Him*. The beast I saw—the thing I told you about at the farmhouse? He looks totally different now, but it's him. I just...I don't know how to explain it. I can just feel it. And he saw me."

"Jen, I think you're getting a bit too close to the edge, dear."

"Close to the edge? You have no idea what we've been through." Jennifer glared at her friend and then headed back to the stockroom. "I can't argue with you right now."

Sara was sitting in a chair, smiling faintly as Theresa finished her hair. Jennifer watched the girls for a moment and smiled. She felt a hand on her arm. A peek over her shoulder found Linda with an apologetic frown.

"I'm so sorry, Jen," she said. "I can't imagine what you've been through. But listen to me—as much as you want to help Sam right now, protecting your girls is the higher priority. I really believe that's what Sam would want."

Jennifer waited for Theresa to finish Sara's hair. It was a rare occasion when the girls actually got to be girls. "Linda, I can't believe I'm saying this, but maybe you're right. Maybe they do need me more than Sam does."

"Well, y'all are welcome to stay as long you want. I kind of like the company, anyway."

The chime of a bell announced that the store had a visitor. Linda headed up front with Jennifer at her tail. Just inside the doorway, two young men waited.

"Jennifer!" one said with feigned surprise. "I thought that was you. How are you doing?"

Jennifer froze, unable to breathe, much less reply. She looked at the young man she'd seen ride by only a few minutes earlier, pulling the barn jacket closer to her body against a chill that had nothing to do with the season. She tried to regain her composure, looking directly at the man.

"I'm very well, thank you, but forgive me if I'm at a loss right now. I don't recognize you."

He nodded sheepishly. "Yes, I suppose that's understandable. Well, I've gone by many names over the years. The most recent—and the one you'll most likely remember—was Steven. He was one of my favorite skins, by far; a gentle-looking fellow with a mild disposition. He had a way of getting people to trust him, to let their guard down."

A hand flew to Linda's mouth. Stunned, and with no other place to go, she stepped behind the cash register and tried to disappear into the background.

"Skin?" Jennifer was saying. "So who are you wearing now?"

"He never mentioned his name, actually. We called him Poe, for obvious reasons. His soul was dark and empty—more malicious and diabolical than any skin I've ever taken. Matter of fact, you're lucky I was there to take him, considering he survived your little fire."

"Oh, yeah? And why is that?"

"Because he would've slaughtered you two by now. Whereas I have no intention of killing you so flippantly. In fact, I might have a use for you older women, yet."

From behind the register, Linda whimpered.

Jennifer flashed her a warning glance. "So, if your name isn't Steven or Poe, what is it?"

"I'm Malphus, but the men call me Captain." With a nod of his chin, he gestured toward his companion, who had gone almost unnoticed until now. "This is Asmodeus, my new second in command. We've combined forces here in Pagosa for a difficult task."

Asmodeus politely extended his hand. "Most folks call me Jack," he confided with a chuckle. "People have too much fun with a name like Asmodeus."

With mouth agape, Jennifer withdrew from the hand in disgust. "Why are you doing this, Malphus?" she whispered.

The young man's eyes widened, his expression stiffening. "Do you really have to ask? You must know that you've played a role in all this from the beginning."

"*Played a role*? I was kidnapped and forced into slavery. I would hardly call that *playing a role*. I've done everything I can to help humanity, on both sides."

"And therein lies the difference between us," Malphus quipped with a grin. "While you're busy trying to help humanity—a complete waste of energy, by the way—I intend to do everything I can to destroy it."

Jennifer felt anger burn inside as she thought back to the previous morning. The sound of the shovel as it sank into cold dirt. The feel of her two girls, stiff and lifeless. She'd taken them from the loft by herself and buried them under a large cottonwood tree across the field from the barn. She'd wept bitterly as she covered them with dirt, followed by river rocks to prevent scavengers from disturbing their remains.

Rage rose within like fire, engulfing even her words. "Why?" she growled. "Why must you destroy? Don't you know how this all ends?"

Malphus smiled. "Yes, dear; I know. My fate is inevitable. But that's the beauty of free will—having the strength and liberty to make our own choices, to turn our backs on our creator and destroy his creations. Yes, I'll burn in the end, but I'll take many more with me."

Jennifer shook her head with tears stinging her eyes. "How can you be so smug about murder? About what you did to my girls?"

Malphus took a moment to consider his conversation with Logos. *A little taste of depravity goes a long way. Killing is highly addictive, like a drug to these animals.*

"My apologies," he said aloud. "That wasn't supposed to happen. But in the end, I must accept the blame; I allowed my men to take things much further than was necessary. That's why I don't take you and your girls now. I made a promise, and I intend to keep it." He leaned forward. "With that said, cross my path again and I might not be so kind."

Jennifer swallowed audibly.

"By the way," Malphus said. "I'll tell Sam that you said *hello*. I'll be seeing him in a couple of days."

At a loss for words, Jennifer could only stare blankly at the demon.

Malphus tipped his hat and turned toward the door, followed by his second. He held the door for Jack and paused with his hand on the old brass knob. He looked back to find both women watching his exit.

He grinned. "Nice touch by the way."

Jennifer blinked, her lips quivering.

"The blonde—it suits you."

CHAPTER 22

The mountain meadow beyond Piedra Pass was a lonely but peaceful place. Sam took his time with the food he had left. He leaned back against the base of a tree and emptied his canteen. Kuruk centered the pack on his horse and tightened the leather straps that held it in place.

"What are you thinking, Sam? If we hurry, we can make Creede by sundown."

"Yeah, I know. But then we won't have any light to scout for our enemies. I'd rather hold off until dawn and ride into town with some daylight on our side. No surprises. Besides, I'm going hunting tonight."

Kuruk sat beside his old friend. "I figured as much. We need to have a powwow with our shadows on the ridge, you realize."

Sam smiled and pulled his hat down low over his eyes. "Yeah, I hear you. Wouldn't want them thinking we weren't neighborly, would we?"

"Absolutely not. I'll have Eli and Ben find us something to eat. My belly's starting to growl."

"Mine's just starting to remember how to growl again. Survival rations ain't cutting it in the high country, my friend."

Sam closed his eyes, listening to Kuruk send his son and nephew on their way. The two seemed to enjoy getting away from camp, stretching their legs on their own. They crossed the meadow and stopped to let their horses water in the creek. Soon they had disappeared into the timber.

Zack stayed at Emily's side and played with her in the shade of an enormous spruce tree. Several ground squirrels kept them entertained, darting from one log to another. The sun was bright, almost hot out in the open, but the air remained crisp in the shade of the big tree. Sam dozed with Tango sprawled nearby in the grass, soaking up as much sun as he could.

Sam twitched and his eyes fluttered, then opened. The sun had fallen from the sky and the orange remnants of the day painted streaks against the clouds above. Eli and Ben had returned with a bounty of five grouse and a rabbit. Kuruk built a cowboy rotisserie using a few well-shaped sticks. The kids were poking at the fire; Sam could see the Apache chief was a little frustrated with the duty of babysitting all afternoon.

Sam smirked and saluted the big Indian on his way to the edge of the creek. There, he knelt to wash his face and fill his canteen. When he returned to the warmth of the fire, Kuruk had just removed the first grouse from the spit. Unsheathing the knife on his belt, he carved meat from the breast and deboned as much of the savory meat as possible. He piled the meat on a makeshift plate he'd fashioned from dried wood and handed Zack and Emily their portions. When the remaining birds were done, he distributed one to Eli, Ben and then himself. The rabbit remained sizzling on the spit. Sam sat at the edge of the fire with nothing to eat.

Kuruk smiled at the mountain man, who looked ready to fight tooth and nail for a bite.

"They killed it, I cooked it," Kuruk said with a hearty chuckle. "Go on, eat the rabbit. We saved the hasenpfeffer for my big hungry friend."

Sam needed no formal invitation; he reached for the spit and stripped it of the rabbit one bite at a time. Before he could even begin to enjoy the meat though, something rubbed against his leg; the high-pitched whine of a large carnivore pleaded for his attention. Sam rolled his eyes.

"You never share with me," he grumbled at Tango. "And I doubt you've missed a single meal in weeks."

"But Sam, he loves you *sooo* much," Eli needled.

"Okay, fine. But a front leg is all he gets." He tossed the wolf a leg and protected the remainder of his meal with one arm, pushing the wolf away firmly with the other.

In a single bite, what might've seemed like a meal for most disappeared.

Kuruk laughed. "That's probably his second or third rabbit of the day."

Everyone ate their fill, and the fire kept spirits high. Sam prepared his bedroll for the children, but Zack protested.

"We'll be fine by the fire," the boy assured him. "You need to rest more than us. You should take your own bedroll."

It warmed Sam's heart that the boy tried so hard to be an adult.

"Thanks, little brother," he replied. "But in a little while, I won't be needing a bedroll. I've got work to do that can only be done when everyone else is asleep. If you and your sister don't use it, no one will."

Zack stole a glimpse at his sister, who stretched and yawned. Reluctantly, the boy nodded and rested his hands on his gun belt like a seasoned fighter. "Okay, but tomorrow I won't take no for an answer."

Sam stifled a grin. "Yessir," was all he could muster with a straight face.

As Zack unrolled the bedding with his sister, he hesitated. "Do you know any stories?"

Sam's brow furrowed.

Zack blushed. "It's just that, um, Em's been having a hard time sleeping. Something like that might help."

Sam cocked his head in thought. When the kids were snuggled in, he pulled the cover up to their chins and settled back against his log. He felt the weight of Zack and Emily's gaze on him, imploring him for a tale worth hearing. Sam smiled. With eyes widened dramatically and voice softening to scarcely more than a whisper, Sam settled into a soothing cadence.

"Once in a while
When the moon is high
And the cold wind moans and blows
A lonely soul by a campfire glow
Can see the ghosts of old

They dance with shadows against the stones
And they run from the light
They twist and turn reaching for the sky
The moon and stars their enemy's lie
They battle and hide from God's own lights
Yet once the fire begins to die
The flames, they must depart
With one last stand
The ghosts grow bold
They flicker
And they fight
Embers blow
Coals grow cold
Sparks vanish with coming light
Coyotes cry on mornings wind
The ghosts must flee sunrise."

Sam fell silent and leaned forward to see if either child was still awake. Both were fast asleep, already content in their own dreams. Sam glanced toward Kuruk, who shook his head.

"Man you almost had me snoring," he whispered. "What was that?"

Sam shook his head, smiling fondly at an old memory. "Something my momma used to recite when I couldn't sleep. It sounded more like a song when she did it, though."

Silence crept in for several seconds. Kuruk's throaty whisper broke the spell. "Sam, what do you think they want with the girl?"

"I'm not sure we want to know."

Sam checked his sidearms and left his rifle in its scabbard. He took a long drink from his canteen and set it beside his saddle.

"I should be back before dawn," he said quietly. "If not, I'll catch you in Creede."

Kuruk nodded. "Watch your six, brother."

Sam departed the camp on foot, following the edge of the woods back to the game trail he'd traveled earlier. Finding tracks in the dark was nearly impossible, even for the best of trackers. Yet the light of the mountain sky was in full force with millions of stars shining down.

Even without a moon, Sam had little trouble navigating. His best bet would be to cut the track where he left it last on the ridge above. Taking a deep breath, he smiled. For the first time in weeks, he felt alive and rested. Blessed energy flooded his veins. He was ready to finish what the enemy had started.

He whispered to Tango, who walked at his side, "It's good to be back, brother wolf."

Half an hour later, Sam topped the ridge. With little effort, he located the horse trail he'd discovered the day before. Knowing the big wolf liked to range far and wide, Sam tapped his leg and used a hand signal to keep Tango close. If the guys following him had packed it in shortly after Kuruk made camp down below, they might not be far ahead. Sam couldn't risk either of them—he or Tango—ruining the surprise.

What about the spy? Sam had to wonder. *What's his role in all this?*

The ridge paralleled Piedra Pass, leaving no doubt as to which way the horsemen had traveled. The top of the ridge itself formed a natural funnel, and the horse tracks were clear and frequent enough to make Sam cautious. He dropped to one knee to inspect another set of hoofprints. Tango put his head under Sam's chin and received a free ear rub.

"What do you think, boy? Are they at the end of this trail, or is this a trap?"

Sam favored his instincts because they rarely misled him. He looked in the direction from which he had come and made a mental note which way he was headed. He tapped his leg once more; Tango heeled and followed Sam off the trail. They walked down to the edge of the woods on the east side of the ridge. The slope wasn't significant there, but it was steep enough to conceal the trail where he'd been.

Sam crouched low and followed the same heading he pictured from the trail. He continued for several hundred yards until the tree line began to drop away, leaving him without cover. He and Tango moved hastily through the open meadow and stopped to rest behind a pair of boulders nestled against a high bluff. Sam tried to get his bearing; if he wasn't mistaken, he was at least a quarter mile beyond his camp in the valley below.

Still no sign of the Jackals.

The moon had risen, illuminating the terrain more clearly. The ridge was beginning to slope downward, he realized. As he and Tango wandered beyond the rock outcropping, Sam discovered a finger of canyon running behind him. Unless he was mistaken, it eventually converged with the valley where his own people were camped. Sam peered into the smaller valley and realized with a start that he was sky-lined with the rising moon behind him; anyone looking in his direction from below would recognize his silhouette against the vivid night sky. He cursed his carelessness and dropped to the ground. He waited there for a few minutes, scanning the canyon below for any sign of life.

Tango lay quietly beside him, obeying every command. They got moving again; once they'd worked their way across the ridge, Sam raised his right hand with palm down, made a fist and bumped his chest twice. This was a command for *covert passive hunt*. Sam had designed this command specifically for hunting people. Once Tango located his target, he was to alert passively and stay out of sight until Sam could catch up.

The dog trotted off with his nose in the air; almost immediately, he trailed the ridge to the north. Sam followed close behind, occasionally breaking into a jog to keep up with the long-legged wolf. His lungs burned in the cold night air; he was about to stop and rest when Tango came to an abrupt halt. The dog faced the front of the ridge, out of Sam's view. Sam took a minute to catch his breath, thinking, *how many times have I told myself over the last few years that I'm too old for this?*

Sam grinned as he caught up to Tango. The thought of walking away from trouble never crossed his mind.

The black wolf was almost invisible at night, but Sam could see him lying in wait, gaze locked on his target. Sam crept up behind the wolf and eased beside him. He tried to follow the trajectory of Tango's eyes, but all he saw were shadows and ambiguous silhouettes; there was just enough moonlight to play tricks with his mind.

He closed his eyes for a moment and took a deep breath. "Let's go right at 'em," he whispered to Tango.

It was after midnight with the moon now almost directly overhead; he didn't like his position in the open, but he was confident they still had the advantage of surprise. He gathered his feet beneath him and gestured to Tango with a closed fist, tapping his nose twice—his signal for an aggressive takedown. The huge dog was gone before Sam had a chance to lower his hand.

Sam drew both his handguns and followed as close as he could. Cresting the ridge, he caught a brief glimpse of Tango as he leapt over a deadfall into the light of a small campfire.

Sam broke into a run, fearing the worst. As he approached the downed trees, he peered over the logs, leading the way with his gun barrels. He was shocked to find Tango sitting comfortably in the clearing, facing two men on their knees with hands bound behind their backs.

"Since when can you tie knots?" Sam asked with a smirk, his chest heaving.

Tango wagged his tail in response.

Sitting across the fire were Tanner and Jamie from the Eagle's Nest. Tanner was searching for his daughter Chasity, no doubt, with the help of Jamie, one of the Nest's trackers.

Sam holstered his weapons and stepped over the log and sat down, still trying to catch his breath from the dash across the ridge.

"What are you two doing here?"

Jamie gave Tanner a sidelong glance. "Tell him, would you? This is your rodeo, cowboy."

Tanner's cheeks flushed; his gaze dropped to the ground. "Well, I didn't mean anything by it, but Jamie came across the tracks you followed and realized that there were kids involved. Then she saw more tracks following you. She came and got me. I figured with the kids' tracks and all, one might be my Chasity."

His breath hitched at the mention of his little girl.

"I thought you might need some help, so we tracked you to the meadow, where you met up with your friends. We figured you'd be okay then. But on our way back, we saw these two fellas shadowing you on the ridge. We caught them a little while ago, sleeping like babies. We were going to bring them down to you in the morning."

"Did you ask them any questions?"

"Yeah, but they won't talk."

"Oh, they'll talk," Sam assured him. "They might even sing for Kuruk. That much I can promise."

CHAPTER 23

Clouds moved into Pagosa Springs from the north at nightfall. What some had taken for an early spring shifted in minutes, a healthy reminder of Mother Nature's fickle temperament. The north wind brought freezing rain that soon turned to sleet as the temperature plummeted. The sleet pelted against the store windows until late in the evening; by early morning, the wind had calmed, and fat snowflakes fell softly to the ice-covered ground.

Jennifer snuck out the back door of the store, carefully working her way across the snow-covered ground to the stable. The storm had hidden the ice under a blanket of white, making her footing precarious. She had borrowed extra winter clothing from Linda's store, along with a small bag of food.

The clouds began to part, permitting an occasional glimpse of the stars overhead. The moon rose over Wolf Creek Pass as she rode from Pagosa Springs, illuminating an incredible scene like something from a snow-covered dream. She planned to follow the main highway across the Pass to South Fork, and then head northwest toward Creede.

Creede was about sixty miles away, yet even with the snowfall, Jennifer was confident she could outpace the company of Jackals and find Sam before they got there. Her horse had belonged to Linda's husband; the thick draft gelding—possibly a Friesian cross—hadn't received much attention since the man's death. Between fifteen and sixteen hands, the animal wasn't huge for a draft, but he was solid. His name was Asgard. He was muscular with a barrel-shaped chest. His head held high, he appeared to be worthy of any Norse god from the land of his namesake.

The animal seemed anxious for a little work. Jennifer let him slip through the main part of town at his own pace. A single bark from a wary dog broke the silence as she approached the San Juan River bridge on the edge of town. With Pagosa behind her, she leaned forward in the saddle and let the big horse stretch his legs. He moved into a lope, and at almost a hundred yards, Jennifer gave him a nudge. She eased him to a canter and let him have his head at about half throttle. The horse's gait was smooth and strong, covering a great deal of trail in a short amount of time.

When she approached the turnoff to Treasure Falls, morning light was beginning to break. She'd been riding for a little over three hours by then, and Jennifer wanted to give Asgard some water. She slowed the animal to a walk and led him down to the creek. Once he'd slurped his fill, they began the ascent up Wolf Creek Pass. The snow got deeper the higher they climbed; by the time they reached the summit, the big horse was plowing through two- to three-foot drifts. The sun had risen over the front range and was now staring Jennifer in the face. The snow would probably melt before Malphus' army arrived at the Pass, she realized.

She urged Asgard down the eastern side of the mountain. By mid-morning, the sun was high in the sky, blasting the mountain with the full warmth of spring. The snow melted even faster than she'd imagined. The rhythm of the horse's hooves on the old paved highway began to take its toll; drowsiness, fueled by sleep deprivation as much as the lull of movement, tugged at her eyelids. The thought of Sam and the army behind her was all that kept her awake and moving. Asgard came to a halt, snapping Jennifer from her daydream.

A mountain stream with dense trees on either side flowed from a small valley on Jennifer's left. She watched Asgard's ears pivot toward the next bend in the road. Something had him on edge.

Jennifer had learned from Sam that horses offered a wealth of information to those who took the time to observe them. It was tempting to push on, but she resisted.

I'd rather be cautious than dead.

Jennifer led the horse off the road and into the obscurity of tree cover. They weaved between trees and underbrush, pushing far enough into the timber that anyone coming in their direction on the road would be unable to see them. Surrounded by towering trees, she stopped Asgard and dropped from the saddle. She kept a firm grip on the horse's reins and stroked his nose to sooth him. After a few minutes, the clap of horse hooves climbed the Pass toward the summit. As they drew near, Jennifer heard someone speak.

"Let's water the horses here," a man said.

She watched from the trees as several men drove their horses down the creek bank and into the water. With practiced silence, Jennifer unsnapped the thumb-break on her holster; she drew the handgun and waited. Since the assassins now operated in disguise, there was no way to know if these men were good or bad. Each minute seemed to crawl by in an eternity as the men chatted. Finally, the horses were satisfied, and the riders led them back up to the highway. Just as Jennifer dared to breathe a sigh of relief, Asgard blew a snort toward the other horses.

She froze, as did the men on the road.

"You hear that?" one hissed

"Wild horses?"

"Nah, we'd have heard them before now. That's somebody lying low."

"Leave them be, then. We've got to find Crow before anyone else gets killed."

At the mention of her husband's name, Jennifer climbed into the saddle and urged Asgard toward the road. "Hey!" she shouted toward the men, who were now on the move.

The riders reined their horses in and turned to face her. She stopped a safe distance from the men with a hand on her Glock. She addressed them with a bit of steel in her voice. "Gentlemen, what business do you have with Sam Crow?"

There were only four men in this group, she couldn't help but notice. The Jackals tended to travel in groups of six. But after all she'd been through, trust was hard to earn. She drew the Glock and held it ready, scanning each man for any hint of threat, as Sam had taught her.

"Hold on, ma'am," one pleaded. "We don't mean no trouble."

"Then talk to me. What is your business with Sam?"

"We're farmers. From Del Norte, ma'am. We've had a mess of trouble, lately. Some men showed up offering to help out, but we don't think they are who they say they are."

"And what makes you think Sam Crow can help you with that?"

"Truth is, we're riding on faith, ma'am. If he can't help, I reckon no one can."

"Tell me about these men."

"Well, they act a little strange. Awkward, like they don't belong. They came in talking like cowboys, but they don't necessarily know things a cowboy ought to know. And then Bill here heard them talking a couple of nights ago; one of them said he wished they'd hurry up and kill Crow so they could start having some fun. I talked to one the other day, and I swear he was on some kind of drugs. His eyes were wild, hands shaking like a tweaker. Thing is, we haven't seen meth around in years. We decided to ride up to Pagosa and talk to Crow about it."

"How many are there?"

"A total of twelve. The first group of six came on a Monday; the others arrived a week later."

"How long have they been there?"

"About a month, maybe six weeks. They showed up during that Indian summer—you know, when the weather got real nice for about a week?"

Jennifer nodded, remembering that was about the last time she had seen Sam. She considered the man's story, poking and prodding it for holes. It seemed to hold water. They must be telling the truth, she decided. The Jackal army behind her wasn't her only problem, and at this point, she was burning daylight. She fixed the man who seemed to be the spokesman of the group with a cool gaze.

"Y'all married? Got kids?"

"Yes, ma'am. We do. But we've had some go missing the last couple of weeks."

Her eyebrows rose. "Kids?"

"Yes, ma'am."

"How old?"

"Six and eight. Both girls."

Jennifer thought back to when the enemy had abducted her. She had just graduated high school and was enjoying a summer of sun and fun on the beach in Biloxi, Mississippi. She'd met Sam at a concert one Friday afternoon. The sun was hot, the clouds few. They'd danced until the sun went down and the music finally stopped. They went out on several dates afterward, though the ritual of courtship had been unnecessary; she'd know right away that Sam was the one.

Jennifer remembered waking one morning on a metal bed in a tiny cell without the slightest recollection of how she'd gotten there. Her captors had gone by many names back then. The national media called them extremists, but in the end? It was just Islam. They'd been stealing children all over the world for centuries, assimilating them into their cult or making slaves of them. Now, their dream of global theocracy had but one obstacle. Her Sam.

But why are they collecting children now?

She glanced back at the group of farmers, who shuffled restlessly, obviously anxious to get on with their trip. "Y'all need to get back home and protect the rest of your families. Your instincts are probably spot on about those men, and in about an hour, an army of them will be coming over the Pass behind me. They'll show no mercy to you or me. Or anyone else, for that matter."

"We can't go to Pagosa?"

"Not a chance."

"What about Sam Crow?"

"He isn't there."

"How do you know?"

The man grew more frustrated with each question, and though understandable, his persistence was beginning to grate Jennifer's nerves. She took a breath to check her irritation. "I know because I'm married to him."

The man gaped for a long moment. He swallowed and then opened his mouth to say something, but clamped it shut again.

From behind him, another farmer spoke up. "What are we supposed to do with the men in Del Norte?"

"Does your town have a jail?"

"Del Norte's grown a lot," the man said proudly. "We have a county jail, a Sheriff and two deputies. The valley is thick with farms. It's gotten pretty big—as towns around here go, that is."

"Well, if I were you? I'd lock 'em up until all this gets sorted out. But you're going to need more than two deputies. A lot more."

Realizing the time was getting away from her, Jennifer holstered her weapon.

"Good luck, gentlemen," she said with a tip of her hat. She put a heel into Asgard's side, prodding the big horse into a steady trot down the Pass. As she rounded a curve, she glanced over her shoulder. The farmers were trailing her. With an army of jackals behind her and a dozen more ahead, she was glad to be turning west soon toward Creede.

And Sam.

CHAPTER 24

The moon was still bright as it snuck behind the western range, and while Sam's eyes showed their age when reading, following a track in the dark remained a simple task. He'd decided to take a chance with the two Jackals they'd captured during the night by allowing them to escape.

Tanner and Jamie settled into their bedrolls, trying to get comfortable close to the fire. Sam skirted the fire to check the restraints on the two men who had been shadowing him. As he moved close to one of the bound prisoners, he stumbled and caught himself on a log near where the Jackals were sitting. Sam picked himself up from the forest floor, deliberately dropping a pocketknife at their feet. He knocked dead leaves from his clothes and pretended to be none the wiser. He gave their bindings a few tugs.

"They're not going anywhere," he announced to the others.

He threw some more wood on the fire and relaxed with his back against a tree, just outside the firelight. He pulled his hat over his eyes and crossed his arms. Within a few minutes, the old deputy was snoring.

Tango trotted to Sam's side and curled up next to him. Sam placed a firm hand on the wolf to keep him from reacting when the men decided to make their move.

Rowdy waited almost an hour. He'd heard the knife hit the ground and covered it with the heel of his boot. Since then, he'd pushed the old pocketknife toward his hands with slow and persistent care. It wasn't long before both men had slipped away from the camp, sneaking east along a game trail. They moved low and quiet, their every move devoted to putting as much distance between them and Sam's group as possible.

Sam watched them slip into darkness with a faint smile. He gave the Jackals a fifteen-minute head start, after which he rose and examined the ground where they'd been tied. The only sign of them was the remnants of their bindings. He studied the soft dirt next to the fire, found the track of one boot and committed the print to memory. He found another partial print near a log they'd stepped over during their escape. He smiled at Tanner and Jamie, who were now sitting up.

"Would you two do me a favor?"

"Yessir," Tanner replied. "You name it."

"When it gets light, ride down to my friends below and tell them I'm trailing the Jackals. I'll meet them in Creede as soon as I can."

Without waiting for a reply, Sam slipped beyond the firelight and let his eyes adjust to the darkness. He tapped his leg twice, instructing Tango to stay at his side.

The night was clear and cool. At this altitude in the Rockies, the stars chased the darkness away. Even without the moon, they were bright enough to cast a shadow. Yet once the moon was completely down, Sam was forced to travel slower with less light. The two Jackals were headed east. They traveled as fast as possible with little regard to the sign they left in their wake. Sam, in turn, had to be careful because he didn't want to spoil the surprise by getting too close too soon. He had to find out where they were going; with any luck, he'd get some answers about why they were taking children.

The game trail was well traveled, pounded flat and littered with elk and deer sign. Every so often, Sam found a boot imprint; the men couldn't have been more than an hour or two ahead of him, he knew. As the trail wound around the valley, it narrowed to the point that Tango was forced to walk behind Sam. They followed the trail over a rise and angled across a ridge into a saddle. On one side was a steep incline covered with loose shale; on the other, the ground sloped almost straight down for a hundred yards before leveling into a shelf clustered with young pine trees.

Sam stopped to looked around. Tango crept next to him and nuzzled Sam's hand with his head. Sam gave his loyal friend a rub on the muzzle. "Sorry, buddy. It just feels like someone's watching."

Finding no sign of anyone, man and wolf continued down the narrow trail as a gray sliver of light appeared on the eastern horizon. To the north, a pack of coyotes howled the start of a new day. Moments like these endeared Sam to the mountains; if only life would leave him alone long enough to enjoy them.

He stopped once more and knelt to examine another track. "Bear," he whispered to Tango. "And he's a big one, too. A grizzly."

Spring wasn't the time to encounter bears, he knew well. They'd be mean and hungry. Coming off a late winter, they'd be playing catch-up on calories.

Sam had no intention of becoming calories.

He stood and tested the wind. It blew down the valley out of the south. That would change when the sun rose, and thermals caused the breeze to reverse. Unfortunately, right now the wind wasn't in his favor; if the bear remained on the trail, Sam's scent would draw it in sooner or later.

The trail angled downhill toward the bottom of the valley, as did the men's tracks. And so did the bear. Sam smiled uneasily at Tango. "This might get interesting."

A lifetime of chasing bad guys prompted Sam to subconsciously check his weapons. He needed only to relax his shoulders and press his elbows against his side to feel the butt of each handgun. The feel of them comforted the old law man.

The sky was getting lighter. Sam knew he needed to get out of the open and move on down the trail. Suddenly, he heard something above him on the slope. Tango growled, but the warning came too late. An enormous mass of muscle and fur had somehow closed in without a sound. The beast was on top of Sam with fangs and claws before he could even interpret what was happening.

The retired marshal's instincts kicked in without thought. He thumbed the release of his holster and drew his Glock 10mm with speed that was uncharacteristic of a man his age. With no time to aim, he jammed the barrel against the huge animal, even as the beast plowed Sam off his feet. Man and bear rolled down the slope, Sam firing shot after shot into the massive predator. The bear roared as each round found its mark.

Both bodies came to rest on the shelf below the trail, the bloody battle ending just as abruptly as it had begun. Moments passed and Sam blinked a few times, then opened his eyes. His gaze swiveled up the ridge, where Tango was pacing back and forth. The wolf looked anxiously for a way down but finally resolved to stand guard from a distance.

Sam tried to catch his breath; he felt as if a huge weight was on his chest. He raised his head to find an enormous arm covered with fur splayed across his upper body. His shoulder was pinned beneath the arm and chest of the bear. He grunted with the effort of pulling himself free. The gamey smell of blood was thick in the air; it wouldn't be long before the carcass attracted attention, he knew. The mountains were full of scavengers that relied on the dead or dying for sustenance.

Sam tried to rise, but gravity imposed its will; the battered warrior fell back to the ground. He lay on his back facing the sky. With shaking hands, he examined his injuries. He was badly bruised, bleeding from several lacerations, but he was in no immediate danger. With some rest, he thought he could continue.

"You need to hurry, Sam."

Sam jerked his head to one side and found Logos kneeling near the bear. The old man lifted a massive paw and examined its claws.

"I don't think I have any hurry left in me, Logos."

"The men you seek heard your shots. They're increasing their lead on you as we speak. Also, the smell of death will soon attract some unsavory guests." Logos held his hand against the bear's paw, comparing sizes. "Truly incredible beasts," he remarked in awe. "You're quite lucky to be alive."

Sam gathered himself onto his knees. "Gotta say, lucky isn't a word that comes to mind, at the moment. Luck ought to involve a tropical drink and a cabana on a beach somewhere. Do I really have to hurry?

I'd rather take a little nap."

Logos chuckled. "Trust me. You don't want those men getting too far ahead."

Sam stood on wobbly knees and took a few deep breaths. While the danger had passed, the euphoria of adrenaline lingered. His muscles would feel fatigued soon enough, and he knew he'd feel that fall for several days. He checked his holsters; the Glock he'd just used was missing. Scanning the ground, he spotted the slide of his weapon protruding from beneath the bear's rear leg. Pulling it free, he examined the gun for damage. It looked fine. Satisfied that it was still functional, Sam fed it a fresh magazine and returned it to his holster. He plucked his hat off the ground and knocked the dust from it.

"Hurry, Sam."

"This is me hurrying after getting my ass kicked by a bear, Logos."

"These men are still dangerous. They can do tremendous harm, if given the opportunity. In this case, distance is time. And time is your enemy."

Sam turned to face Logos, but as was often the case when the old man had spoken his peace, the messenger was gone. Sam squinted up the slope to where Tango remained. It would be impossible to climb in his condition, he knew. With few options, he followed the ridge east toward his adversaries. Soon, he located a path heading in their direction.

The trail was narrow with a cliff face on one side and a sharp drop on the other. It angled dangerously around the ridge. Sam hoped it would eventually intersect the main trail, yet he was keenly aware of the present danger; one misstep would send him into a fall that he wouldn't survive.

For goats only, he thought.

Sam stopped to gather his breath, still exhausted from his fight with the bear. He leaned against the canyon wall and glanced across the valley below. At its head were two waterfalls that flowed from a glacier atop the divide. Water from the falls converged at the center of the valley in a serpentine creek, splitting the land in half. Sam's trail paralleled the creek below. As he looked down to the valley floor, he spotted two figures on a road next to the creek, moving briskly away from him.

They'd covered far more ground than he'd expected and were likely to increase their lead. They were on an open road, after all, while he was still bushwhacking down the mountain.

Sam headed down the trail with more determination. Confident that Tango would soon catch up, he picked up the pace. The goat trail finally leveled out on flatter terrain; Sam was glad to find firm ground on either side. When he stopped to drink from a spring, he realized how long it had been since he last ate. His empty stomach growled in protest.

"No time," he grumbled to himself.

He pushed on. The trail finally emerged onto the valley floor, where he promptly located the old road. He found fresh tracks left by the men and figured them to be a little more than an hour ahead of him, now. Emboldened, he increased his speed on the road, realizing that if the men reached pavement before he caught sight of them, he would lose any ability to track them.

The Jackals had left a conspicuous trail in the dry grit of the road. As Sam rounded a curve, he saw an expansive bridge in the distance with two figures crossing it.

The Rio Grande.

Instinctively, Sam stepped into the shadow of a tree, in case they turned to check their backtrail. Breaking into a jog, he tried to stay on the side of the road, which offered some cover. The men were close to the highway now, he realized, somewhere southeast of Creede. This didn't just mean pavement; it meant more people from whom the Jackals could steal horses and weapons.

The men disappeared from the bridge. Sam scowled, knowing that if he crossed the bridge he might well be spotted. Yet there wasn't time to wait for nightfall. Practically on tiptoes, he approached the bridge and peered to the other side. Beyond the bridge, the road curved behind a group of trees; the men were nowhere to be seen. Throwing caution to the wind, Sam jogged across the bridge and ducked into a copse of willows on the eastern side of the Rio Grande.

He slipped from tree to tree, using the riverbank for cover. He took his hat off and peeked over the edge of the bluff; the Jackals had reached the paved road and were now heading southeast. Sam smiled. They were headed toward a chokepoint in the road—one he knew well. A rock bluff awaited them, creating a gap just wide enough for the road and the Rio Grande.

Wagon Wheel Gap.

Sam watched from a distance as the men walked down the highway. When they approached the narrowest point of the gap, they stopped on the side of the road. Someone must've been approaching from the other direction, Sam realized. Sure enough, the men scampered from the road to hide behind a pile of boulders. There was no cover to aid Sam in getting closer, so he watched from afar.

It was difficult to hear much over the roar of the river, but Sam could see the men sizing up their next victim. A rider came into view. A woman, he thought. When she approached the boulder pile, her horse grew agitated. The big animal refused to go any farther. She planted her heels firmly into its flanks to no avail. When she tried plow-reigning the animal to the left, to get its feet moving, Sam caught his breath.

Dear God...

His stomach clenched as if he'd swallowed a hot coal. It was too far to recognize her face, but he didn't need to. He recognized her frame, the way she moved. There wasn't a doubt in his mind.

Jennifer!

CHAPTER 25

The horses twitched and raised their heads at the hiss of burned coffee dousing the coals of last night's campfire. A cloud of steam billowed into the sky as Kuruk kicked dirt over the wet embers. He'd waited on Sam as long as he could. It was time to go. The horses were saddled, and everyone was anxious to move. He was about to lead the group out of the valley toward Creede when a voice startled him from the near distance.

"Hello, the camp!"

Kuruk pivoted on his saddle, sweeping back his coat to reveal the revolver on his hip. Large fingers wrapped around the handle as two riders approached on horseback. His first impression was that neither posed a threat, yet they led Sam's horse. Kuruk scanned the woods behind them, not about to be fooled by ambush or distraction.

"State your purpose," he bellowed when they reached the campsite. "And tell me who you are."

Tanner introduced himself and Jamie, and then explained Sam's intention of following the two Jackals they'd captured and allowed to escape. He advised Kuruk of Sam's instructions to meet him in Creede. Minutes later, Kuruk's group—now two riders larger—was headed north, moving their way up the valley. Kuruk let Eli and Bendigo lead the way, hanging back to look beyond the mountain in the direction Sam was apparently traveling.

"What are you up to, old man?" he muttered under his breath.

Kuruk had saved Sam's life prior to the Battle of Washington, and they had become fast friends. The Apache chief had recognized the origin of visions that had come to them both, back then. He'd known immediately that God was leading the way and had therefore followed without question. Sam had been a little stubborn, on the other hand; when it came to believing that God would champion or even speak to the likes of him—Samson Crow—he had a hard time. Even now, with no more visions to rely on, Kuruk believed wholeheartedly that he and Sam were still being led. The paths before them were plain as day.

As the sun rose, it broadcasted warm rays across the valley, clearing the mountains. Kuruk started north to follow the rest of his company but hesitated with an ear cupped eastward. He thought he'd heard the distant report of a firearm.

There. There it was again.

And then, again.

Four, maybe five shots in all.

He looked to Tanner and Jamie, who peered back from the tail of the group. "How long has Sam been on the trail?"

Tanner shrugged. "Three or four hours."

"Show me where you camped last night. And hurry."

With Tanner leading the way, the horses dug hooves into the trail and the group climbed through the timber. With Sam's horse in tow, Kuruk followed diligently. The sun was high overhead when they finally reached the camp. Tanner directed Kuruk to the spot where he'd last seen Sam, and Kuruk nodded. Kuruk spurred his horse on to find Sam's trail. Tanner tried to follow, but Kuruk stopped him.

"Thank you, but I can't ask you to go any farther. In fact, I would prefer if you didn't. Too many people stomping around the same patch of woods draws a lot of attention."

The expression on Tanner's face revealed much to Kuruk; the man was clearly in pain.

"I'm sorry," Kuruk added, "but you really should go home now."

"Sir, my little girl—her name is Chasity—they took her over a week ago."

Kuruk nodded and offered a stoic smile. "I will keep both eyes open for your little girl." Without another word, Kuruk turned his horse east and got moving.

"She's five!" Tanner shouted after him. "Red hair and green eyes!"

With a quick wave, Kuruk acknowledged the message and spurred his horse into a trot with Shadow close behind.

The shots he'd heard were now over an hour old, and Sam had been trailing the men for more than three hours by then. Kuruk had much ground to cover. Fortunately, the sign Sam had left was blatantly obvious. Kuruk was confident that he could find Sam, but would he find him alive?

As much as he hoped so, he wasn't sure.

The path was a heavily used game trail that followed the canyon ridge. At times, it became so narrow that he was forced to walk ahead of the horses. The trail eventually opened onto a plateau, where Kuruk immediately recognized bear tracks. He dismounted to examine the bear sign.

Based on the depth of the tracks, as well as the distance between them, Kuruk surmised that a bear had collided with Sam and tumbled down the slope. Near the bottom was a shelf of gray shale where a carcass lay in a heap of bloody fur. Kuruk tied a rope to his saddle, tossed his hat over the horn and rappelled down the slope. Crows had already staked a claim on the carcass; they protested loudly at his arrival before fleeing to the safety of nearby trees.

Kuruk found several spent rounds of brass on the ground around the bear. He identified where Sam had struggled to his feet and then stumbled toward a narrow trail that led east. The big Indian smiled.

"One tough son of a gun," he chuckled.

Grasping the rope, Kuruk started to climb.

The sun was now at its peak, the day about as warm as it would get. Sweat poured from Kuruk's brow as he stepped back onto the Jackal's trail. He drank from his canteen and poured some of the cold water down his face and neck. He plucked his hat from the saddle horn and dropped it on his head. He gave the brim in front a slight tug to secure it in place and then stepped back into the stirrup. Kuruk glanced to one side and stiffened as he swung into his saddle.

Someone was sitting on Sam's horse.

Though startled, Kuruk didn't feel threatened once he'd looked his visitor in the eye. "I know you," he muttered. "I see you sometimes, usually when I'm not looking at anything. I catch a glimpse of you from the corner of my eye, but when I turn to look at you, no one's there."

"And I know you," the old man in the white bathrobe replied. "I have followed you for many years."

"Why have you come?"

"Oh, I try to find every excuse possible to experience my Father's creation. I've actually never ridden a horse before. Do you mind if I ride along for a while?"

"Do you know how to ride?"

"Well, of course not," the old man replied with a laugh. "Why would I need to learn to ride a horse?"

"I suppose you do have a point," the Indian ceded.

"I imagine the horse will just follow you, and that's all I need for now."

Kuruk chewed his lip. "Again—why have you come?"

"The enemy is close, and his horde is closer."

"Are you talking about the Jackals?"

"I'm talking about everything that is evil—Satan and those who fell with him today, those who follow him and the lost who follow no one. Even those who choose no side have chosen a side."

"We thought we were done with that bunch."

Logos sighed. "Evil never leaves. It hides and waits for complacency. Its patience has no end. Evil will exploit the slightest crack in a man's defenses, the tiniest flaw."

Kuruk's gaze fell to the ground as he contemplated the old man's words. "What was our flaw?"

"Everyone assumed the war was over when the last battle ended. How many times has evil been soundly defeated only to return stronger?"

Kuruk was at a loss for an explanation. "So, what's the answer?"

"Watchful vigilance. And remembering that the enemy is always there, always waiting."

Kuruk led his horse down the trail. He recognized one of Tango's tracks and knew that he could follow the wolf to Sam. He stole a glance at Logos and found the old man smoking a pipe. "Glad to see you're still with me," the Indian confided.

"You know, this horseback riding thing is quite relaxing. Sometimes—not often, but sometimes—you humans manage to refine creation. This really is very nice."

Kuruk continued to follow the wolf tracks along the trail as it wound down into the valley. "It's funny—I feel like I've always known you, yet I still don't know your name."

The old man chuckled. "I am Logos."

Kuruk nodded and gave his horse a scratch on the neck. When the path took a steep turn, he glanced back over his shoulder to check on his new friend. "Put your weight in the stirrups and lean back," he suggested.

"What's a stirrup?" Logos pleaded with desperation.

Kuruk laughed. "The thingy you put your feet in."

"The foot thingy? You're having way too much fun with this," Logos chided.

The Apache shrugged. "Guilty as charged. But let's focus on the reason you're here. What's next? More war? Eliminate evil again?"

"Evil was never eliminated, my friend. You must accept that humans weren't given that power."

"So we're fighting a battle we cannot win?"

Logos took a deep breath and sighed heavily. "No, I didn't say that. Humans weren't designed to eliminate evil, but that doesn't mean you can't defeat it."

Kuruk frowned. "You're not making any sense."

"Evil will not be completely destroyed until the very end. That is my father's job. Even then, it will still exist. The enemy and those who choose him will last forever. They won't like where God puts them for eternity, but it will have been their choice."

"Ah, I get it now—Revelations. The lake of fire thing. So we must battle evil our entire lives, with no relief?"

"Well, there is relief. Battles will come and go, but even after a victory as monumental as Washington, you must not let your guard down. Even before you've won a battle, the enemy is already searching for a new angle of attack. Before the smoke has cleared, evil is already regrouping."

"I was afraid you were going to say something like that. So what do we do now?"

"Keep moving forward. Recognize the enemy and know his ways. Deception and lies are the tools of his trade."

"I get that. What I have issues with is that these Jackals or assassins have bought into this belief that God actually approves of their behavior. Many seem to genuinely believe that their god is the same as mine, that they're doing God's will. How can they believe things that conflict so blatantly with God's word?"

"Ah, that is the deception, indeed."

"What is?"

"Their misguided belief. Just because you want to believe something doesn't make it true. They choose to believe in a god who promises them an eternity in paradise, where their reward satisfies lust. Any religion built on violence and intimidation is the invention of man. And one that promises soldiers seventy-two virgins is especially suspect."

"So you believe their religion is a deception?"

"I know it is. The whole basis of their doctrine stems from the notion that God made a mistake."

"How so?"

"They believe their god is the only god. Correct?"

"Yessir."

"They believe their god didn't have a son. Correct?"

"Yes."

"Think it through, then. For their belief to be true, the gospels must be mistaken—the word of God must be a lie. Do you agree?"

"Of course."

"So, for their religion to be based on truth, the Bible must be in error; Jesus simply cannot have been the son of God. Do you believe God is capable of making a mistake?

"No, I don't."

"So, for one religion to be true, the other must be a lie. One worships the true creator, the other a false god. By definition, a false god is an agent of deception, yes? And who is the father of deception?"

"The enemy… Satan."

"Which leads us back to God versus Satan. Who would benefit from discrediting the gospels and the deity of Christ?"

"Satan."

Logos smiled and gave Kuruk a confident nod. "Ah, we've arrived."

"What?"

"Sam is there," Logos said with a finger trained ahead. "At the bridge."

Kuruk followed the old man's finger to a tiny figure crossing a bridge; the structure spanned two ridges that formed the very valley they'd been following. Grinning, he turned to Logos. "I see him!" he exclaimed to an empty saddle.

CHAPTER 26

The roar of the Rio Grande was deafening from mountain snow still melting in June. Sam watched two men advance on his wife as she fought for control over her horse. One removed something from his pocket and shared it with his cohort. Their faces disappeared into the palms of their hands, where they appeared to lick or snort something. Seeing an opportunity in their moment of distraction, Sam leapt from cover and made a dash toward Jennifer. The men were facing her now, unaware that Sam was coming.

Jennifer finally saw the men when they were mere feet away. Their presence agitated her horse even more. One snatched the reins to settle the animal as the other tried to pull Jennifer from the saddle. With the reins torn from her grasp, she kicked desperately at her assailant. The horse finally settled as Jennifer was pulled to the ground. She attempted to clamber to her feet but froze with her gaze trained beyond her attacker.

"Take your hands off my wife, you inbred cur!"

The men turned to appraise the broken and bloody man who dared to confront them in the middle of a highway. One snickered at the old cowboy and shook his head; unimpressed, he returned his attention to the woman. He bent over at the waist to grab her by both arms, forcing her to her feet. He held her at arm's length, standing behind her with only his head exposed. He seemed surprised when Sam stepped forward. With a wicked smile, the Jackal unleashed a cackling laugh.

"You're kidding, right? Best mind your business, old man. You don't want to take on the two of us."

"I'm not here to take on either one of you. I'm here to kill you both."

With a flick of the wrist that neither man saw, Sam drew his Glock and squeezed off a shot. The man's head jerked back awkwardly, a hole gaping just to the left of his nose. His arms relaxed and fell to his side as he slumped to the ground. Sam drew his second Glock in his free hand and leveled it on the other Jackal, who still held the reins of Jennifer's horse.

"Raise your hands."

The Jackal smiled and put both hands in the air. "That was fast. Damn. Where'd you learn to shoot like that, cowboy?"

"In shootin' school, stupid. What's your name?"

"Rowdy."

Sam chuckled and shook his head. "Good name for a bad guy. Where's the rest of your team?"

"My team?"

Sam lowered his head and glared at the younger man from beneath the brim of his hat. "Look, I know who you are, and I know what you've done. You and your idiot minions attacked me and killed my horse. You've caused a lot of trouble for a lot of folks, and I'm done dancing around the truth. Tell me what I want to know or die where you stand."

"You're Crow, aren't you?"

"That'd be me."

Rowdy paused for a moment and closed his eyes tightly. Twisting his head, he pressed his chin against one shoulder. He opened his mouth as if to yawn, and then returned his gaze to Sam. "Oh, yeah… that *Push* was a good one." His body shivered for a few seconds as if nursing a chill, and then settled. "Now, where were we? Oh, yeah—you just killed my friend."

Sam recognized the change in Rowdy's behavior, the influence of a drug. The old marshal held his guns at the ready as the man's demeanor grew more brazen. The Jackal still had his hands in the air, but he'd begun to inch forward. Sam took three steps toward the man and planted the end of his ten-millimeter barrel against Rowdy's head. The lone Jackal closed his eyes, expecting the worst. It would've been easy to pull the trigger, but Sam resisted. Instead, he swept Rowdy's legs with a vicious kick, sending the man hard to the pavement.

"I've tracked you sons of bitches since you killed my horse and left me for dead, and I know about the kids you're stealing. You better talk or die."

Rowdy winced; the painful impact on his body had weakened the man's surly demeanor. "They'll kill me if I talk," he whimpered. "Please..."

Sam shook his head, glaring pointedly at the Jackal. "*I'll* kill you if you *don't*. Tell me where the children are. Last chance."

With a hiss between stained teeth, Rowdy relented. "There's a camp on the river about a mile south of here. They're keeping the kids there."

Sam withdrew the gun barrel from the man's head. He lowered it with the intention of letting Rowdy go, but then a thought struck him: every break he'd given a Jackal had always—without exception—come back to haunt him. He raised the gun again.

"Mister, please—I don't want to die."

"Neither did my horse."

The assassin looked into the eyes of Samson Crow and knew there was no appeal. The click of the trigger, the fall of the hammer—these were the last sounds Rowdy would experience before death claimed him.

Sam holstered both guns and turned to Jennifer. She reached for him with tears in her eyes, wrapping him in her arms with all her strength. "I thought... well, I wasn't sure if I'd ever see you again."

Sam held her close for a long moment and then gave her a gentle smile. "There've been a few times lately when I wasn't so sure myself."

Jennifer took a step back to admire the man who had been through hell for the last two months, taking in his tattered clothes, the blood and cuts from the bear attack. Thin and bearded, beaten and worn, Sam looked more like a bandit than a retired marshal. Yet even now, with evil closing in, the man stood ready to move forward.

"My God, I almost didn't recognize you," Jennifer whispered.

Sam smiled and pulled her close. "What, it's not like I colored my hair or anything."

Jennifer laughed and batted her long eyelashes. "You know what they say, hun. Blondes have more fun."

A sound caught Sam's attention from behind. He turned just in time to catch a giant ball of fur in his arms. Tango howled with delight at being reunited with his brother. Sam scratched the black demon dog's belly and then looked to the west.

Jennifer followed his gaze. "Who is that?"

"Must be Kuruk," he replied, squinting into the distance. "With my horse, too. Aw, the poor guy must be worried about me."

Jennifer eyebrows furrowed. "That doesn't look like Patton."

"Hun, the Jackals killed Patton. These two were part of the team that attacked me. They ambushed me almost two months ago, just below Turkey Creek Lake. Shot me and Tango in an ambush. Patton, too."

"Did you tell her about the grizzly?" Kuruk chimed in as approached.

Sam cocked his head to one side and skewered Kuruk with a taut grin and angry glare. "I'm almost glad to see you, old friend. Almost. I kind of hoped to save that one for a campfire, or sometime a little less dramatic."

Jennifer blinked a few times and lost the smile she'd worn so happily for the last few minutes. "You fought a *grizzly*?"

Sam casually took Shadow's reins from Kuruk and stepped into the saddle. "It's not like I went looking for a fight. He started it."

Jennifer's eyes widened

"Relax, hun. It wasn't even much a fight."

"Not much of a fight? It was a grizzly." Jennifer swung her leg over Asgard and settled into the saddle, eyes flashing angrily.

Sam cleared his throat. "Well, no. He charged me and pushed me over a cliff, so I shot him."

Jennifer slumped in her saddle and stared at her husband with mouth agape. "He… *pushed you*? Over a *cliff*?"

Kuruk snickered as the couple argued, doing his best to hold back a guffaw. The Apache chief knew there was much more to be said about the Jackals, as well as the battle ahead. But he also figured the next few hours didn't have to be quite as intense as the last two months. "Okay, you two lovebirds. Let's save reunion time for later. I'm glad we're all back together, but we've got to get moving."

Sam's smile faded. "You two go on to Creede. I want to take a look at that camp down the road."

"Nah, I go where you go, Kemosabe," the chief retorted with a smile.

"And don't you think for a second that I'm going to let you out of my sight," Jennifer snapped.

Sam laughed as they oriented their horses southeast. "Okay," he mumbled. "Hi-Yo, Silver. Away."

The sun had begun to slide behind the western slope. Clouds gathered in the southwest; the hint of a storm was in the air.

Sam smiled, looking fondly at his wife. "Kuruk told me you and the girls went to the reservation. What are you doing here?"

Jennifer turned away from Sam to hide her expression.

Sam waited for an answer, but none came. Something was clearly wrong.

Jennifer had been dreading this day—the day she'd have to tell Sam about Elise and Tiffany. And now it was here, without warning. She tried to gather herself, taking a deep breath. "We never made it," she said, her mouth suddenly dry like desert sand. She tried to hide beneath her hat, fighting a losing battle against tears.

"What is it, hun?"

"So much has happened," she said in a wavering voice. "Theresa, Elise and Tiffany were in one canoe. Me and Sara were in the other. We got separated and I… I didn't find them until the next morning. They were at the farmhouse past Chimney Rock. Jackals had taken the home, killed the family." She swallowed hard and rolled her lips. "By the time Sara and I got there, they'd taken the girls, too."

"What?" Sam asked, his heart leaping in his chest.

Jennifer choked off a sob and wiped her eyes. "Elise and Tiffany—they didn't make it, Sam. I'm so sorry."

Sam looked at Jennifer, felt her pain. Wiping his own eyes, he took a deep breath. "It wasn't your fault," he said. "Whatever happens, you can't blame yourself for what these… these sons of bitches have done."

Jennifer nodded without reply, thinking, *easier said than done, my love.*

"What about Theresa and Sara? Where are they?"

"They're at the general store in Pagosa with Linda. She'll take care of them."

Sam took his hat off and glanced back at the falling sun. "Let's pick up the pace a bit."

"Sam," Jennifer added, "they have a new leader. And he's really bad—worse than the others, even. Not human."

Sam's grieving frown deepened. "Not human?"

"He's a demon. They call him the Captain. He was at the farmhouse when they took Elise and Tiff."

Sam gave Shadow a tug on the reins, bringing him to a stop. He turned the horse to face Jennifer head on. "Where's this demon now?"

"I saw him in Pagosa two days ago. He stopped at the store. Somehow, he knew I was there. He said he'd made a vow to leave the girls alone, but he was coming after you. He knows you'll be in Creede, Sam."

"How many?"

"There must be about eighty by now. He and another like him have joined forces. The other's name is Asmodeus, but they call him Jack. He seems to be the second in command."

The wheels in Sam's weary head began to turn. "Four against eighty."

Jennifer shook her head angrily. "No, you can't. Not going to happen, Sam."

"It's inevitable, hun. We have to take a stand. No one else can stop them."

"You can't fight him," she insisted. "I watched that devil walk through fire like it wasn't even there! You can't beat him! Don't you see? No one can." Frustrated, Jennifer dug her heels into Asgard's side and let the horse stretch his legs down the side of the highway.

Sam pulled alongside Kuruk and watched Jennifer ride away.

The Apache frowned. “What are you thinking?”

“The Battle of Thermopylae.”

Kuruk’s eyebrows rose. “Wagon Wheel Gap?”

“Exactly. I think with good cover and enough ammo, the four of us can defend a pass like that.”

“I guess we’ll just have to see, won’t we?”

They caught up to Jennifer and approached the camp, which wasn’t far off the road. The place had the look of an old fishing village—the touristy kind, where people had vacationed before the Fall. People milled around without a care in the world, as if everything was normal. A series of cabins lined the southern side of the highway. North of the road, numerous travel trailers were parked near a cinderblock building.

“What’s the plan?” Kuruk muttered.

Sam gave him a sidelong glance. “Let’s go right at ’em.”

CHAPTER 27

A battalion on horseback wound its way down the east side of Wolf Creek Pass. Logos sat on the hood of an old hearse next to a vacant church, watching the procession draw near. Nearby on horseback, Malphus approached his old friend with a smile.

"Ooh!" he crooned. "I like your ride. It definitely feels appropriate."

"Well, unfortunately it doesn't run. A tragic waste."

Malphus chuckled. "It's funny that you even tried to start it."

"Yeah, I know," Logos laughed. "An angel driving a hearse—who would've thought?"

Malphus broke from the procession and walked his horse a few steps closer to the angel. "Have you ever driven a car before, Logos?"

"Actually, no. It's one of the many things that I've failed to accomplish in my career. Of course, I'd never ridden a horse either, until yesterday."

"That is precisely why I do what I do. These opportunities to experience Father's creation are incredible. So many times, I've found myself wishing to be human."

"It's unfortunate that humanity comes with such a hefty price, my brother."

Malphus nodded solemnly. "Yes. That's true. And I wish you'd stop reminding me."

"What are you up to now?"

"Oh, I'm headed to Creede. Hoping to say *hello* to Samson Crow."

Logos dropped from his perch on the hearse and landed on the ground beside Malphus's horse. Giving the horse's neck a rub, he looked into the eyes of the young man Malphus wore as a skin, peering at Malphus himself. The demon was scarred and deformed, made ugly by eons of evildoing.

Logos shook his head sadly. "Are you sure you want to go there?"

"Why do you ask, Logos? Have you forgotten our deal?"

"No, I haven't forgotten. I just know there's more to you than you like to let on. You love this place. It's obvious, and I understand why you do what you do. But my friend, you still hold the foundation of being an angel close to your heart."

Malphus opened his mouth to dispute this, but hesitated. He looked toward his battalion, and then to the mountains as the sun kissed the summit of Wolf Creek Pass. He dropped his head to his chest as if to ask for forgiveness. "You know me too well, Logos. Yet even though I'm torn, I remain forever bound. You know our brother Lucifer would never let me go, and Father no longer wants me. There's no reprieve, no liberation from my predicament. When we were in Father's home and I saw His incredible creation, I was filled with envy. I desperately wanted to experience it all—the taste and feel, the sights and sounds. The textures and scents."

Malphus raised his head toward the sunset along the peaks. He spread his arms wide and took a deep breath. "Can you smell this air? Can you see the beauty all around us? All this He created for humans—mere skins with souls—yet, I wanted it for myself."

The two friends regarded each other in silence for a long moment.

"It's ironic that now, as we approach the end, I'll gain nothing but eternal agony. Once, long ago, I had two choices. I could stay with you and Father forever or follow our brother to this wonderful place. Lucifer was so convincing. I didn't know where it would lead, much less the darkness I would embrace. But I made my choice all the same, and soon I will pay the price. I can only hope that throughout the coming torment, I might cling to memories of my experiences here."

Logos nodded sadly at his friend. He could offer no words of comfort; only a goodbye. "Farewell, brother."

"Farewell to you, my friend."

The demon turned his horse to face the battalion. He urged his horse to the front of the line and halted the procession, ordering his second in command to make camp. He peeked over his shoulder for a final glimpse of his old friend, but Logos was already gone. Malphus smiled with melancholy.

I will miss you, my brother.

Darkness fell, and the moon rose. Campfires soon winked from the open fields beside the Rio Grande. Malphus sat beside the water, listening to the music of Earthly night.

Jack approached from the other end of the camp. "Hey, boss. A lot of my guys are running out of *Push*. Will we be able to get a new load in soon?"

Malphus considered this in silence for a few seconds. One of his teams had been manufacturing the drug at a camp near Creede. Now that he thought about it, he hadn't heard from them in a while. Apparently, production had fallen off as well.

No matter. They would soon be close enough to get as much as they wanted. Malphus had shared the lab's location with no one, because once these fools got a taste of the drug, they would never stray far from its source. The highly addictive intoxicant combined methamphetamine with heroin, often referred to as a *speedball* in pre-Fall drug-abuse communities, avoided by most experienced addicts because of its tendency to kill the user. In the post-Fall apocalypse, these men had become convinced they were chosen, blessed by Allah with an immunity to the drug's adverse side effects. Others, disillusioned by the religion, maintained use of the drug as a numbing agent against their evil deeds, just as the Hashashins had done with their drug of choice during the Nizari age of Islam.

The Nizari Ismaili had struck terror into all who opposed their sect of Islam during the middle ages, along with anyone else unlucky enough to cross their path. They were the original assassins, the renowned medieval warriors of Alamut—named for the fortress of their leader's home,

Alamut Castle.

Malphus had been part of the training, back then. He missed the days of the blade, when men were unapologetically ruthless, barbaric without a hint of remorse. When contests were won on strength, stamina and skill.

Alas, the birth of firearms had changed everything. Guns gave equality to the inferior. Even he, a demon with otherworldly powers, had been held at bay by a woman with a rifle.

Jack cleared his throat. "Uh, sir?"

Malphus sighed, torn from his reverie. "Tell them tomorrow. We'll have more tomorrow." He left Jack and retreated to a stand of trees, away from the noise of the battalion. He sought solitude, a separation from the chaos that had become the norm. He scowled at the thought of his men. They weren't warriors. They didn't share his passion for their mission. They were driven by selfishness, petty desires of the flesh. The honor of battle, the thirst for war—neither was in them. Malphus craved both.

He raised his head to the sky. "These fools have no guts, no spine!" he glowered. "They want only to satisfy themselves. The ancients might've followed a lie, but at least they fought like tigers for their misbelief."

"It's a sad day for humanity," a voice from behind.

Malphus stiffened. "Who's there?"

"Brother, it is I. Lucifer."

Malphus relaxed. "I was beginning to wonder where you've been. It's been a long while."

"I've been distracted on all fronts, Malphus. The Battle of Washington exposed a weakness in our plan; many who bought the deception have since turned to the light. I've been busy coaxing them back to into submission."

"Do you still believe we can win Earth for ourselves?"

"Of course. God will make a new heaven and Earth for his children. A third of heaven's angels will be ours, along with what remains of humanity. I will be the Allah they've sought so relentlessly, and they will be our slaves."

"But that isn't what the word says."

"Do you doubt me?" Lucifer demanded with a smirk.

"I don't doubt you, my brother. But God's word hasn't failed him yet, and you haven't explained how we're to escape judgement and the lake of fire."

"Father will forgive us, brother. I have no doubt. Our fall was part of the plan. How else was He to weed out the unworthy?"

Malphus gazed down the river and enjoyed a moment of peace. He nodded silently. "Thank you, brother, for your patience with me."

"No worries. I must go now, but I'll see you soon. Carry on the battle!"

Malphus found a fallen log beside the river and made himself comfortable. He listened to the rush of the Rio Grande and peered into the darkness. As the night embraced him, he felt his melancholy turn to bitterness.

He lies even to me.

CHAPTER 28

Jennifer dug her heels into Asgard's flank as she charged the fish camp. Her hat flopped behind her, allowing beautiful blonde locks to flow in the wind. Few men in the high country had seen anything like her in years; the Jackals were no exception. As her big horse rushed the main cabin, she swung off him in a cloud of dust.

Two men spilled through the front door to meet her while three more darted in from the cabins across the road. Jennifer panted for breath as a man made a grab for her arm.

"Rowdy will have that hand if you touch me with it," she snapped.

The man hesitated. "Rowdy?"

"Yeah. I'm his old lady now."

Another Jackal stepped onto the front porch and leaned against the doorframe, lighting a cigar with an old Zippo lighter. "Where exactly *is* Rowdy, old lady?"

"He needs help. Somebody ambushed us back toward Creede, at the Gap. He sent me for help. He's holed up in those big rocks beside the road."

"Your too pretty for Rowdy," the cigar-smoking man remarked.

"Well, junior, I'll let you take that up with him."

"I may not be that handsome, but I'm not Rowdy, either," Sam chimed in as he stepped through the door with both handguns drawn. "Raise your hands, gentlemen."

"Well, heck," Jennifer exclaimed. "You're not Rowdy!" She gave her husband a wink. "But I guess you'll do in a pinch."

"If I was Rowdy, I'd be dead."

Sam holstered one of his Glocks and snatched the cigar from the man's mouth. "Nasty habit. Makes your breath smell like an old campfire."

One of the men standing behind Asgard snaked a hand inside his beltline for a small handgun. Without warning, and before Sam registered the movement, the man clutched his chest and fell forward. The thunder of a high-powered rifle echoed through the valley a split-second later.

"Well, I guess he's about a quart low by now," Sam joked, shaking his head. "Anyone else dyin' to prove his stupidity?" He took a moment to look each Jackal squarely in the eye. "I presume that addresses any other plans to reach for a hidden weapon?"

He paused for effect, drilling the men with cold eyes.

"Alright, then. I assume y'all have accepted your role in this little exercise. You're the prisoners, and we're in control. Any questions?"

Sam searched each of the men for weapons while Jennifer covered them with her rifle. When he reached the man who had been smoking the cigar, Sam's jaw clenched involuntarily. Inside the man's pocket, he found an old folding knife with a straight-edged razor blade. Sam tucked it into his own pocket and moved on to the next Jackal.

Kuruk approached from a spruce grove west of the main building with Sam's .300 magnum cradled in his giant hands. Following closely behind was the big black wolf.

Sam greeted his friend with a knowing grin. "You okay, big fella?"

"Yeah, but this thing's like field artillery; got a whole lot of bark with that short barrel. Bite ain't so bad, either."

Sam and Kuruk escorted the Jackals into the main building and ordered them to lie on the floor, face down. Anchored on one wall was a series of large hooks from which an assortment of handcuffs, leg irons and belly chains dangled. Once the tools of law enforcement, these were now being used to deny people their freedom, Sam realized.

With Kuruk's help, each Jackal was shackled with cuffs looped through belly chains to reduce his range of movement. As an added safety precaution, Sam positioned the men in a tight circle with their backs to each other; he used extra cuffs to join the men at their belly chains. They sat immobile in the middle of the room, imprisoned by their own chains.

"I'm almost afraid to ask what they're doing with all of these chains," Jennifer whispered.

"Follow me," Sam replied.

They walked quickly down a corridor lined with rooms on both sides. Each contained six bunk beds endowed with leg irons at the end of their mattresses.

"What's going on here?" Jennifer asked when they reached the end of the corridor, her cheeks pale.

"Isn't it obvious?" Kuruk said bitterly. "Islam has never heard of the Emancipation Proclamation."

The corridor ended at another door; Kuruk opened it warily. Beyond was a huge room that might once have been used as a common area for guests of the camp. The furniture had been replaced with rows of tables, each surrounded by children. The tables themselves were covered in trays lined with slabs of a clear substance.

While the older kids broke the slabs into uniform crystals, the younger ones packaged the final product into small baggies for distribution.

The entire room fell silent at the sight of new faces intruding on their horrible little universe.

"My God…" Jennifer whispered, a hand flying to one cheek.

Stripped from the waist up, each child wore a face mask to filter the air. Small surgical gloves covered their dainty hands to protect them from chemical burns. The children were marked with angry lacerations across their backs, evidence of abuse and torture. There were twenty in all, ranging from six to twelve years old.

"It's okay," Sam told the children, trying hard to force a believable smile. "We're here to take you home."

As Kuruk helped the children remove their masks and gloves, Jennifer began to examine them. Many had been beaten, their torment mapped on their skin by ugly scars and bruises.

"Chasity?" Sam called to the group. "Anyone here named Chasity?"

No one spoke for a moment. But then, a little girl who had been hiding timidly at the back of the group raised her hand.

"Chasity, my name Sam. I met your parents a few days ago, and I'm going to take you to them."

The girl peered shyly from behind another child, not quite ready to trust another stranger. Another man. She was barely six, her matted and tangled hair hiding most of her face. Sam took a step toward her.

"Your mother told me to tell you that she loves you. She can't wait to see you. And your daddy, Tanner? He's been turning this world upside down trying to find you."

From behind her tangled hair, Chasity's eyes widened. For three long seconds, nothing happened; the girl merely stared at Sam, petrified.

At once, she ran to him. Tiny arms wrapped around his leg, trembling with hope. "Please, take me home," she wept over and over again.

Sam lifted the girl and held her against his chest. "Where's your clothes?"

She pointed to a closet at the far end of the room.

They spent the next few minutes sorting through clothes and getting the children dressed. In the meantime, Kuruk headed outside, where he rounded up six of the Jackals' horses and tethered them next to his own. He returned to the room minutes later, gesturing for Sam to follow him. "You need to see this," he muttered when Sam was in earshot.

Sam followed the Apache through the back door and past a barn that stood behind the main building. There, a pile of partially burned trash buzzed with flies. On the backside, lying amidst gobs of melted plastic and charred lumber, were the corpses of two children. They'd been thrown out to burn, discarded after outliving their usefulness.

Sam took in the scene with tears in his eyes. He bent to examine the mutilated body of a girl, recognizing the telltale lacerations of the *death by a thousand cuts.* The children had been the victims of incredible abuse.

"Their throats were cut, Sam. And there are bite marks, like they were sacrificed in some sick ritual."

Sam reached into his pocket for the knife with the straight-edged razor blade. A blade like this—perhaps this very one—had been used to cut these children to ribbons. Sickened, he threw it as far as he could. His anger fueled a fire that had burned for more than a decade; this was but a dried twig added to the flames. He looked away to the setting sun, amazed that such beauty and ugliness could exist in the same world. This mission had taken far longer than intended, yet as his gaze returned to the bodies of the children, he knew it wasn't over yet.

To Kuruk, Sam muttered, "Let's find a shovel, brother."

The sun was almost gone when they returned to the hall. By then, Jennifer had the children ready to go. They left just as darkness fell. For the first time in a long time, the kids felt the excitement of freedom. Each was placed on a horse with an older, more experienced child in front to drive. No more than three to a horse, with Sam and Jennifer carrying one child each. Chasity sat behind Sam with tiny hands clenched tightly around the old marshal's gun belt.

They left the camp in flames. The firelight illuminated their way toward Wagon Wheel Gap in satisfying flickers. No one appeared to be bothered by the roar of the blaze, much less the Jackals' screams as the building collapsed. No one mourned the men who had made the camp a place of evil.

Tango trotted by, sniffing two makeshift crosses that overlooked the river west of the cabins. At a bend in the river where the current became placid, Sam and Kuruk had buried the two young children, each burned beyond recognition. But for the crosses, their final resting spots were unmarked, for no one knew their names. The slower flow of the river cascaded down shelves in bedrock and trickled between boulders; the sound was soothing and tranquil.

Sam whistled to Tango. Within seconds, the wolf had caught up with the caravan and taken his place beside Sam and Shadow.

CHAPTER 29

The sun was setting behind the western range. At best, they had about an hour of light. With darkness and the cold of night closing in, Sam began to look for shelter for the children. He paused at the entrance to Wagon Wheel Gap, looking at the sunset and considering the remaining three-hour ride to Creede.

"What are you thinking, old man?" Kuruk inquired.

Sam peered over his shoulder to check on Jennifer; she was preoccupied with the child on her horse. "The battle of Thermopile will have to wait," Sam whispered. "Our priorities have changed." He gestured toward the children. "I want you to take Jennifer to Creede and leave her there. We'll meet up at Piedra Pass in two days."

"She'll hate us for that."

"Kuruk, she lost most of her life as a slave to this bunch. I won't let that happen again."

Kuruk sighed. "How will I sell it?"

"Leave that to me."

The caravan approached the bridge over the Rio Grande. Sam gave Shadow's reins a tug and brought the pale horse to a stop. He walked his horse to Jennifer's side.

"I'm going to take the kids about a mile and a half south of here on Goose Creek. There's a house there. At sunrise, we'll take Fisher Creek trail over to Piedra Pass."

"I'm going with you," Jennifer insisted.

"I'm sorry, babe. I wish you could, but I need you for something else. I need you to pick up Zack and Emily in Creede and take the long way around to Pagosa. Kuruk will pick up Eli and Ben, and we'll all meet at the Pass."

"I don't understand why we can't all go to Creede."

Sam knew that if he didn't convince her quickly, she'd win the argument.

She always does.

"Look, if we all go to Creede, the entire army tracks us there. It'll be a handful against eighty without the slightest tactical advantage. But if we split their forces here, I can wear them down in the mountains. And Jen, I need you to take Zack and Emily to safety. They'll trust you. You can follow the long way around to Pagosa and we'll meet you there in a week. I need Kuruk, Eli and Ben at Piedra Pass."

"He's right, Jenn," Kuruk added.

"Why don't we just take these kids the long way around? Can't we outrun them?"

"We won't be able to outrun them as a group on an open road, Jen. We can't move fast enough with all these children. By now, the Jackals know I'll be with the kids, and I can assure you the mountain trails will slow them down."

Jennifer knew Sam was right. Reluctantly, she nodded. She helped the child on her horse onto another and walked Asgard to Sam's side. She leaned over and kissed him on the cheek. "I love you," she whispered. "Please come back to me."

Sam gave her a gentle smile, gazing into her eyes. He reached across the empty space, pulled her close and kissed her full on the lips. "We'll be done with this soon, and then we'll run away," he promised. "Nobody will find us. Not even Kuruk."

"Like hell," Kuruk interjected as he passed Sam his saddlebag. "I'm coming, too."

"What's this?" Sam asked, eying the saddlebag.

"Jerky. Maybe enough to get you through a day with that bunch, but that's it. Still, it's better than a growling gut."

Sam thanked the big Apache and then led the children across the bridge over the Rio Grande. Jennifer watched the caravan until it was out of sight, a hand cupped over her mouth.

The children were quiet as darkness closed around them; Sam knew it was time to find shelter when a boy started to cry.

Sam sidled next to the boy's horse. "Hey, buddy, I know this is no fun. But we have to be tough and get through this, okay? We want to get you back to your family. You want that don't you?"

Sam could see the boy's glassy eyes in the low light of the rising moon. The boy nodded and wiped his cheeks.

"Good, then. We'll find a place to rest soon, and I'll see what I have in this pack to eat."

Even with the moon only a quarter full, it illuminated the road before Sam like a beacon. Soon, he was able to make out the rooftops of buildings he'd seen on his recent trip down the valley. As they approached one, Shadow grew restless, nickering several times. Sam patted him on the neck to settle him and addressed the home from the road.

"Hello, the house. Anyone home?"

He waited for a few seconds and tried again. When no reply came, Sam dismounted and tied Shadow to a hitching post beside the front gate.

"You guys wait here and try to be very quiet."

He stepped onto the porch and rapped his knuckles on the front door.

Seconds passed with no response. Sam turned back to the horses but froze. He could swear he heard something behind him. Then again, it might well have been his ears reminding him just how old he was. He pivoted back toward the door just in time to see the latch rotate.

The door creaked open wide enough to reveal an elderly man inside wearing overalls and a fedora. He gestured for Sam to come closer. In one hand, he held an oil lantern; in the other, a Bible. The flickering light of his lamp cast an eerie glow. He held it high enough to illuminate the porch and took a minute to assess the rough-looking man on his doorstep.

"Boy, you look like you saddled a cyclone with teeth," he observed in a gravelly voice. "I've been expecting you, but y'all took so long, I fell asleep."

"Expecting us?"

"Yeah. I have an alarm system set up down the road. Gives me a good thirty-minute warning if someone's riding in on horseback. It's motion activated, so the minute y'all started into the valley, I was watching you on a computer monitor."

"Pretty high tech for an old guy," Sam remarked with a chuckle.

"Not really. Just an old hunting trail cam we used back in the day to locate elk herds for high-paying clients."

The old gentleman held the lantern off to Sam's side and looked beyond his broad shoulders at the mob of children. He made his way past Sam and down the porch steps to where the children waited on horseback. "My word," he wheezed.

He took a tentative step toward Shadow. The horse nickered and moved closer to the man, checking his scent. He nickered again, then nodded his head up and down.

"Well, would you look at that," Sam mumbled to no one in particular.

The blue roan lay his head across the man's shoulder and whinnied. The old man laughed and beamed back at Sam.

"Glad to see this old boy survived. I raised him from a colt."

Sam grinned. "You raised a good one. Saved my bacon up there in the high lonesome. There was a whole herd with a big boss mare."

"Bay Roan? About seventeen hands?"

"That would be her."

"Well, I'll be. I can't believe they're still around. Most folks who survived the disease left the ranch. It was just me and my wife for a decade. And now, it's just me. I turned these guys out a few years ago. Couldn't take care of them anymore." He stroked Shadow affectionately on the neck. To Sam, he offered his hand and shuffled back to the porch.

"I'm Joshua," he said as they shook hands. "And you must be Samson Crow."

"How'd you—" Sam started to ask.

"Not many people travel with a black wolf; nor do they look and smell like they've been fighting in a bear's den for days on end. Hard to mistake you for anyone else with calling cards like that. Now, let's get them kids down and bring them inside."

One by one, the children dropped from the backs of their horses and allowed Sam to corral them into the cabin. They stood wordlessly in the entryway, piling up in the space. Sam and Joshua watched the kids huddle together with heads bowed, eyes trained on the floor.

Joshua motioned toward the fireplace. "Make yourself at home, guys. Go warm yourself by the fire."

The children were timid at first, but when one boy dared to brave the first step, the rest swarmed behind him toward the fireplace.

The cabin's entryway opened into a large great room decorated with game trophies. There were several bear skins and a mountain lion next to the hearth, not to mention a mountain goat and elk heads mounted on the walls.

"What's wrong with them?" Joshua wanted to know as Sam followed him into the kitchen. "They seem a little… out of it."

"They've been through a lot. I guess you know about the guys up the road at the fish camp?"

"Yeah, we had a run-in a time or two. I finally agreed to work a deal with them just so they'd leave me alone; I keep their horses trimmed and shod. It's worked out okay so far, I guess. Haven't had any problems since."

"Josh, those guys are part of the same bunch I've been fighting for the last few years."

"You mean ISIS? I figured they were all worm-bait by now."

"Well, most are. Those who survived got lost in the crowd. Many lost their faith. Consistent failure has a way of doing that to a cult. Plenty joined up looking for a free meal ticket; it didn't take long for them to find another cause to cling to. The Battle of Washington knocked them to their knees, but the survivors escaped to regroup somewhere. And now this bunch in the Rockies may be all that's left."

"What are they doing here?"

"Can't be sure, but my money's on oil. Eventually, the country will get back on its feet. When it does, they'll try to get their clutches in by controlling the oil supply."

"I'd like to say that's ridiculous, but it makes a little sense. I thought these fellas were just some old cowboys who liked to raise a ruckus every now and then."

"You aren't alone. They've fooled a lot of folks. They figured out how to infiltrate our communities. We forgot 9-11 pretty easily, and in this age of little or no technology, it's almost as easy to forget their little invasion a few years ago. After Washington, they found a place to hole up and learn new tactics. Completely changed their mode of operation." Sam scratched his chin thoughtfully. "I don't have any proof of this, but I suspect they watched old movies to study how to look, how to walk and talk like a cowboy. 'Yes ma'am' and 'yes sir' will take you pretty far out here, and they've been using the kindness of good mountain folks to infiltrate small towns all over the Rockies. Eventually, they'll convert or kill everyone they meet. They started with me and my family."

"I'm sorry, Sam. What happened?"

"I'd been ambushed in the wilderness, left for dead, when they attacked my home. They got two of my girls. Killed them in cold blood."

Joshua paled. "My God. We've lost too many good people to evil, lately." His gaze shifted back to the great room. "What exactly were they doing with these kids?"

"Pretty much anything they wanted, I'm afraid. They were mostly using them to cut and package dope. They've been slinging something called *Push* to their compadres out of those cabins by the lodge." Sam shook his head sadly. "Funny thing—they started this mission a thousand years ago, and all the evil they danced with ate them alive. Now they're nothing more than a bunch of thugs thirsty for a bullet."

"What's your plan?"

"I have to get these kids to safety. Any help you can give would be much appreciated."

"Where are you headed?" The old man chewed his lip uncomfortably. "I'll help however I can, but you can't stay here. I'm sorry."

"Yeah, I understand. Come morning, about eighty men will ride up this valley. I'm sorry, Joshua. I didn't think anyone was back here."

"Sorry, nuthin'. We'll fix 'em good, but let's get these kids some food now so they can rest."

"You have food to spare?"

"Tons. My boss prepared for everything, except for what he couldn't see. Damn Pandemic killed him. He built a bunker beneath this place that could house his whole family, as well as his employees—almost twenty-five people. I rarely touch the food stores because I prefer fresh game. Elk, deer, trout."

"I hear that."

"Anyway, I'll heat up some stew. They left gallons freeze-dried in the bunker."

It wasn't long before the smell of beef stew filled the air. A small head peeked into the kitchen. Sam smiled and motioned for the little girl to enter.

"I'm hungry," she said, rubbing her eyes.

From the stove, Joshua flashed her a grin. "It's just about ready, hun."

"Joshua, this is Chasity. She's been helping me ride my horse."

"Nice to meet you, Chasity. Would you like some stew?"

She nodded slightly, walked to the kitchen table and sat down as if the cabin had been her home her entire life. Sam called the other children into the dining area, where they ate until the entire pot of stew was gone. Lounging in the comfort of the fire with full bellies, it wasn't long before the kids fell sound asleep on the floor. Sam and Joshua walked the horses over to the corral and hung their saddles and tack on the fence.

Sam gazed at the placid moon. "We'll get these kids moving about sunup. That should give us a head start by a few hours."

An hour later, Sam found a sofa to stretch out on. As hard as he tried though, sleep eluded him. He rested his head, closed his eyes and tried to design a plan that might buy him enough time to get the kids to Pagosa. Fatigue eventually found the old marshal, drawing him into a time and place very far away—a time before history.

Sam watched from a distance yet seemed to see everything as if it was right before him. He could almost reach out and touch the dream.

The village was centuries old, its location clearly chosen for defense. Dozens of homes were carved from the mountain wall, no less than twenty-five feet off the valley floor. Ladders were dispersed here and there, each shared by multiple households. The village's inhabitants wore animal skins embellished with carved bits of horn, claws and elk ivory.

The villagers moved about the valley without concern, women washing clothes in the stream, children playing among the trees. Most of the men had traveled far from the valley to hunt deer, elk and buffalo. They lived a hard life, but it was all they knew. Rarely did a villager see forty summers.

A butterfly caught the interest of a young boy, who made chase with little hesitation. His mother called after him, but just as young ones have challenged their parents since the dawn of mankind, the boy ignored his mother and continued to run. No longer interested in the butterfly, he was now running and laughing just to be rebellious.

The boy's mother abandoned her busywork to chase after him, calling his name repeatedly. Her eyes shot to a line of tall posts that marked the boundary of their territory.

The boy ran even faster, thinking it all a game. As he approached the end of the valley though, his step faltered. Animal skulls and hides were displayed on posts there, marking the otherwise invisible edge of safety. He was too young to understand the rituals that kept their valley safe. He simply couldn't imagine the evil he was about to unleash on his people.

And so, he ran on.

His mother stopped and fell to her knees, sobbing and pounding her chest with clenched fists. Her child had stepped beyond the boundary, where she could longer pursue him. She cried out for his return and heard him just beyond her line of sight, still laughing as he ran. Suddenly, a shriek echoed through the valley. And then… silence.

The Wood Demons.

Sam stood by in awe as the woman returned to her village alone, her body racking with sobs. He saw her clearly, yet he could somehow see through her eyes as well. Though distraught with shock and grief, she took only a moment to compose herself. Outwardly, she appeared to accept the loss of her child as if she'd lost an article of clothing. A moment later, she passed the women on the creek, who continued about their chores as if nothing had happened. She slowly meandered through the trees toward one of the ladders. Just as her foot came to rest on the bottom rung, a scream erupted from behind her, followed by manic shouting.

"Climb!"

She launched up the ladder with others on her tail. She didn't dare turn to catch a glimpse of the chaos. She stumbled into her home in the cliff face and buried her head in a pile of fur bedding in the corner of the room. She covered her ears to muffle the screams of those who didn't make it up the ladders in time.

Squinting, Sam peered beyond the doorway of the home as villagers frantically pulled up the ladders and laid them behind the ledge. It dawned on Sam that he wasn't merely an observer; he was part of the dream. Yet when he tried to help, his feet refused to move, as if lodged in the rock itself. Try as he might, Sam was unable to move in his own dream.

On the ground below, villagers young and old were being dragged away by creatures he didn't recognize. They were humanoid, only huge. Tall and lean, but incredibly muscular. One turned to look Sam directly in the eye; it was then that—for all its human qualities—the creature revealed just how inhuman it actually was. Its face was more or less human in shape, but that's where the similarities ended. With the eyes of a raptor and a short, muzzled mouth like that of a large cat, this creature was built for one purpose.

An ultimate predator.

The creature's jaws protruded like a vice; when it opened to hiss at Sam, two rows of shark-like teeth were revealed. Sam had a sense that this creature would top the food chain on any continent.

Thank God it was only a dream.

The beast unleashed a screech that seemed to alert the others. In unison, they bolted for the ledge where Sam stood. As they closed in on him, Sam realized just how huge these beasts really were. Much larger than any human he'd ever seen, the nearest was at least twelve feet tall while others behind him stood at least a foot taller.

Sam noticed a ladder was still in place next to the woman's home; he started to pull it up himself. The creatures picked up speed, covering ground faster than Sam could've imagined possible. The nearest made a leap for the ladder as Sam gave one last heave. Claws scraped the bottom rung of the ladder but mercifully slipped off. The creature fell to the ground with a squeal of frustration. It stood completely upright and glared up at Sam, baring long, pointed teeth.

He's almost human.

"What on God's green earth is that?" he gasped.

"Nephilim… Wendigo!" came a voice from behind him. The woman stood at the entry to her home, pointing at the creature with a trembling finger.

"Nephilim… Wendigo!" she said again, repeating the phrase over and over with eyes wide and full of grief.

Sam turned to face the creature again, but it was gone; the leaves of nearby shrubbery wavered in its wake. Adrenaline surged through his system, stealing his breath and sending tremors down his body. Sam tried to settle himself, turning to the woman who wept behind him. He wanted to comfort her, but she'd begun to fade into black. The shaking in his limbs worsened until suddenly—

At once, Sam awakened with Joshua shaking him by the shoulder.

"Sam! Wake up! They're coming!"

CHAPTER 30

The moon shone behind the two demons, Malphus and Asmodeus, as their battalion rode toward Creede under the cover of night. When the formation approached the fish camp, Malphus knew at once that something was wrong. Asmodeus noticed as well. The acrid odor of burning trash and human flesh spurred both demons into a gallop. Within minutes, they'd reached what remained of the fish camp lodge.

Malphus pointed at several men, his jawline tightening. "Check the other cabins," he spat. "See if the labs are still intact."

The Jackals broke rank and ran to the cabins by the river. They returned soon after with poor tidings. The labs had all been destroyed; nothing was left.

Malphus turned angrily on his second in command. "Jack, this was all of the *Push* we had left. These men are coming down soon, and they'll be coming down unbearably hard. I need them on the hunt soon."

"Where do you want me, Captain?"

"Crow's guys have been here. Send a scout to find their tracks. I want to know where they've gone."

"Can we not wait until daylight?"

"Don't question me, Asmodeus. Just do what I say."

Jack nodded. "I'll do it myself, then. These humans can't see worth a damn in this low light."

He spurred his horse into motion. Once he was beyond the fish camp, he began to examine the ground. The pavement was old and worn, covered with dust and mud in some places. Tracking wasn't difficult for Jack; he was patient, and he knew what to look for. The road went on for a mile with nothing but pavement. Yet there were fresh scuffs on the blacktop where a horse had dragged a hoof or perhaps stomped at a biting fly.

With a cliff face to the right and a river to the left, the only route possible was forward. Unless… there *was* that bridge.

*****

Malphus appraised the rest of his men, his gaze bouncing from one to another with waning confidence. He found himself looking into the eyes of his brother, who he'd willingly followed out of paradise. "Along for the ride, or will you actually be doing something this time?" Malphus grumbled.

Lucifer smirked. "Getting a little cocky for a subordinate, don't you think?"

"I wouldn't call it cocky. I just find it frustrating that you demand so much of your men, only to show up when all the work is done. Convenient, wouldn't you say?"

"Little brother, aside from destroying their only motivation, it doesn't look like you've accomplished much for my men. Why would I bother to take credit for doing nothing?" He shook his head, then flashed a sly grin. "Would this have anything to do with your meetings with Logos?"

"No, not at all. I think I've been emphatically clear to him that my path does not waiver."

"Then why do you question my motives and our fate?"

Malphus crossed his arms. "My brother, since the day we were cast out of our father's home, you have had but one driving force, and that is destruction. I followed you because I longed to experience Father's creation. I didn't mind the games at first; it was like a chess match for the souls of these pathetic little humans, not to mention the freedom to play dress-up with their beautiful skins."

He smiled almost wistfully; a split second later, his features hardened again. "I've grown weary of your deceit. Deceiving humans is one thing, but your own kind? You've lied to me many times, brother, and I'm done pretending that creation will one day be ours."

Lucifer frowned with exasperation. "I can't believe you doubt me now, when we're so close!"

"Close to what?" Malphus demanded. "Our demise? Why do you lie to me? Creation will never be ours! I have chosen to follow you for eternity, for better or worse. Yet your compulsion to lie to me—your own brother—tells me all I need to know. Father doesn't lie. Deceit isn't in him. Yet you are filled with it... even toward me. I'll finish this mission, but then I'll be leaving."

Lucifer smiled faintly. "I don't think you will."

"What's that supposed to mean?"

"Malphus, I can only imagine the seeds of doubt Logos must've planted in your mind; they've grown into rebellious behavior."

Malphus couldn't help but laugh at the irony. "I am becoming you."

"In what way?"

"You doubted Father and rebelled. Now I, your second, doubt *you* and face the same fate."

The men waiting behind their leaders had become nervous. While they couldn't see Lucifer or hear the conversation, the entire battalion felt the turbulence emitted by the angry demons. Perhaps of more immediate concern, the soldiers were beginning to feel the crash as their most recent hit of *Push* metabolized from their systems. Some had developed a twitch; others picked at sores that weren't there. Soon, they'd be completely useless.

"So, my brother—what now?" Malphus asked with a smirk.

Lucifer glared at his second in command with an intensity that could only be interpreted as a threat. The fallen angel turned his horse and rode into the darkness. Malphus watched his brother until even the moonlight seemed to retreat from the demon.

A figure appeared on the darkened horizon a moment later, heading toward Malphus at a gallop. Just when it looked like the rider might crash into Malphus, Jack skidded to a halt at his feet.

"Two sets of tracks," he announced. "Two horses headed toward

Creede. Eight more turned left at the bridge and crossed the river."

"Was there any wolf sign?"

Jack nodded. "Across the river."

Malphus sighed as he watched the moon glimmer from the back of his horse. He looked at Jack and nodded toward the scene. "Peaceful, isn't it? Asmodeus, do you ever tire of this mission?"

"Not at all," he replied. "I despise these human animals. They're filthy and weak, not to mention ignorant beyond all understanding. I suppose if I've grown tired of anything, it's wearing their skins. I detest their stench."

"Well, I doubt they'd accept us in our true form, however evil their hearts might be." Malphus watched a dot glide across the sky and smiled. A satellite. How quickly mankind had lost all they'd worked for. It had been truly heartening at the time. Now?

"Look through the cabins for enough equipment and precursors to piece together a lab. We need to manufacture some product. We still have a few hours to kill; let's try to give these animals something to live for."

As his second headed for the cabins, Malphus swung from his saddle and dropped to the ground. Scowling, he started toward the river.

I've got to escape this madness, somehow.

He was caught on the wrong side of Lucifer, stuck babysitting human idiots. They'd sell him out in a second for a single fix of *Push,* he knew. It wasn't merely the most powerful drug on the planet; it was the only remaining currency for men who had lost all interest in the simpler pleasures of life.

What a job, he thought. *With not much of a payoff, either.*

The demon fell into stride next to the Rio Grande, walking briskly until he stumbled on two fresh graves. He gazed at the crosses. It wasn't hard to imagine the story of two children, conditioned by abuse and snuffed out when their usefulness began to dwindle.

They're probably better off now.

He walked around a bend in the river and silently rejoiced that he was beyond the sound of the camp. He sat on a rock and watched the water cascade over a series of boulders. The peaceful sound reminded him of better days.

"Nice, isn't it?"

Malphus groaned. "You're intruding, Logos. I'd prefer to enjoy this without your commentary."

"Very well. I just wanted to warn you."

"About what?"

"Your second in command has his eyes on your job."

"It's that obvious, is it?"

Logos nodded. "I'll leave you alone, for now. Enjoy your solitude. But watch your back tomorrow, my friend. You are no longer in Lucifer's favor."

"Always, brother. Thanks for the warning."

Again, Malphus found himself alone, which was precisely as he preferred it. No betrayal. No babysitting. No uncertainty.

Sadly, the only being I can trust is my enemy.

Abruptly, the demon heard shouting, followed by a set of cheers. Someone had built a large campfire in the parking lot of the old lodge. With a mighty sigh, Malphus rose and strolled back. Backlit by the fire, a group of his Jackals stood at the edge of the old trailers, bouncing around like children. Asmodeus stood nearby with a bag of *Push*. The one-gallon freezer bag contained a hundred or more individual baggies, ready for distribution. Even from a distance, the creamy white crystals were unmistakable.

Jack caught the Captain looking at him and smirked. He began to pass out the drug to its many addicts. "We're back in business, my brother," he said with a sinister grin. "Undoubtedly, one of your men here at the camp was holding out."

Malphus rewarded this with a blank expression. "Well, it's irrelevant now, considering they're all dead. Besides, who's to say someone was holding out? He could merely have been planning for the future. And I, for one, think it's damned fortunate for us that he did."

Malphus turned to leave once more, flustered by Asmodeus's insolent attempt to call him out in front of the men. He took a step but paused. Over his shoulder, he shouted, "Have the men ready to move two hours before sunrise."

"That's in three hours," Asmodeus protested.

"Precisely. Is there a problem?"

His second scowled and bit off a snide retort. "No."

"Good. And I want you to advance the valley with a scout as soon as possible."

"But—"

"Are you questioning me?" Malphus roared.

There was a brief hesitation with eyes smoldering. "No."

"Very well. I expect a full report before we ride." Malphus left his second in a rage. *I will end this trivial nonsense tomorrow*, he promised himself.

From a distance, he watched the men grow more and more intoxicated as the evening progressed, with no regard for the day that lay before them.

Idiots.

He was aware that, in light of recent events, he should prepare for more than one battle. And this Samson Crow was becoming more than just an irritant; a relentless and resourceful animal, the man was. Malphus closed his eyes and tried to concentrate on the calming sounds of the Rockies. The river seemed to whisper nearby; the night wind whistled a love song through the trees. Yet spoiling it all was the obnoxious yaps of his Jackal army. Opening his eyes to look skyward, Malphus realized time was getting close.

Where was Asmodeus? They should've been ready to go by now.

The demon stood and approached the fire, where his men still raved from the powerful drug coursing through their veins. Their senses were on high alert, their bodies burning energy at an alarming rate. Their heartrates surged, their blood pressure spiked. Malphus could sense this, along with their mindless joy. Yet how long their feeble bodies could tolerate such abuse was beyond him. He was about to address the group when the clap of hooves approached in the darkness.

Asmodeus climbed from his mount and addressed his commander in a tone that was considerably humbler than his previous state. "Sir, Crow's only three miles from here," he said. "They were still bedded down when we left. For the moment, we have the advantage."

"Are you sure?"
"Yes, sir. One hundred percent."
"Ready the men," Malphus ordered. "We leave in ten minutes."

CHAPTER 31

Sam almost fell from the sofa when Joshua dropped a large backpack at his feet. The old man moved among the children, trying to wake them. Sam pulled on his boots and set his hat on tight. Joshua disappeared into the bowels of the house and returned seconds later with a stack of wool blankets.

Sam looked at Joshua, still shaken from his dream. "Have you ever heard of the Nephilim or Wendigo?"

Joshua's eyes widened. "Well, the Nephilim is a word the Bible uses in the Old Testament to describe giants. They were thought to be the offspring of fallen angels who lay with humans. Wendigo is a name American Indians gave to evil forest spirits. The wendigo supposedly craved human flesh."

Sam thought about the dream for a moment, about the mother who had used the names interchangeably. "Could they have been one and the same?"

"I guess it's is possible. There are a lot of similarities in stories from different cultures."

"What do you think happened to them?"

The old man shrugged. "Humans are here; they are not. I have to assume humans got tired of being eaten."

Sam chewed his lip contemplatively. "I can't explain how this works, Josh, but every now and then I have a dream that means something. I think my dream last night was specific enough to be a message. I just have to figure out what it means."

Handing out the extra blankets to the children, Joshua nodded without a hint of skepticism. "It's cold out," he said. "And it's gonna get colder as we head over the mountains. I don't have any children's clothes, so these blankets will have to do."

"What's in the backpack?"

"Jerky, dynamite, grenades. Some tripwire."

Sam shook his head, rubbing the lingering exhaustion from his eyes. "Grenades? What's a horse ranch doing with grenades?"

"Boss was a prepper. Why, you don't want 'em?"

"Oh no, you're not getting these back," Sam retorted with a grin.

Joshua locked the front door and wrapped an old belt around a cluster of dynamite sticks. He nailed the belt to the entryway floor to keep it from moving. Next, he retrieved a spool from his coat pocket and ran a length of wire to the doorknob. The other end was secured to the pin of a hand grenade he'd taped to the dynamite.

Sam watched the older man still wearing his overalls and fedora. "Is there something in your history you should be telling me?"

Joshua grinned. "Let's save the small talk for later. Everybody out the back door."

*****

The *Push* high was at its peak; a few of the men struggled to focus on the task at hand, yet they scrambled for their horses without hesitation. However restless, the entire Jackal army was ready to ride in minutes.

The moon had dropped behind the western ridge when eighty riders crossed the bridge at Wagon Wheel Gap. Most knew to trust their horses in the darkness, and for them, the old road was an easy ride. Others had a rougher time, bumbling and grumbling in the absence of light. Nevertheless, the army pushed on.

As the sky began to turn gray from the break of dawn, the Captain spied the ranch ahead. "Which cabin is it?" he asked.

"The big one in front. There was a flicker of firelight inside earlier. Smoke from the chimney, too."

"Have the men surround it. Assemble a team of six to breach the front door."

Asmodeus gave the orders and his men reacted rapidly, for they could taste the coming battle on the tips of their tongues. Poison flowed through their veins without restraint, bending their already weakened minds toward evil desires. It took mere seconds to surround the house. The selected squad of men approached the front door. Asmodeus glanced up at the chimney, from which smoke still plumed in the moonlight.

Something didn't feel right.

"Jack," Malphus hissed to Asmodeus. "Come here."

Jack rode back to where Malphus was waiting. Frustrated, Asmodeus opened his mouth to address his commander. In that moment, a member of the entry team shouldered the front door open. A sudden flash of light engulfed the cabin as it exploded. Wooden shrapnel pelted the two demons while the blast itself spooked their horses. Malphus managed to gain control of his animal. When he turned his attention to his men, he found several on the ground, dead or dying. Splintered wood and slabs of smoldering timber were scattered in all directions.

Asmodeus looked at his superior, whose gaze remained on the burning cabin.

"How did you know?"

What little structure was left of the cabin was now engulfed in flames. The entry squad was nowhere to be found. Malphus glared into the maw of destruction for a long moment, seething, and then turned to Asmodeus.

"I didn't know," he finally replied. "Crow just seems to be one step ahead of us at every turn. They must've seen or heard you coming."

"Impossible. We never came within a hundred yards of the home."

"Nevertheless, they're gone. And we're down at least a dozen men."

Asmodeus bared his teeth in frustration. "What should we do with the wounded?"

"Finish them," Malphus said dryly. "We have no time to delay."

Asmodeus nodded.

"Get your scout and find their trail. They're still close; I can feel it."

CHAPTER 32

With the horses saddled, Sam helped the children onto their mounts. When he hoisted Chasity onto Shadow, the little girl paid him with a smile that warmed his heart. He caught a glimpse of Joshua approaching from the stables on a beautiful palomino. Across the old man's back was an ancient Remington 742 Woodmaster. On his side, a Colt 1911 .45 was holstered.

Sam grinned. "Clinging to what works, I see."

"Yessir! They haven't failed me yet."

"Josh, did you used to guide this country?"

The old man nodded. "All the way up Goose Creek Valley to South River Peak."

"Can we get over the top there?"

Joshua cringed. "No, it's too steep. The only way over is up Fisher Creek. Pretty rough country, either way."

"Can we get to Goose Lake?"

Nodding, Joshua gave his mount a scratch on the neck. "The trail beside Fisher creek will take you straight to Goose Lake."

"Well, that's where we're headed, then. We'll move pretty quickly, as long as the road lasts. I need you to pull up the rear—don't want to lose any kids." Sam nudged his heels against Shadow's flanks and led the caravan away from the horse ranch.

The stars alone illuminated the road well enough for the horses to find their way. They followed the road for about an hour, chewing up a lot of ground at a brisk pace. Suddenly, a distant thunderclap rumbled up the mountain. Sam halted to check over his shoulder.

Joshua flashed a cocky smirk from the rear of the caravan, giving Sam an emphatic thumbs up. "That'll keep 'em busy for a bit!"

Sam nodded with enthusiasm but urged the caravan into a quicker pace. "We better move a little faster from here on out. They'll be coming harder than ever now." He eyed the clouds gathering in the north. "Hopefully we'll get some rain to wash out our tracks."

"Sam, it's still early enough in the year for snow up where we're headed."

Sam nodded grimly.

Chasity clenched the belt around Sam's waist as they traveled. Soon, they were forced to slow as the road faded into a game trail.

It doesn't take long for Mother Nature to reclaim what was hers, Sam reflected.

The western horizon brightened at the approach of morning. Saplings and shrubbery grew between the ruts of the old road. It didn't take long in the morning light for Sam to realize they were nearing a body of water. Sure enough, the trail opened up beside a lake. Sam admired the untouched beauty as a flock of geese rose from the water ahead of them. A cow elk bounded from the shallows into the woods with a calf on her tail, leaving gem-studded rings in the lake. Riding through the wilderness, seeing the abundance of wildlife, the children seemed to relax, gasping and whispering at the exotic sights.

No matter how serious life got for Sam, a ride through the high country always made his troubles seem insignificant. Seeing the children experience it for themselves tugged at the corners of his mouth. Still, while Sam relished the soothing whisper of the wilderness, he knew all too well they couldn't let their guard down, not even for a second.

As they reached the end of the lake, the valley narrowed. The old road began to ease upward and soon withered to nothing more than a faint game trail. The group had a clear view of the creek below, and Sam was grateful they didn't have to deal with any deadfalls. When the trail leveled onto a small plateau, Sam and Joshua helped the kids dismount to stretch their little legs. From Joshua's backpack, Sam divvied out a handful of jerky to each child. By now, they'd gotten used to the wolf trotting beside them; one of the boys gave his share of jerky to Tango.

Sam smiled. "I'm sure he appreciates the gesture, but we have to be careful, guys. This meat needs to last us a while."

"He gets hungry too, Mister Sam," pointed out one of the older boys.

Sam almost laughed at the young man's sincerity. "I can assure you that he won't miss a meal out here. He's probably wandered off and eaten twice just since we left."

Sam offered some jerky to Joshua, but the old man waved him off.

"Don't worry about me, I have plenty in my pack. This old boy don't miss many meals, either."

"Good. Now look, I'm heading back to that narrow run down the trail to plan a little surprise. Be back in a few."

It didn't take long for Sam to pick the perfect spot. He carefully laid out three grenades in a tidy daisy chain. He set a tripwire well beyond the point of explosion to maximize destruction across a wider area. On his way back, he stopped beside an old spruce and unpacked the last grenade. He ran another tripwire across the trail, this one set to detonate at the point of contact. If everything went according to plan, the Jackals would be down another third by dusk. They'd have to slow their pace to search for more booby traps.

Satisfied with his work, Sam returned to the caravan. Joshua had already helped the kids back into their saddles. Everyone was ready to ride. The sun was bright and warm now, but Sam was ever conscious of a cloudbank that approached ominously from the north. It wasn't long before he felt the wind shift. A sudden chill covered him as the clouds obscured the sun.

The trail continued higher, and soon a cold shower bombarded them. Two of the children began to cry. Sam stopped and dismounted. He unpacked the blankets he'd stored in the pack behind his saddle and handed them out to the children. Trying to encourage them, he smiled warmly at the group.

"We might get a little cold and wet here, but we've got to keep moving," he explained. "We'll find some shelter and get a fire going as soon as we can. If things go our way, we'll be home in a couple of days."

Sam caught Joshua looking at him and imagined he could read the old man's thoughts.

Don't make promises you can't keep.

Another hour found Sam and his caravan at the fork of Goose and Fisher Creeks. Sam took in the rugged terrain that lay ahead with a frown.

Joshua eased beside him and spoke in a low voice. "I didn't say this would be easy."

Sam considered the climb ahead with unease, knowing it would be tough enough without children to look after.

"It's not as bad as it looks from here," Joshua assured him. "Follow me."

The first leg of the climb was the most difficult. The trail was steep, narrow and rocky. Sam would've been a little less worried if the kids were in car seats with safety belts, yet they somehow managed to cling to their mounts. From there, the path became easier to navigate. It was clear to Sam that they weren't following the same trail that paralleled Fisher creek. This one was leading them up the crest of the ridge; they were now well above the stream.

Sam could feel Chasity starting to shiver against his back and patted her hand gently. "Hang on, sweetie. We'll get you a fire soon."

Sam couldn't tell how late it was, but he knew it wouldn't be long before dark. The clouds darkened and the drizzle was rapidly turning to snow. Small flakes at first, but as they continued to climb, the snow grew heavier and quickly blanketed the ground.

Sam whistled for Joshua's attention. "Hey, we need a place to bed down. Soon. This could turn into an all-nighter."

"Trust me, Sam. I got this."

Minutes turned into another hour. The horses climbed steadily, and the children fought on without complaint. Sam was amazed at their resilience.

If I was alone, I'd have thrown a fit a long time ago.

It wasn't long before the mounts trudged through several inches of snow. Even the riders were covered in the white powder. Sam worried about their safety. Hypothermia, sickness. Possible injury. With every minute in this weather, the risk seemed to rise.

Sam whistled again. "Josh?"

"Just a few more minutes."

Sam shook his head as the old man led them into a stand of trees. The trail was harder to read, snow-covered in relative darkness. From what Sam could tell, it led over a knoll and into a hidden meadow. At the edge of the meadow, tucked against a small bluff, was a cabin. Roughly made from logs, mud and indigenous stone, the shelter looked like heaven to Sam.

They led their horses to a stall behind the cabin. Joshua disappeared into a small loafing shed and returned moments later with a bag of feed. As he poured it onto the ground, the horses scrambled eagerly for the pellets.

"How old is that feed?" Sam wanted to know.

"Maybe a month. They make it down in Del Norte. Those Jackals brought me a load to pay for some of the work I did on their horses."

"You brought it up here alone?"

"I pack it in first chance I get. There's no hunting seasons anymore; I have to survive all winter on what I can hunt."

"But isn't there enough game around your house?"

"Maybe. But if I hunted there first, I'd probably push the game out of the area. I prefer to hunt close when the weather gets bad."

Sam nodded. "Fair enough."

The kids had dismounted at their first opportunity to take shelter inside the cabin. When Sam and Joshua opened the door, they found the children huddled together inside, trying to warm themselves by their proximity to each other. Against the wall beside the fireplace, more than a rick of firewood was stacked. Joshua set about building a fire with expert precision. Soon a fire was roaring, and the children were content to crowd as close to the flames as they could bear. Their faces glowed from warmth, their eyelids drooping from the effort of their day.

Sam slipped outside as night finally consumed the land. Snow continued to fall, which eased Sam's mind; their trail would now be completely covered in white powder. Their pursuers had their work cut out for them.

Confident that the children were safe for now, Sam headed back inside the cabin. As his hand grasped the doorknob, a clap of thunder rumbled from down the mountain. Three consecutive blasts that echoed through the valley.

"Gotcha," Sam muttered.

Back inside, he claimed a corner as far from the fire as possible and hung his hat on a rusty nail. He leaned into the corner, watching the children sleep. He smiled at the sight of their innocent faces, realizing that with only a day and a half behind them, he'd already come to care for them deeply.

Is this how God feels about us? he wondered.

By the flickering light of the fire, Sam put his hands together and prayed.

For the children. Amen.

CHAPTER 33

The sounds of an old cabin in the high country were enough to make sleep difficult, even for one so travel weary as Sam. The creaking of wooden clapboards in the wind combined with the sound of tiny animals scurrying beneath the floorboards left Sam in dire need of more dream time. Nevertheless, Sam opened his eyes for good just before dawn. His right arm had fallen asleep. When he tried to move it, he found that at some point during the night, Chasity had mistaken his arm for a pillow. Her head rested against his arm, tangled hair spilling down her cheeks.

The fire was almost out. Sam slowly lay Chasity on the floor next to the other children and rose to stoke the flames and add more wood. He stepped over and around the sleeping kids with care and began to feed kindling to the remaining embers. Soon, flames crept up the small pile of wood and filled the small cabin with warmth again.

Sam tiptoed to the door and slipped onto the front porch. The sky was clear, and at this elevation, the multitude of stars put on a light display unrivaled by anything Sam had ever seen. The ground was covered in a thick blanket of snow. The air was crisp and cold. Joshua was perched on the edge of the porch, watching the spectacle unfold. Tango was curled next to the porch with a layer of snow on his back.

"How long have you been up, old man?"

Tango awoke and stretched at the sound of Sam's voice.

"This time?" Joshua laughed heartily. "At my age, I can't sleep more than a couple of hours. If I did, I might wet the bed."

Sam chuckled. "Where do we go from here?"

"There's an old game trail that starts over in that corner of the meadow," he said, jutting his chin toward a small break in the tree line. "It'll take us down to Fisher creek and up to Goose Lake." Joshua pointed toward the opposite end of the canyon. "It's just over that ridge there."

"I've almost come full circle, then," Sam remarked in amazement. "That ridge is where all this began."

"So you know about the trail at the upper end of the lake?"

"Yeah. That's how I came over from the Piedra. But this isn't the canyon I followed out; I wouldn't have missed your ranch."

"I'm betting you crossed the saddle between Fisher and Copper Mountains and came down Pierce Creek. That would put you below my ranch in the valley."

Sam nodded and glanced back toward the cabin door just as an explosion sounded in the valley. "Time to go," he said. "That's our alarm clock. How far back is that?"

"Four miles, maybe."

The sun had just peeked over the mountains. With fresh snow on the ground, the kids took turns looking out the window. Sam smiled at their youthful excitement. It didn't take long for them to be trail ready.

They gnawed on jerky as they rode. The first leg of the trail led them downhill. There was no way to conceal their tracks after the heavy snow, so Sam relied on speed and easy travel to put distance between his caravan and the enemy. Even in the best-case scenario, the Jackals were down to sixty men; that meant slow, uphill travel in the snow. It would be unlikely for the Jackals to overtake them before they reached Goose Lake, Sam knew. And once his caravan was over the top, Sam was confident they'd have no problems outrunning the Jackals to Pagosa.

The snow melted quickly with the sun beaming from a cloudless sky. They made it to the bottom of the valley in good time and by mid-morning had begun their ascent. The horses responded well to the food and rest. At their current pace, Sam was optimistic they'd be over the top by early afternoon.

As they continued up the trail to Goose Lake, the terrain leveled onto a shelf that Sam recognized. He examined the aspen trees lining the trail for confirmation; it didn't take long to identify the marks he'd blazed on the tree trunks. Soon, he topped a knoll and froze.

This was the spot where Patton had died.

He looked to his right; just inside the tree line, his saddle remained on a log, marking the location of his last ride with his war horse.

Sam patted Shadow on the neck and smiled, wiping a rogue tear from his cheek. "We're almost home, big guy," he said under his breath.

Looking back on the children, Sam smiled. They all seemed to be enjoying the ride, despite the cold. A flicker of movement caught his attention on his side of the canyon in the valley below.

"Joshua, there—in that meadow, about an hour back."

Sam wheeled Shadow around and spurred him into a trot. The other horses followed his lead. The trail was steep and slick, and the horses fought hard to put ground behind them. Soon, their efforts were rewarded as the entire caravan crossed the saddle between valleys. Sam followed the trail downward, relieved that the horses had all made it safely with the children. Around two in the afternoon, they broke into a meadow just below Piedra Peak with only the Pass before them. They rested at the creek and let the horses wade in to drink their fill.

Joshua remained on his palomino and handed out more jerky to the children. "Sam," he hissed, nodding up the valley toward the Pass.

A small elk herd had spooked and was running across the valley. Sam's heart fell as no less than a dozen men on horseback filed out of the woods from the east. He looked to the north; there were nearly twice as many already waiting there. Two men had set themselves apart from the larger platoon. Sam assumed they were in charge.

"How on earth did they beat us here?" Sam lamented.

"They must've gone around," Joshua replied. "They had to come up by Spar City. That's the only way."

"Pushed us across the top with a small group on our tail," Sam grumbled with a cold gaze. "Can't believe I fell for it."

One of the children began to cry.

"Hey, fella. No need for that. These guys just don't know who they're messing with. What's your name?"

"Timothy," the boy squeaked, trying for all he was worth to hold back a sob.

"Well, Timothy, I'm going to go have a talk with these guys, and we'll soon be on our way."

"I want to go home," the boy moaned.

"I know you do, son. I intend to make sure you get there." He turned back to Joshua. "What's left in your pack?"

"Three sticks and a grenade."

"Hold on to those. I'm going to buy us some time. If you manage to get the kids through the Pass, blow it."

Tango trotted with Sam for a moment, but Sam brought Shadow to a stop and signaled for the wolf to sit and stay.

Sam rode Shadow toward the two men, slowing to a stop when he'd split the distance between them. He placed a leg across the saddle and rested his arms on the horn to wait for the two men to approach.

Seeing that Sam had offered an invitation, one of the men came forward. As he drew near, Sam realized the captain of the platoon was far too young to have earned so much responsibility. "You must be the demon," he surmised.

"I'm Malphus. Or you may call me Captain. Whichever you prefer."

"Why are we here, Malphus? What is it you want?"

"That's a good question. It's funny—for thousands of years, I've sought retribution relentlessly; yet for some reason, it doesn't feel all that important today."

Sam's brow furrowed. "Retribution? I don't understand. Retribution for what?"

Malphus sized Sam up with surprise. The human didn't seem fearful, nor did he plead his case to be let go.

"Many things," the demon replied. "Things that cannot be undone."

Sam tilted his hat back and looked directly into the eyes of Malphus. "What troubles you, demon?"

Again, Malphus was surprised by Sam's reaction. "Nothing that should concern you."

"Well, there must be something that concerns me, or you wouldn't have surrounded me and these children with your army."

"My troubles are not your concern. However, you've been a thorn in our side for so very long, and I've grown weary of these games."

"Okay. Take me and do what you will, but let the children go. One time offer."

"That sounds like a fair offer. If only I was the deal maker, I would gladly let the children go, Sam. But this is beyond me. I answer to my brother, and if I fail him now, he'll send me into the abyss."

Sam thought for a moment, looking deep into the eyes of the demon. At once, the meaning of his dream resolved in his mind. "Wendigo," Sam muttered.

Malphus gaped. "What did you say?"

"The Wendigo, the Nephilim—they were your children?"

Caught off guard, Malphus was no longer able to meet the cowboy's steady gaze. He looked to the ground for a few seconds, and then back at Sam. "Yes," he finally relented. "The Nephilim were our children. We had wives, one I dearly loved. But this world wasn't meant for us as tenants, nor were your women meant to be our wives.

"As our children grew, it became obvious they weren't normal. They could never be normal, never accepted by humans. Some were worse than others; they craved human flesh. Others seemed ordinary enough but grew to abnormal size. When humans rebelled, we discovered that our offspring weren't immortal. Our children were stoned, driven off cliffs, burned at the stake. We could do nothing but watch and grieve the genocide of our children."

Malphus squeezed his eyes closed.

"She was so beautiful, Sam. Much like your Jennifer. Long, flowing black hair. Smooth, flawless skin that smelled like honeysuckle in spring. The humans took her. They took her for being my wife, called her a witch and a sorcerer for having my child. They stoned her first and then burned her at the stake. Those are the things that cannot be undone."

Sam listened intently to the demon. When he was through speaking, they faced each other in silence. The demon had nothing left to say, and Sam was left speechless by the demon's confession. He'd never expected to see such human emotion from a fallen angel. Malphus began to turn away.

"Wait," Sam said in a low voice. "I can't pretend to imagine what you and your wife went through, but I have to believe we can do something—reach some kind of arrangement to let these innocent children go home. When does this suffering end?"

"It doesn't, Sam. Suffering and torment will be mine for all eternity. The choices I made long ago left me where I am today, and I have to accept that."

"That doesn't mean you have to destroy the lives of helpless children."

"I know that, now." The demon looked back at his men, zeroing in on his second in command. He was surprised Lucifer hadn't arrived yet, but he knew his brother must be close by. He was always present for events of this magnitude.

Malphus faced Sam again. "Samson Crow, not once in this conversation have you shown any interest in saving yourself, and that surprises me. Most humans are petty and selfish. Nothing at all like you, in fact. I'm equally impressed that you've shown more interest and compassion for your enemy than yourself. I won't take you or the children today, but you must leave. Now. And be quick about it."

Sam watched in silent amazement as the demon turned away and rode back to his platoon. He signaled for his men on the south side of the meadow to follow and, without a word, led them past the children in the creek.

Wheeling Shadow around, Sam planted his heels into the horse's flanks. The pale horse carried him across the meadow, where he stopped long enough to coax the children out of the creek and send them galloping south toward Piedra Pass with Joshua.

A loud crack resounded through the valley, causing Sam to flinch. His first thought was that someone had fired a rifle. Yet when he turned to face Malphus once more, he saw that Lucifer had arrived and was holding his little brother off the ground by the neck. With a flick of his wrist, the Prince of Darkness used an enormous claw to decapitate Malphus. The demon's severed head flew from his body, discarded like a piece of trash. At once, the head and body dissolved into nothing.

Lucifer rubbed his palms together as if to wipe a bit of dirt from his hands. He glared across the meadow at Sam, pointing a long, gnarly finger at the man.

"Take him," the devil commanded. "Take him now. And hunt down those baby skins, too. Yes, kill them all."

After two days of maintaining their high on *Push*, the Jackals were finally turned loose to engage their depravity. Sam spurred Shadow into motion and let the horse have his head as they raced toward the Pass. Tango followed closely, the wolf matching the horse stride for stride. Sam could see Joshua ahead, coaxing the children along as fast as they could go. But for all their efforts, there was no way the children would outrun this army of madmen, Sam knew.

I've got to buy them some time.

Sam turned Shadow to confront the Jackals bearing down on him. He let go of the reins and drew his handguns and opened fire. The eyes of the closest Jackal widened as a bullet to the chest knocked him off his mount. His body was trampled by the horses of his own army. The assassins had been ordered to pursue, and in their drug-induced insanity, they hadn't been expecting resistance—certainly not a from a one-man army. Not one had bothered to draw his weapon; within seconds, a dozen men were dead or dying in the meadow, their blood smearing against lingering drifts of snow.

It didn't take long for Sam to empty his guns. When their slides locked to the rear, Sam knew he'd never reload in time. They were practically on him by then. He let his guns fall to the ground, unsheathing his Bianchi Nighthawk and leapt from his horse, knocking his closest attacker off his mount. Their bodies struck the ground with a bone-jarring thud. Sam pulled the knife from the Jackal's chest just in time to plunge it into another. He twisted and dodged the enemy, flaying skin in passing.

Tango leapt over a horse and took down its rider by the neck.

Sam rolled to dodge one horse as another charged from a different direction. He prepared to sidestep a horse on his right and slash the abdomen of its rider, but a distant crack of thunder sent the rider to the ground at Sam's feet. Again, thunder echoed through the valley.

At once, the remaining horsemen began to retreat.

The old marshal wheeled to find an army approaching from the trail to Piedra Pass. He brandished his bloody knife as thunder shook the valley yet again. The remaining assassins fled in haste. The sounds made sense almost in tandem with the sight of TJ blazing onto the field with an American flag waving proudly in the wind. Sam saluted the patriots as they approached, some on horseback, others on foot. They had ridden in with TJ, ready to battle again for the very freedom that had cost them so much.

Soon, a smattering of gunfire sounded from the opposite end of the valley. Sam pivoted in reaction, smiling with relief as Kuruk, Eli and Bendigo emerged from the north tree line with their own guns blazing.

The battle was over in less than a minute. When the last of the enemy had fallen or fled, only Lucifer and Sam remained standing in the clearing. The Father of Lies crossed his arms and glared at the old marshal.

"My, fortune does seem to favor you, Crow."

"I get a little help from upstairs."

Lucifer sighed with feigned indifference. "No matter. Your deadline will come soon enough, old man."

Sam gritted his teeth angrily. "Don't you worry. Others will follow in my footsteps."

Chuckling, the devil gave Sam his back and sauntered back toward the woods. "Until next time," he said over his shoulder.

"I'll be waiting!" Sam barked, but his voice fell on thin air. Lucifer had vanished.

The adrenaline had come and gone, leaving Sam weak. He collapsed to the ground, managing a grin. TJ slid off a horse nearby and rushed to his side.

"I think I'll just lay here for a while and take a nap," Sam muttered with a dazed smile. He struggled to rise and slid back down.

TJ took him under the arm and helped him up. "I've met you twice now, young man, and I've had to help you to your feet both times. I think it's time you retired from this 'saving the world' business. You ought to be a CEO by now. Take a vacation, or just call it a day."

Sam laughed. "Done. I was too old for this when it found me the first time."

Kuruk and the boys greeted Sam and handed over Shadow's reins.

"What took you so long?"

"Well, my friend, that's a long story starring Jennifer and a kid who's almost as stubborn. Don't tell her I said that."

"Did they finally go to Pagosa?"

"See for yourself." Kuruk nodded toward the tree line at the north end of the meadow. Jennifer, Zack and Emily emerged from the woods on horseback and trotted across the field.

"We had a heck of a time avoiding this army of tweakers."

Jennifer slid off Asgard before the horse had time to a stop, lunging to greet her husband. She threw herself into his arms and held him long and tight. When she stood back to look at him, she frowned.

Sam shrugged. "I know, I look like hell."

"Yes, there's no denying that. But you're alive, Sam. Thank God."

TJ patted Sam gently on the shoulder. "We can't thank you enough for what you've done, Sam. Chasity is safe and on the way to her mom. Her dad is somewhere amidst all this mess. He refused to stay back when he heard you were here alone."

"And Jamie?" Sam asked.

"She wasn't happy about it, but it was her turn to pull duty in the tower."

Sam grinned. "Well, you and your patriots saved my life today. You also saved the lives of those children."

"They wouldn't be here without you, Sam. And I'm not sure if we saved your life or just reduced the number of Jackals you had to kill. It looked to me like you and that dog of yours had things pretty well in hand. And just so you know, we have room at the Eagle's Nest for you and your family. I mean it. Y'all are welcome any damn time."

"Thanks, brother. We'll talk it over, but it's hard for me to see us anywhere but the Moon Dog Ranch, for now."

The sun began to set as the last soldiers from the Eagle's Nest made their way through Piedra Pass toward home. Sam, Jennifer and their friends made camp in a high meadow, just beyond the Pass, and settled in to prepare for travel the next day.

Leaning against a fallen log, Sam watched the setting sun turn the sky into a spectacle of colors. For the first time in a long while, Samson Crow felt peace within.

EPILOGUE

There wasn't much to discuss. Both Sam and Jennifer knew without a doubt that the Moon Dog Ranch was the only home for them. They invited Zack and Emily into their family, and by the end of that summer, their friends from the Eagle's Nest—along with Kuruk, Eli and Bendigo—had helped them build a new cabin. It wasn't the enormous lodge that they had lived in before, but it had room enough for everyone. Sara and Theresa each claimed one of the smaller cabins that survived the fire, yet they chose to spend most of their time with the family in the new home.

Logos never returned to talk with Sam again, but throughout the years that followed, Sam would occasionally catch a phantom scent of pipe tobacco on the wind. The smell would never cease to leave him with a smile.

ABOUT THE AUTHOR

Will Kinnebrew is a retired Deputy United States Marshal of twenty-seven years. He and his family reside in rural Oklahoma outside the town of Claremore. He graduated from the University of Southern Mississippi with a degree in Criminal Justice and pursued a career in law enforcement that spanned more than thirty years. His credentials and training certifications are many but his most coveted award was graduating at the top of the class at the Federal Law Enforcement Training Center Firearms Instructors School. He was assigned to the Violent Crimes Task force for many years and finished his career as a Senior Inspector in charge of sex offender investigations.

> "*We sleep safe in our beds because rough men stand ready in the night to visit violence on those who would do us harm.*"
>
> *-George Orwell*

CPSIA information can be obtained
at www.ICGtesting.com
Printed in the USA
LVHW012341180720
661024LV00005B/314